# Hedone

J.C. Morgan

SRL PUBLISHING

SRL Publishing Ltd
London
www.srlpublishing.co.uk

First published worldwide by SRL Publishing in 2023

ISBN: 978-191507326-6

1 3 5 7 9 10 8 6 4 2

A CIP catalogue record for this book is available from the
British Library

SRL Publishing is a Climate Positive publisher offsetting more
carbon emissions than it emits.

*For Dylan, my partner in crime.*
*And for the hedonists — be careful what you wish for*

*Man is not free to avoid doing what gives him greater pleasure than any other action* — Marie-Henri Beyle (Stendhal)

# JULIAN

# One

Allow me to bring you back to London.

Oxford, more specifically. A place where the weather is as dreadful as the traffic, where danger looms thick in the air, lurking around every corner, slithering along black alleyways, scratching about in the dark, plotting another depraved act, masturbating into a handkerchief—whatever it is we have to do to keep ourselves sane. Or the opposite, depending on how you look at it. I look at it like this—some of us do insane things to keep ourselves from becoming insane, while some of us don't need a reason at all.

Allow me to bring you back to *us,* Matt and I, and our connection that bled more than it soothed.

Our lives were cast in a heavy shadow of loneliness before we met, lusted, obsessed, and drained one another dry. I often thought about how things would be if we never met when he was fifteen. How normal, how terribly boring. Perhaps we could have found ourselves on a path to forgiveness rather than encouraging one another to walk closer to hell, but perhaps you can't be forgiven if you aren't bothered either way. If I was to make a list of my regrets, it would be a journal of additional misadventures I never got to do. More blackmail, more power, more boys.

That's not to say I don't have any regrets, because I certainly do.

If I could rewind time, I would have tormented Matt and myself for longer; continued playing the game of cat and mouse until neither of us could run anymore. That's what I loved, after all. That's what it's all about. The chase, the thrill, and the first time I gave in to it— anything beyond that is dessert. I would have done the same with Will, chased him for longer; earned more of his trust; plotted my moves more carefully, like a master of chess. And I *was* a master, a master of my own game. With Will I was younger and new to the rules—I acted on impulse, allowed the internal lust to take over the rational part of my brain, resulting in one of the best, most depraved nights of my life, the night we had sex in my car when he was fourteen and I was twenty-seven. I often wondered if Will would still be alive had I not let Matt get too close to the truth. Was there something a little less drastic that could be done? Without Matt in the picture, I could have talked Will down, made him see sense and remember he was as consenting as I was. I could recall that night frame by frame, as accurately as a video recording, and I certainly didn't hear any complaints. When he came looking for answers I would have soothed his anger, fed him the lies I knew he wanted to hear...

*Your memory is a bit washy, that's all. You know I'd never hurt you, not intentionally. I cared for you the moment I saw you, Will, and you were just so beautiful, there at the back of my classroom with your thick head of chestnut brown curls. I had to have you. Blue eyed boy. Can you blame me? You loved every second of it back then, don't you remember? It broke my heart when you moved away, I had to move too. Everything reminded me of you…*

Weighing on the past is pointless unless you're willing to learn from your mistakes, and I'm not sure I was capable of correcting mine. Oh, how easy it is to lose everything, it happens so fast you don't know it's over until you have nothing left.

Matt killed Will before I got a chance to see him again and offer an explanation. He saved me from becoming the exposé of the year, and for that I had to be grateful, right? Perhaps I would have shown gratitude, had Matt actually told me what he did. But he didn't tell me. I had to find out on *Facebook*, of all places, that a body was found in the Thames, and that the body belonged to William Smithers, my ex-pupil, my ex-lover. I'm sure you remember. He was murdered on the night of Halloween at just twenty-eight years old, the same night Matt came home covered head to toe in blood and I failed to probe deep enough as to the reason why. I helped him burn the evidence in our back garden, in the firepit next to the fish pond. Weeks later, when I stumbled on the Facebook post and finally discovered the truth, I went home to confront Matt. There, he told me the truth—Will came to Oxford in search of justice and Matt gutted him as punishment for it. Then, he nearly gutted me in the aftermath.

We had the tendency to let things escalate, and that night was just one of our many acts of perverted justice against one another. Everything was heightened, our senses in a frenzy, both of us on the floor, naked and fighting for the Stanley blade. I remember the heat of my own blood as it seeped from my chest, a stream of dark red chaos. Hades, begging for another soul. Matt, ready to deliver. I always thought it would end that way—death by a lover's hand, but it turned out Matt was as much of a liar as I was. I gave myself to him, closed my eyes and prepared to wade into the quiet, and Matt put the blade down. It was all part of the game. I unintentionally called his bluff. He realised he was lucky—no other person in their right or wrong mind would continue to love such a callous hellion. No one else would feel safe sleeping next to him at night, nor would they gaze into his baby blues with nothing but adoration, even when he has a knife to their chest. Not to say I never punished him for it— believe me I did, again and again. He would let me, he would stay, because without me and the acceptance I brought and my own hidden impulses, he would be alone. All on his lonesome, prowling the city in search for a warm body and a quick fuck before rendering them lifeless and disappearing into the night like a ghost. Poof, and he's gone, he was never really there. No one to confide in, and, with the exception of the dead, no one to share his secrets and lies. Without each other, we were lost ships on an ocean in which we did not belong. Our chances of survival were better together.

So I asked Matt to marry me. It was something I always wanted for myself, the romantic pipedream to complete the perfect facade. Besides, what better way was there to have Matt truly belong to me than to give him my name? Matt & Julian Blake. It's got a ring to it, I think, and speaking of rings, we had them engraved. They said in elegant script: *If my love for you wanes, kill me*. I know you think we're insane. I suppose if you didn't there would be something wrong with you, and you won't ever admit that, will you?

The wedding ceremony was perfect, quiet and private, just how I liked it. No one mentioned my sister's absence, but it was noticed, nonetheless. Not even Matt made a snide remark. I pretended for the whole day it didn't bother me, like I hardly noticed Ashley was missing, but deep down I wanted to find her and scream in her face. It was raising eyebrows, whispering itself around the castle. My own sister for crying out loud.

Yes, things were rocky with Ashley since she caught Matt and I, when he was sixteen and breathless over my coffee table, and yes, I admit it must have been a tough image to erase—even I thought about it constantly, the memory, the distraction, how young he was, how stupid I was—but however shocking a scene it was to see, surely Ashley's reaction was a little excessive. Was it truly enough to make her despise Matt and I? I needed answers, and once we were home from Greece and we came down from our honeymoon high, I decided to use my last free day off work to visit my sister and niece.

Upon my arrival, Ashley handed me a black envelope with *Jules* written on it, and the card inside had been thoughtfully personalised. The outside had a picture of the Grim Reaper holding a scythe, and the inside read: *Congratulations, Brother, on signing your life away. Rest in peace. Lots of love, Ash x*

'Hilarious, sis,' I said, tucking the card into my coat pocket. I was already agitated and tired from the early flight home the day before, and I could feel how unwelcome I was within seconds of being there, so I knew it would be a short visit. Ashley didn't sit either, instead she stood in her lounge doorway while I leaned against the staircase. Everything about her body language told me I wasn't invited another step closer.

She said, 'You could've called.'

'I tried. You never pick up.'

'I've been busy.'

'Great.'

'What are you doing here, Jules?'

'Where's Annabella?'

'You *never* come to see her—'

'Because you never let me, Ash.'

'The only reason you've asked about her is because you're here to throw a tantrum over the wedding,' she said. 'Don't pretend it's for anything else, Jules. Just save it. You don't really give a shit.'

'How can you say that? She's my niece. I love her.'

'Yeah, well, you have a fantastic way of showing it.'

'What am I supposed to do?' I asked. 'You just

admitted you never answer the phone when I call you. How am I to keep a relationship with Anna, or you for that matter, when you refuse to give me the chance?'

Ashley sighed, knowing I was right, and said, 'Anna's out with her friends, she's not here, and she won't be back until ten.'

'What the hell do you mean she's *out* with her friends. She's a kid—'

'Nearly fourteen. I know my own daughter's age.'

'Oh I know that for Christ sake. I'm just saying, you know.'

'Yeah, well. How about you try keeping a teenager in the house, and let me know how it goes for you.'

'Isn't ten a little late?' I asked. 'Don't you worry about her?'

Ashley chuckled. By the look on her face I could tell she was about to be a stone-cold bitch.

'Sure I do,' she said. 'But I mean... by your standards, technically in two years she could be in bed with a man older than her father.'

*Technically she could be now...* She wanted a reaction which I held back, stayed silent to force her to continue so I wouldn't have to respond. 'Let's just get this over with. I know you didn't come here to see Annabella and I *certainly* hope you aren't here to offer your insightful parenting advice. Remind me how many kids you've had again?'

The question struck me like a bolt of lightning. I almost gave her an answer.

'I didn't come here to argue. Why do you have to

make everything so difficult, Ash? All I want is for us to be able to have a conversation that doesn't end in a fucking nightmare. Can't we just talk?'

Ashley shook her head. 'No, we can't just *talk*, because the minute I mention that brat boyfriend—sorry, *husband*—of yours, you turn into a twat. He's dangerous, and you're blinded by him, Jules. He's changed you into this egomaniac, and I don't like it one bit.'

I'd be lying if I said she wasn't right. Yes, I did get defensive when someone, *anyone*, spoke of Matthew in a negative way. But is that not typical in a partnership, a marriage? Yes, Matt was the most dangerous person I knew. Yes, I was blinded by him, but Ashley didn't realise she was as equally blinded by me. I almost felt sorry for her, how she could apparently sense Matt's darkness after only a handful of times meeting him, and yet have no idea about the one that had resided in me since the moment I was born.

'This is who I am. It's who I've *always* been,' I said. 'And don't call Matt a brat. You've never given him a chance, you don't know him.'

'Do you see what I mean? This is what you always do. You ask questions you don't want the answers to. You came here to confront me, but you can't stand it when I confront you back. There's something wrong with Matt, Jules, and I'm scared. I hate thinking that one morning I'll wake up to the news he's killed you.'

'Oh for Christ sake, Ashley. Stop being so bloody ridiculous.'

'I've seen your scar. I know it was him.'

10

'What are you talking about?'

'Stop denying it! The scar on your chest. I know the bar fight was just an excuse, I know when you're lying about something. Since when do *you* get in bar fights?'

'Think what you will,' I said, shaking my head. 'You're being ridiculous.'

'Oh, you can deny and deny all you want. I don't trust him and I never will. You know me, Jules, I'm honest and I'll never lie to you. You want an answer as to why I wasn't at your wedding, and that's my reason. I refuse to celebrate someone I detest.'

'I never liked your ex-husband either, you know.'

'And what? What's that got to do with *anything*?'

'Well, I was still at your wedding, was I not?'

Ashley went quiet. I straightened up from leaning against the stair railings and cleared my throat to announce I would be leaving. We weren't getting anywhere, and we never would—Ashley would be hateful until I changed my mind and left Matt, and I would never leave him, and he would never leave me, because we would kill each other before either of us got the chance. What more could I say to her? I knew exactly who Matt was, and I did not care. I was not in danger, I was a part of the danger.

'I'm leaving,' I said. 'Thanks for the card, sis. I'll leave it here, if you don't mind.'

'I'd rather you didn't.'

I left the card on the stairs and turned to leave anyway.

Ashley said, 'Has anyone bought that house for sale

by you yet?' The question was completely out of the blue.

'What? Why?'

'Just answer the damn question.'

'Yes, I think so. I saw a sold sign a couple days ago…
Why? You want to be neighbours now?'

'Funny,' she said.

'How did you know it was up for sale?'

'I saw the listing online. Is that a crime?'

'Goodbye, Ash.'

I closed her front door behind me before she could
say anything else, knowing she wouldn't go out of her
way because that would be showing weakness, and she
was the most headstrong woman I'd ever known, closely
followed by Catherine. My old colleague, my best friend.
The best friend who caught Matt and I in the office at
work and paid for it in death. My wishes were Matt's
commands, after all, and he loved having a reason to get
his knife wet.

I arrived home after dark, just in time for dinner.
Matt cooked despite his broken wrist—the result of a
drunken stumble in Greece. We spoke about our days
over wine: I told him about what happened at Ashley's;
he told me about the moving vans at Graham's old house
that I missed during the day. According to Matt, they
were full of *just stunning* shabby-chic furniture. The house
had been up for sale for ages, and despite it being a
gorgeous house in a good neighbourhood, it seemed no
one wanted it. Matt joked about the house being a bad
omen, haunted by the memories of Graham's
extracurricular ventures with underage boys.

We finished dinner and I washed up, while Matt continued talking about the furniture. He was fidgeting with energy the way he did when he wanted to say something that would disrupt the atmosphere of easy domesticity. I raised my eyebrows as if to say, *come on then, what is it?*

Matt said he met the people who bought the house while I was out. It was a couple and their teenage son, and he went over to say hi and welcome them to the street like the noble young man he loved to pretend he was. The couple's names were Lara and Melissa, their son was called Tyler, and Matt said living so close to him was going to be a problem for me. You're probably wondering what he meant by that, or perhaps you see exactly where this is going.

'What do you mean?' I said.

Matt smirked. 'You'll see.'

On my way to work the next morning, I drove past the house as I always did, and I immediately understood what Matt was talking about the night before. The kid was beautiful. Muddy brown hair, glassy blue eyes, that invincible energy often found in teenagers. From that second, I knew he'd have a magnetic smile, soft hands, a bright and inquisitive mind. I knew he'd set my world on fire, and I would gladly walk through it. It was like seeing a ghost, an intense Deja Vu—he was leaving for school, and in his green and gold uniform he looked exactly like Will did at that age.

# Two

The first time I met the kid was a couple of days later. I pulled up on my driveway and there he was, sitting on my garden bench and scrolling through his phone like all teenagers his age tended to do. He didn't look up from the screen as I approached him. I loved the ignorance of youth. Too ignorant to be scared and too stubborn to back down. In the callowness of adolescence, they imagine they're inventing the world for the first time, and their vulnerability shines because of it. As the thought struck me, I wondered at what point in my life I became so twisted.

Tyler's cheeks were blood red, his breath hot and unfurling like smoke into the crisp air around him. He must have been freezing, and immediately I had to stop myself from offering him inside for a hot chocolate. It was a friendly gesture, no ill intentions, only good ones. I wanted to warm him up from the winter chill, put the fire on and wrap him in a weighted blanket, keep him there, never let him go, run my fingers through his hair and work my magic, make him mine, my Will reincarnated.

*No. Behave, Julian, you're married.*

I walked up to the boy confidently; he was in *my* garden, after all, and I could feel my inner predator clawing to get out.

'Well, hello there.'

'Oh, hi. I'm Tyler,' he said, looking at me with curious eyes. 'Your car is really cool.'

'Thanks, it's actually really old now, I can't bring myself to part with it.'

'Old cars are still cool,' he shrugged.

'Perhaps I'll take you for a drive. I don't get to take advantage of her speed a lot.'

The boy smiled. 'Really? That would be totally cool. I just moved across the road a couple days ago. Me and my mums, I mean.' He was well spoken yet shy. Full of promise.

'I'm Julian. It's a pleasure to meet you. You've met my husband, I believe.'

'Yeah, uh… shit. I'm not good with names. Don't tell me. It's um… Matt. Matt, right?'

I found myself chuckling, equally loving and hating how endeared I was. 'You are correct,' I said. 'So, what brings you to my garden, Tyler?'

As it turned out, the boy lost his football. He was playing in the street when he kicked it a little too hard, and it landed in the back garden. He said he tried to open the gate but it was locked, so he thought he would wait for someone to come home. He apologised for trying to break in, so I laughed, wanting to reassure him.

'Please don't apologise, it's not a problem. I'll go get it for you.'

I unlocked the gate and went out back to find the missing football. It was in the fish pond, floating on top of the water as the Koi tested it for food. I returned the ball to Tyler and his face lit up.

'Thank you, sir.'

'You're welcome. You can call me Julian, or Jules. Most people call me Jules.'

'Cool, I like Jules.'

'Thanks. I like your name, too.'

'Really?'

'Yes.'

'Cool… So do you like living with another guy? I live with my two mums. It's kinda cool.'

'I do, yes. Matt and I got married a couple of weeks ago. We just got home from Greece.'

'That was where you went on your honeymoon?'

'Yes, it's my favourite place.'

'That's cool.'

'You're funny.'

'Me?'

'Yes.'

'Cool.'

'Cool…' I mimicked.

'Wanna know something kinda weird?' he asked.

'Always. I love weird.'

'My parents got married recently, too.'

'That *is* weird,' I said, humouring him. 'Do

16

coincidences unsettle you?'

'Nah, they're actually pretty cool.'

Of course they were. Everything was cool. The kid was so laid–back he was sleeping, and I was never any good at leaving sleeping puppies lie. The wolf in me was stirring. Tyler was malleable and warm and soft, the gooey dough to my baker. I wanted to get my hands inside him and press him into all the shapes he could bear, and he wouldn't complain because it was *cool*, it was fine, and he didn't want to kick up a fuss. Relaxed souls hate confrontation. That's why I portrayed myself as such, despite the storm tearing through my mind and body. Pretending to be fine with the coincidences when in reality they unsettled me. The most disturbing of them all was his striking resemblance to Will. There was the house, once haunted by the memories of underage boys, but now occupied by one, while another lover of transgression lurks in the shadows of the house across the road. There was his hooded sweatshirt with his name written on the front in small black letters, *T. Williams*. Of all the surnames in Britain, his had to be fucking Williams. I didn't know if it was fate or a sick joke. William Smithers, Catherine Williams, my rapidly declining *will* to control myself.

Tyler thanked me for retrieving his football again, I said it wasn't a problem. It was only a friendly neighbour getting a ball back. At least it should have been. It should have been easy, simple as one two three. Hand the ball back, say goodbye, watch to make sure he gets home safely. But it was freezing out, bitterly so, and the boy didn't have a hat, nor gloves, and he had been sitting on an icy bench for god knows how long, having the respect and patience not to force entry by waiting for someone to come home instead, and besides all that, I was quite enjoying his company.

*No, no, no.*

Contrary to your probable belief, I was a changed man. I'd learned how to internalise the unstoppable lust within me that told me to transgress. I had Matthew for that—I didn't need to drag any other poor soul up the top of our mountain of bodies. On the drive with Tyler so close, I warned myself of the consequences, the spiral, the punishment I'd be begging for, and the life I would be risking.

'I'd better get inside, it's my night to make dinner,' I said. The boy asked what I was making. 'Veggie burgers, tonight.'

'Why veggie ones?'

'Matt's a vegetarian.'

'Cool. Sounds good,' he said, and I could tell—while wishing it wasn't true—that Tyler didn't want to go anywhere. *Cool.* Absolutely fantastic. He said, 'My mums aren't home yet, they both work late. I'll just be out here kicking the ball some more. But that's cool.' It felt like he was trying to get me to invite him in. No way. Was he? More importantly, should I?

I could see into the near future already, saw myself attempting to stay distracted by chopping vegetables and shaping burgers. I saw Tyler behind me, next to me, offering to help, making a mess of my kitchen, asking questions and being a downright nuisance. I saw myself indulging in the thrill it would give me, saw how I would effortlessly worm my way into his head, plant my seeds of seduction and blame him for it when they bloomed and flourished. No, it was not going to happen. I swore up and down it wouldn't.

'Oh, really?' I said. 'When will your mums be back?'

'I'm not sure.'

Of course he wasn't.

'Okay. Not a problem.' I had no idea what to say. I'd held myself together and there he was forcing himself into my home. I know it sounds dramatic, but when you've worked hard at keeping the monster within you at bay, all for it to stab you in the back anyway, it's really fucking frustrating. 'I can wait out here with you, I suppose, and…' What was I supposed to do? 'I mean, I guess you can sit in the lounge while I make dinner. I'll make you a hot chocolate, might warm you up a bit.' I could have screamed.

'Hot chocolate sucks,' Tyler said. 'I like tea, tea's cool. Do you have tea?'

I rubbed my eyes. Who in Oxford did not have tea? And what kid didn't like hot chocolate?

'Yes, we have tea. You can watch something on the telly while I cook.'

'Thank you, Jules.'

My name on his lips softened my every edge. *Jools.* I hadn't known a better sound. 'Are you sure? Do you mind?'

Like I had a choice in the matter. Like I could tell

him yes, in fact I do mind, go home, stay away from me, I am not the good older neighbour that you have convinced yourself I am, with no basis other than a five-minute conversation with my pathological husband.

'Not a problem at all,' I said, and I hated myself for it. I was angry at life, at him, because even when you do everything right things will still go wrong.

Inside, Tyler sat on the armchair with a piping hot cup of tea, sweet as him, and I focused on dinner in the kitchen. I cut the vegetables into small chunks; carrots, parsnips, kale, spinach. I added sweetcorn, garlic, chilli, and garden peas, setting them in the oven to roast next to a tray of black beans. While I waited for the timer to ping, I told Tyler I was going to the study room to send out a couple of emails, which I did. I had no interruptions by the time the timer pinged. When I was using a mixer to blend the vegetables together, that's when Tyler came in, and he set his cup next to the sink, asking if he could help with anything, like I anticipated. I asked him if he knew how to make vegetable burgers, and found myself almost laughing at the absurdity of the whole thing. The boy told me no, he didn't, he actually didn't know how to cook anything except toast. I mixed two eggs with the vegetables, added some chickpeas, and I asked him if he would like to shape the mixture into burgers.

'How many?'

'Three, please. Put them on here when you're finished.' I handed him an oven tray, and he washed his hands before touching the food, which quietly pleased me. Then he went to work, moulding the burgers into shape. I busied myself with the bread rolls, slicing them in half, buttering their insides like I wished to butter his.

'You can stay with Matt and I for dinner, if you'd like,' I said. 'Are you hungry?'

'I'm starving, yeah.'

'Me too.'

The only thing I wanted to devour was him. I wanted every other freckle on that face. I wanted him to get out of my sight and yet never leave my vision again. I set the three buttered rolls down on the counter and watched as the boy put the last formed burger on the tray.

'Oh,' he said, as if he was embarrassed for not realising something. 'The third one was for me.'

I smiled, said, 'Seems we have a detective,' and when he giggled my mind slipped out of me. It floated to the ceiling so I could see myself from above—looming over him, a thousand yard stare.

'So what's with the Egyptian stuff in there?' he said, referring to the Greek ornaments in the living room. I belly-laughed at that, and the kid looked suddenly wounded. 'Sorry, was that a stupid thing to say?'

'No, not at all. I'm laughing because they're Greek philosophers, and no one's ever compared them to Egyptians before. It's funny because you're totally right, and it never crossed my mind until now.'

'Well, they're cool. I guess you like Greek phil…osophers? That's a hard word.'

'It is indeed,' I said. 'I don't *like* them so much as I *teach* them. I'm a lecturer at the university—'

'The posh one?'

'The posh one.' Both of us laughed at that.

'So you're like, a professor of Greek stuff?'

I grinned as I slid the steel tray into the oven, and then I sat on a stool at the kitchen island. I tapped the one next to me, saying, '*That* is my exact job title. Professor of Greek stuff. I'm keeping that one.' It reminded me of Matt when we first met; confident and quirky in the cafe as he pretended not to know what I taught over breakfast. *Something to do with the words 'Ancient', 'Philosophy', and uh… 'Greeks'.*

Tyler laughed at me, the desired effect, and said, 'You don't act like a professor.'

'Oh, no? And how does a professor act?' I mused.

Tyler shrugged. 'Dunno… snobbish, I guess. Like they know everything.'

'Well, I certainly don't know everything. I do know some people that fit the type you're referring to, though. Up themselves, is how I like to describe it.' He flashed me a smile, one that read of warmth and gratitude. However much I detested that part of my makeup, I understood teenagers, and Tyler was no different—they have a concoction of feelings and hormones churning inside of them and no idea on how to express them. When they try, their parents or grandparents or teachers tell them to get over it and stop acting so hard done by, *When you're older you'll understand, cut it with the talking back or you're grounded, your attitude is unacceptable, stop asking so many questions.* You would be surprised at how easy it is to get a teenager on your side—all you have to do is let them be themselves, listen, and reassure them their feelings and thoughts are as valid as yours, even when they're not.

Tyler repeated to me, '*Up themselves*. I'm keeping that one, it's cool.'

'It's yours,' I said, and I meant it. Everything, all of it.

I glanced at my watch—Matt wouldn't be long. I knew I was in trouble when my heart filled with disappointment. I swivelled the stool around and checked the fridge to see if we needed anything from Tesco. We didn't, so I had to come up with something else, but what? I looked at Tyler, who was reading a book Matt had left on the counter that morning, and I took a picture of him to send to Matt, along with the text, *Look who we have for dinner tonight. His parents are in work til later. Would you pick up some snacks on the way home please, baby? Dinner is nearly ready.*

I joined Tyler back at the island, hoping my attempt at a diversion worked and granted me more time alone with him. When he was standing up he looked tall for his age, but sitting next to me on the stool, Tyler's head was not yet past my shoulder. I was paying attention to all the wrong things but it was too late to do anything about it, nor did I want to. It was an internal struggle, stop, go, yes, no. Tyler was enticing, handsome yet not outstandingly so, which made him all the more outstanding. He was cheeky and cocky and so very Will. I snuffed every urge to touch his wind-swept hair and ignored every word the voice inside whispered.

*If you don't, you know I will. Let me out. At least plant a seed. You know you really, desperately want to.*

I asked, 'Do you like to read?' and the boy nodded, closing the copy of *Orfeo* by Richard Powers. 'That book was inspired by the myth of Orpheus. Ever heard of him?' Tyler shook his head, so I continued. 'He was the greatest musician in Greek mythology, and a prophet and poet, too. Matt's a musician, hence why he's reading that and there's a massive piano in the other room. He's almost finished his Master's degree, and pretty soon he'll be a music teacher.'

'So he'll be a professor like you?' Tyler asked.

'Not quite like me. He's had enough of university now, so he hates the thought of working at one. He'll be a private music tutor, he's already got around ten clients lined up for when he starts next summer.'

'Does he have to pass the degree to do it? What if he doesn't pass?'

'He'll pass.' Tyler smiled at my confidence in him, and I smiled, too. Sometimes it was easy to forget just how remarkable Matt was. How remarkable it was that he was mine. 'That's where he is now, practice makes perfect.'

'Doesn't he have a broken hand?'

'Yes, he does. It's his wrist,' I said. 'He fell in Greece.' In my head, a flashback. Matt's pain, my pleasure. 'It's hard to stop Matt from doing the things he loves, though. Especially playing the piano. He'll do it one handed if he has to.'

Tyler asked if the university Matt went to and the one I worked at was the same one. I said it was complicated. Technically, yes, we were both at the same place, but location wise, our faculties were a mile apart.

Tyler said, 'That's cool. I'm not too good at instruments.'

'Yeah, me neither.'

'Maybe he'd teach me, what do you think?'

'I'm sure he'll be more than happy to teach you.'

'Cool! Thanks so much.'

It was only a passing comment, something you say to be polite. I did not want him in my house more than he had to be.

'Anyway, enough about us,' I said. 'So, you like football?'

'Yeah, I guess so. My mums like it too, it keeps me active or whatever.'

'If you enjoy it then keep at it. There's a football club about a five-minute drive from here, Oxford City. They have a youth team who train twice a week. You should join.'

'Thanks,' he replied. 'I'll talk to my mums about starting there. They work late a lot though, so it's probably a long shot.'

'It's only a fifteen-minute walk.'

Tyler laughed, 'Yeah. Try living with two women. They won't let me go anywhere alone, especially since we just moved here.'

I hummed, thinking and agreeing. 'Well, I guess it's good they're protective of you. And they're right, you know? It's a dangerous place out there.' The irony of my own statement was not lost on me, and the boy rolled his eyes, like I was another boring, overprotective grown-up.

It was fine, I had plenty of time to get him back in my lane.

'I'm *not* a kid,' he said, moody.

'Tell you what, if you get permission from your parents to go to football, I'll drive you there until you're used to the streets around here.'

He looked at me in disbelief, like I was full of it.

'Really?' he said eagerly. 'Twice a week?' And even the good guy in me smiled.

'Yes. Of course. Your parents work late, but I don't. I usually finish by 6pm every day and football training starts at 7pm. Plenty of time to get home and pick you up.'

The seed was planted. I could tell he didn't truly trust me, but I would damn sure prove myself. After all, it really was my pleasure. The thing about pleasure is that no one tells you it will kill you if you let it.

'Thank you,' said Tyler. 'That's really cool of you.'

'So you don't think I'm a snobby, know-it-all, up myself professor, then?' I joked, and when he laughed that time I couldn't help but ruffle his hair at the back. I was endeared, what was I supposed to do? You see a puppy, you pet it.

The front door opened, bursting my dangerous little bubble. Saved by the bell, I suppose. Matt came into the kitchen with a plastic bag full of junk for Tyler, and a bottle of gin for him and me to share.

'What's going on in here?' Matt asked.

'Burgers,' said Tyler.

'He's been helping me make dinner,' I said.

'I'm sure he has.' Matt looked at Tyler. 'Will you be joining us?'

'Uh, yeah, if it's okay. I mean, Jules said it was cool, so—'

'Oh, I bet he did,' Matt said, and then he looked at me and smirked. 'How kind of you, Jules.' His act was frustrating, it always was, but I suppose Matt felt the same way about me.

'Well, his parents aren't home. I didn't want to leave him outside in the cold.'

'Don't you have a key to your house?' Matt asked Tyler.

'Yeah, I do, but I forgot it this morning when I went to school.'

'I see. Do your mums know where you are?'

'They won't mind.'

'Matt, are you done interrogating the boy?' I asked.

'Sure,' he said, opening the bottle of tonic water from the fridge. 'Hey, Tyler, want a glass of gin, mate?'

Before Tyler could answer, I interrupted. 'Matt, I don't think that's appropriate.'

'Your definition of *appropriate* isn't appropriate.'

I shot him a look that told him to stop.

'If he wants one I say he can have one.'

'Not everyone lives by your rules.'

'They *should*. Everyone would have so much more fun.'

'I don't want to rub his parents the wrong way. I think we should ask first, that's all.'

Matt rolled his eyes, said, 'Stop being such a bore,'

then looked at Tyler, who was laughing. I suppose we looked like good-cop-bad-cop. The last thing I wanted was to come across as boring. I wanted the kid to see me as mysterious and intriguing without knowing why, wanted him to think I was *cool*, as he'd say, before revealing the real me when it's too late for him.

'Fine,' I said. 'But if we get women with pitchforks at our door tomorrow, it's on you.'

Matt poured Tyler a glass of gin and smugly gave it to him.

The three of us ate over casual conversation and Matt asked Tyler, 'So, is that your football by the front door?'

'Yeah, I accidentally kicked it into your garden and Jules got it for me.'

'You need better aim.'

'Jules said he's going to take me to football training. I'm gonna ask my mums tomorrow. I really hope they say I can go.'

I caught the look that crept onto Matt's face before he could stop it. It was just a second, but I saw it, the look of amusement, like a child trying to bite back a laugh after hearing a swear word.

'That doesn't surprise me at all,' he said. 'He *loves* helping you youngsters out, don't you, Jules?'

'I don't like seeing the future generation being held back, that's all. If I can contribute in a positive way, I'll do it.'

'You're admirable, darling.'

Tyler's phone rang, it was his mother—I didn't know which one—and he explained where he was, that he was having burgers with Matt and I and he would be home after that.

When the call ended, he said, 'Mum says to thank you both for having me.'

'Is she alright with you being here?' I asked.

'Oh, it's totally cool. She seemed a bit shocked I guess, but she met Matt the other day and she likes him. Have you met my mums yet, Jules? They're total opposites.'

'Chalk and cheese,' said Matt.

'I haven't met them yet, no. But I look forward to it. I'm sure they're wonderful.'

Once the three of us finished eating, Matt volunteered to take Tyler home before I could and it was not lost on me that it was intentional. In the five minutes I was alone in the house I cleared up the plates and wiped the counters down and poured another glass of gin, neat. I thought of how I had attempted to deter the boy and how he ended up in my house anyway. I thought of his smile, his surfer hair, how everything was *cool*, how he had no care in the world and how he put himself in danger because of it. I thought of Matt, how I could never tell what he was up to, if anything. I thought of Will, above me, beneath me, the lack of space in the car as he rode me like a bucking bronco. Perhaps I pictured Tyler there instead. Perhaps I was slipping already.

*Do not be that guy, not again,* I told myself. *He is just a kid.* Just a kid who had no business imposing on his new neighbours while his parents were at work. Just a kid who looked like Will. Just another kid to get me in trouble, another Will for Matt to murder when the time presented itself. Just another vessel for me to act on my depravities and just another reason to get the fuck out of Oxford. I knew deep down it wasn't going to end well at all, but if I had known exactly what would happen, I would have left town that night and dragged Matt with me by the hair and drove to a cottage in the middle of nowhere. It was something I often thought, buying a place only we knew about, somewhere for us to hide. A second chance. I suppose I only had myself to blame; I had the opportunity to make the right choice and start over more than once, and never seized it. Sometimes I think we want to repeat our past mistakes, and that's why we cannot stop making the decisions we know will ruin us.

When Matt got home from walking Tyler across the road like a personal childminder, he came back into the kitchen and stood there, arms folded, watching me with a grin. I finished my gin in one swallow and slammed the glass down on the counter.

'Please wipe that look off your face,' I said.

'You just couldn't help yourself, could you?'

'It's not like that. He was cold and hungry and his parents weren't home. What was I supposed to do, Matt?'

'Not offer to take him to football training, that's for sure.' Matt wasn't angry, nor was he jealous or upset. He didn't care about Tyler, he didn't care about the football training. What he cared about was making me squirm. He was playing with me again, trying to get a rise out of me, and I refused to let him win this one. I walked past him and headed upstairs, ignoring the laughter coming from the kitchen. I didn't want to think about it. Not the men whose lives Matt could end in a heartbeat, not the young boys I wanted but couldn't have, and not the new kid on the block, pretty as he was poisonous. Forget it all, especially him. Denial, denial, denial.

# Three

Falling behind on work was something I despised and yet seemed to be an expert at. Since the wedding I was off my game, so to speak, and I made a promise to myself to knuckle down and focus. I was spending too much time glancing at the house across the road in the hopes of seeing Tyler. Work served as a distraction, but I realised rather quickly that I didn't *want* a distraction at all. I wanted free reign, I wanted any excuse I could find to use my time in a wicked way; ignore my problems just to cause new ones.

I couldn't get the kid out of my damned head, Tyler and his football and his quirky smile, and when he was on my mind you bet Will was, too. They came to me as a pair, and so did the desire, hitting me twice over in an intense ripple. The brown curly hair; the frosty blue eyes, like the sea in winter. It was terrifying how alike they were, and no, I know what you're thinking, I thought it too—they weren't related. I admit it would be quite the twist, unfortunately I remembered Will's parents, Ron and Linda Smithers, and Will was their only child. It was nothing but a coincidence, a coincidence that brought all those feelings and memories from my time with Will floating to the surface.

I was in the office after a day of meetings and lectures, about to read through some assignment submissions from my students, when my phone pinged with a text message. It said, *Hey. It's me.*

Whoever it was, I didn't have their number saved in my contacts, so I replied with: *And who is 'Me'?* I stared at the screen, hoping to get an answer swiftly, but no reply came. I put my phone in my desk drawer, closed it, and opened my laptop to get on with work.

*The symbolism of Greek dramas: the role of animal personification,* by Natasha Lewis, was an excellent observation on why human beings have always relied on being connected with nature and animals to create compelling visual imagery. *The significance of competitiveness as the basis of ancient Greeks' way of life,* by Jack Cairns bored me, but was otherwise academically great—he would have top marks. *Principles and philosophies still relevant today,* by Freya Morriston took me by surprise, because Freya usually put as little effort into her assignments as possible, but that one was full of zest. My favourite of the class was, *The origin and evolution of love, sex, and up-bringing—an analysis of an ancient world,* by Kimberly Richards. I always did have a soft—or hard—spot for the slightly controversial. I liked seeing my students have the balls to write about something they were passionate about, liked knowing I wasn't alone in my fascination for the immoral.

I read through some more papers, responded to a couple emails, and my phone chirped from inside the desk drawer. Another text.

*Guess!*

I sighed, texted back: *I'm sorry but I don't have the time nor energy for games.*

The halls outside the office were dark and vacant and my desk light flickered. A chill ran down my spine as the next text came through: *Come on, just guess.*

I texted back: *Matthew?*

—*Wrong.*

—*Sister?*

—*No.*

—*Well, I give up.*

I expected a speedy reply but the sender left me hanging, again, so I got back to work, again. The history faculty was deserted, and combining that and the mysterious texts, I felt vulnerable. I wanted to get out of there all of a sudden, so I closed my laptop and locked it in my desk, got my coat, and left the office. My phone pinged in my pocket, so I took it out as I rushed from the building, breathless and trying not to allow panic to win.

The text said: *Fine. Still not gonna tell you.*

I locked the faculty's main door behind me, relieved to be out of the dark halls, but the car park wasn't all that more inviting. I'd been late that morning, so I ended up with a shitty parking space right at the far end of the car park. I typed out a text, *Fine by me*, and sent it before braving the walk to the car. Visions of being followed plagued my every step, the burning feeling that someone was watching me sent goosebumps over my skin. I got to the car safe and sound, cursed myself for being such a paranoid idiot, asked myself what it was I had to be paranoid about. I checked my phone again, an impulse now, and sure enough, another text: *Good night. Hehe.*

I didn't know what the hell was going on. I drove home and Tyler was there again, sitting on the bench, long legs swinging under him. I felt excitement spike my blood and had to close my eyes, compose myself, give myself a warning. *Do not engage with the boy, ask him what he wants and go straight inside. Not inside him, not with him, alone.* Of course, I didn't listen, I never did. What did I know? Same as you, same as everyone else: nothing. Perhaps there was nothing wrong with just talking to the boy, perhaps it would be enough to sate my appetite. I knew as soon as it crossed my mind that it was just another excuse.

'Hello there,' I said as I locked the car.

His phone was in his lap and his eyes were glued to the screen, and he didn't look up at me when he said, 'Hey, Jules.'

Some people hate that, they think it's ignorant, but, well, I'm an entirely different kettle of fish. I liked defiance. I liked it because I liked challenges, and I liked it because I liked forcing defiance's hand. I did it to Will, and I did it with Matt, over and over. Granted, Matt never surrendered quite as easily. He was my biggest opponent, and perhaps that's why we were still together, perhaps it was the challenge of surviving one another that kept our flame burning. Sometimes I thought about what would happen if our flame blew the wrong way in the wind and started another Great Fire of London. Tyler was the breeze, he was the threat of an almighty blaze, and yet I could not settle the urge inside me to move into its heat. It was maddening, how a simple *Hey, Jules* could make me want to risk it all and willingly set my own life on fire.

'How can I help you this evening?'

Tyler's gaze met mine and he smiled, sheepish little thing. He said, 'Football. Sorry,' and I rolled my eyes in a comical manner.

'You want to put that ball on a leash,' I mused.

'I know, sorry—'

'It's fine, silly. I'm only messing with you.'

'Oh, cool.'

'Tell me something,' I said. 'How many other gardens have you kicked your ball in since you moved in?'

I don't know why I asked him that, just that I did. Perhaps it was because I knew the answer.

'None. Just yours.'

I swear Tyler bit his lip. Or did he? Either way, he said it himself. Just mine. Was he doing it on purpose? It was a bizarre thought, and one that I actually dismissed despite wanting to hold on to it. I couldn't go down the road of taking a mile when he gave me an inch. I needed to be sure before I would entertain the idea. It was pointless risking my life for a boy if I wasn't going to win him.

'Cool,' I said, smirking. Tyler laughed, and if I could have caught the sound and put it in a bottle, I would have gotten drunk on it every single night. I went to get the stranded football and returned it to its rightful owner.

'Thanks,' he said, smiling. 'I, uh, I appreciate it.'

'Not a problem.' *Anything for you.*

Before he left he turned around and looked me up and down, saying, 'You look really good today, by the way.'

'Oh, uh, thank you, kiddo.'

'No worries. See ya.'

He walked away, football under his arm, but I did not yet go inside. I couldn't. I watched as he crossed the road and didn't take my eyes off him until his front door was closed, and even then I stood there, frozen, waiting for my heart to return to its normal pace. *See ya.*

I *did* look good that day. I had on my black Ralph Lauren Oxford shoes, black trousers, a striped lilac shirt Matt had bought me, and my Versace overcoat. But why would Tyler say something like that? In what world does a fourteen-year-old boy tell an older man he looks good? I stood there for a minute or so before going inside, refusing to entertain what it meant.

When Matt arrived home shortly after, I didn't say a word about it. No reason to, really. It was no big deal, none whatsoever, and it was fine, totally cool, probably nothing, maybe something, but probably nothing…

It was a struggle to quiet my thoughts. Matt gave me a bottle of red and I finished the bottle before bed, forgetting all about the unknown texter.

The next morning I woke to three texts from the same unknown number. The first said, simply: *Hi.* The second: *Good morning!* The third: *It's me again.* Matt was asleep next to me so I didn't wake him, there was no need for him to get up on his day off. He only had a couple weeks left of university, and he'd already written his thesis and produced a spectacular piece of music to go with it. I slipped out of bed, padded quietly out of the room, and headed downstairs for my morning coffee.

I sent a text back to the annoying stranger: *If you don't tell me who this is I'll have to block your number.*
—*You're no fun!*
—*You're starting to piss me off.*
—*That's cool. Still not telling.*
I decided to leave it at that, so I put my phone down on the coffee table and returned my half-empty cup to the kitchen. I put the milk back in the fridge and that's when I noticed both Matt and I's phone numbers were on the door. I forgot Matt liked to keep things on it: our address; notes on baking; photographs of us together; more photos of us with the guys, and one of Josh's dog, Aphrodite; the Wi-Fi password; our schedules; piano chords on a post-it-note; a shopping list that changed every week; upcoming events; our phone numbers. It was organised chaos, just like his brilliant mind. Whoever it was that was texting me must have been in the house and taken my number from the fridge. But who? I ran into the lounge to get my phone, and brought the messages up, and it immediately smacked me in the face. *That's cool.*

*Still not telling.*

Cool. Fucking *cool*. I showered and dressed for work, and kissed a sleeping Matt on the forehead before I left. I didn't go to the car immediately, instead I walked across the road, towards the sound of a football being kicked. I stood outside Tyler's garden, watching him, waiting for him to turn around, notice me. He was in his uniform, all ready for school plus time to kick his football about and text my phone like a total creep. The ball rolled towards the road, towards me, and he saw me. He froze, let the ball come to a stop at my feet, and I smiled, said, 'Good morning.'

'Hi, Sir.' Tyler chewed his lip, looked at anything but me. He was the polar opposite of the boy I had seen the night before, as if he was a different person altogether. I thought I was losing my mind, but you can't lose something you have already lost.

'You can call me Jules, remember?' I said, and the boy nodded enthusiastically.

'Yeah, sorry.'

'It's fine. I just don't want you thinking I'm a snobby know it all professor.' The boy smiled at that, as was my intention.

'Up yourself,' he grinned.

'Listen, I've got something I need to talk to you about.'

It was going to go one of two ways: I could act upset with him, tell him off for playing childish games and hopefully deter him from contacting me ever again, via phone or in person; or I could play along, not make a big deal out of it, show him I had the upper hand by adding him to my contact list. *Thanks for giving me your phone number so easily.* I usually had to work much harder than that. It was the decision of a lifetime, the crossroads that won't let you turn back once you choose, no matter the cost.

Tyler was anxiously awaiting my next sentence, probably expecting the former option of ridicule and anger, but that's because he didn't know me. He had no idea.

I said, 'I checked the football training timetable. If you're still interested, and it's alright with your parents, I'll pick you up on Monday.'

Relief washed over his face as he sighed. 'Yeah, yes please.'

'I'll see you on Monday, then,' and I kicked his ball gently back to him as I turned to walk away.

'Wait, Jules.'

'Yes?'

'What time should I be ready? What should I bring?'

'I'll text you,' I said.

His face was priceless.

'Shit. Sorry.'

He was obviously embarrassed, and I *obviously* wanted to make him feel better.

'It's fine, don't worry about it,' I said.

He had to have the last word, typical of all kids his age. Setting their own boundaries while ignoring everyone else's. And it was really just one word, his favourite, it seemed.

'Cool.'

I went to work, and when I got there, I saved him in my contacts as *Ty*. I sent him a text: *Guess who*, and locked my phone in my drawer. It was the last day of my classes before the weekend, so I tried to push the audacious boy from my mind. The more I told myself to forget him the worse it got, and after my last lecture I turned my phone off without checking for any messages and drove to the closest Tesco to buy two more bottles of wine.

Knock, knock, knock on a Saturday morning. My skull felt like it had been cracked in half with a machete while I slept. The wine the night before had ended with Matt dragging me to bed, and, regrettably, I had a hangover from hell when I needed to be at the Keysmith's later on to watch Matt play. He groaned into my chest when I moved out of bed to answer the door. *Don't go, ignore it.* He was sleeping again by the time the second knock came, so I checked the time—10am—and headed downstairs. I stumbled over Matt's boots which were left right at the bottom step, cursed him under my breath, removed a newspaper from the letterbox, and opened the door. It was a woman, blonde, friendly looking, holding a foil covered oven dish. I was suddenly very aware of my morning hair, having not been brushed it must have looked like a bird's nest. The woman smiled. I was very confused.

'Oh, good morning. I'm sorry if I woke you, am I imposing?' she seemed apologetic and startled, which only confirmed my concern over the state of my hair.

41

'Not at all,' I replied, trying to hold back the nausea. 'My husband and I needed to get up anyway.' It was a polite lie, to this stranger at my door with an oven dish. 'How can I help you?'

'Sorry about that. I'm Melissa. I just moved in across the road, I met your husband last week? My wife and I wanted to thank you for taking care of Tyler the other night. Both of us are nurses, and we usually work late, so we really appreciate it. Ty said that you made burgers? He loved them, and it saved me from cooking late. Anyway, I won't keep you long, it's starting to get colder, isn't it? I made this for you as a thank you. It's vegetable lasagne; Ty said that Matt's a vegetarian?'

I was expected to answer, but which part? It was too early for so many questions. I didn't know if I was supposed to offer her inside for a cup of tea or be terrified of her presence.

'Oh, thank you so much. There was no need to do that. But thank you, I'm sure it will go down a treat.' I accepted the lasagne from her with a smile. 'Would you like to come in?'

'Oh, no, thank you. I just came over to thank you and Matt, I won't keep you.'

'Well, Tyler wasn't a problem at all, don't worry. Anytime he needs anything from us he's welcome. You and your wife, too.'

Why did I say that?

There's this thing about being a Brit—we are often too friendly for our own good. We are taught to be polite, and to love thy neighbour. We all want easy lives, we all just want to get along and have a sense of belonging. The thing is, no one tells you what to do if you don't want to be bothered by anyone. If I had told Melissa to go home, keep Tyler away from me, to stop trying to make friends with a man who has a hair trigger when it comes to her son's age group, I'd have been the bad guy. It's funny when you think about it—damned if you do, screwed if you don't.

Melissa thanked me again, and before I could shut the door she said, 'Oh, um, one last thing before I let you go, Julian, sorry.' I nodded, holding the door open. 'Tyler mentioned you offered to take him to football training, is that right?'

'Yes, that's right. If I overstepped, I apologise.'

I thought for sure that was it, the reason she came over. To tell me off for taking it upon myself to say such a thing without consulting her first.

Melissa said, 'No, not at all. I wanted to thank you for that, too. Because Lara and I work silly schedules, sometimes Ty misses out on things like that. Not that I wouldn't let him go on his own, but he doesn't know the streets here yet, and I just worry myself to death.'

'I understand completely. As long as you're okay with it I'm happy to help. At least until you and your wife are comfortable with Tyler being out and about by himself.'

'You're a lifesaver, darling.'

'It's lovely to meet you, put a face to the name.'

'You, too. Thanks again for looking after him.'

I shut the door and saw my life spiralling out of control, second by second. I put the dish in the fridge and on the way back to the stairs I caught a glimpse of the main headline on the newspaper I'd tossed aside when Melissa knocked.

CHILD, 8, KILLED AFTER BEING STRUCK BY CAR IN LONDON HIT-AND-RUN

I thought of the parents of that child, the grief they must be experiencing. I thought of Annabella at that age, how it would have devastated my sister beyond repair if that happened to her only child. I felt hate for the person behind the wheel of the car responsible for damaging a child beyond repair, and I projected that hate onto myself. Was that not exactly what I did with Will? Damaged and confused him into looking for answers years after I buried our moments together. Was it not the same twisted pattern I could see myself following with my newest, youngest neighbour, whose mother baked a vegetable lasagne to *thank* us for taking care of her son, the replica of Will, the boy I damaged, the boy I met at my first job in a school, the boy I unwittingly drove into Matt's Stanley blade. Suddenly I found myself sympathising with the driver of that car, carrying a secret that heavy on their aching shoulders. I knew it all too well, and the familiarity was unbearable. I turned the newspaper over. Back upstairs I snuggled into a sleeping Matthew, wilfully ignorant to the horrors of the world beneath me, around me, inside me.

On the way to the Keysmith's that night we picked Jimmy up, who text me earlier in the day asking to tag along. Despite how much he got on my nerves, it was good to have a friend there. I was not expected to socialise with Matt's boss if I had my own company.

Matt was driving, using mostly one hand, so I could have a couple of glasses of wine, and when Jimmy got in the car he banged his head against the door frame. He was clearly drunk. Matt called him a lanky bitch, which made me chuckle as I put the seat back and resumed my place as passenger in the car, but Jimmy didn't find it funny. He was cradling his head in his hands as if he'd almost been decapitated, saying, 'I *hate* these fucking two-door cars.'

'Technically, it's three doors,' Matt said. 'Driver side, passenger side, and the boot. But I guess the windows could be doors too, if you tried hard enough.'

'*What?*' Jimmy said, still rubbing his head. '*Why* do you always say such weird, cryptic things?'

'If you want a different vehicle to take you there, then get out,' Matt said. 'Drive yourself there.'

'Well I *can't*. I sold my car.'

'Why on earth would you sell your Porsche?' I asked, convinced he was joking around. Jimmy loved that car.

'I needed a *change*.'

'Why?'

'Get off my back, Ju-Ju. There doesn't have to be a *reason* for everything.' The three of us sat in silence for a beat. Matt struggled to change gear with his left hand and Jimmy noticed the brace. 'What on *earth* have you done to your hand?'

Matt and I exchanged a brief glance, one of mutual understanding—He would tell Jimmy the lie to save me from the consequences of truth.

'It's my wrist. It's fucked.'

'How are you *working*?'

'I'll manage.'

'What happened?'

'Fell over, didn't I. Drunk as a teabag.'

'*What?*' Jimmy said, while Matt laughed and offered no explanation. Instead, he brought it back to Jimmy.

'Did you crash your car into the river on a coke binge? Is that why you sold it?'

I thought it was funny, but Jimmy didn't respond. He remained unusually silent for the remainder of the drive, his face glued to his phone.

There was a bottle of champagne in a bucket of ice at the table that Luca, Matt's boss, kept reserved for me every Saturday. It was in the perfect place, right by the window and in direct view of the piano, but I didn't get my preferred seat because Jimmy slumped into it before I could. I rearranged the other chair, and by the time I did this, Jimmy broke into the champagne. Matt was behind the bar talking with Luca before the show, probably about his injury. A total accident.

'What's going on with you?' I asked Jimmy.

'Nothing.'

'Are you doing anything for your birthday on Saturday?'

'I *forgot* it was my birthday.'

'*You* forgot about your birthday?' I asked, genuinely surprised.

'Ju-Ju, I don't want to talk about me.'

'What? Since when?'

'Since *now*. Christ.'

'Has someone died?'

'Fuck *no*, Jesus, Ju-Ju. Nobody died. No one *died*, and I didn't *crash* my car. I'm just not feeling like myself, and I bought a new car to try and cheer myself up.' Jimmy downed his glass of champagne and poured himself another, avoiding eye contact with me, glancing nervously around the bar.

'So, about your birthday,' I said, deciding to leave him alone for the time being.

'Yeah. Let's have a party.'

Matt walked from the bar to the piano, through the tables full of people whistling and cheering him on, and when he sat at the piano, the bustling bar suddenly went quiet, like the volume had been manually cranked all the way down. Everyone had their attention locked on Matt, eagerly awaiting the moment he set his fingers on the keys. The one-handed pianist. A sharp spike of guilt hit the middle of my heart, and I wondered if there was anything I could have done to prevent his pain. The answer, of course, was yes, I could have, but then I wouldn't have witnessed true beauty, or tasted the salt of his genuine tears.

Matt looked so different, tall even though he was sitting, his posture far more professional than it had been when we met, his natural hair darker, brightened with silvery blonde highlights. He looked so different and yet entirely the same. Sixteen, twenty-two, still the love of my darkened life. Still the same debauchery ridden little creature with that same deviant Cheshire smile. And I was still, if nothing else, totally captivated by him. My desire was salivating that night. Starved, primal, and in need of sating. I suppose it always was. I was starting to realise it always would be no matter how hard I tried to fight it. I tried to convince myself that the desire I felt was because of Matt, but Tyler's face wouldn't leave me be. My phone vibrated in my pocket, and it was a text from none other than *Ty*. It said, *Hey! Did you eat what Mum made for you and Matt?*

I fought with the urge to text him back. It should have been black and white, yes or no, do it or don't. He texted me first, so it would be rude to leave him hanging, and yet the notion of answering him somehow felt worse. I had a husband in front of me, an ex by the side of me, and I still couldn't get my eyes off the brand-new prize. Perhaps it was the alcohol, because it certainly wasn't me: I slid my phone back in my pocket without replying.

I realised I zoned Jimmy out completely after seeing the text from Tyler, and when my attention settled back into the conversation he was saying, 'Is that it, Ju-Ju? Have I missed anyone?'

'Missed anyone?'

'For my *party* on Saturday. Have I forgotten anyone?'

'No, not at all. You got them all. I'm impressed.'

'Can I stay with you tonight?' Jimmy asked, sighing, like our conversation was exhausting. Of course he could stay with Matt and me. I ordered us another bottle of champagne, and thought about Tyler's text, sitting there on my phone with no response.

The soft sounds of the piano began to fill the room, and I looked at Matt, allowing myself to be enthralled with his every press of the keys. I was fascinated by him more so in these moments. When he was connected to something, when he belonged somewhere. When he was human.

'I did something horrible.'

Jimmy's words came out of nowhere.

'What do you mean?' I said, keeping my voice low. 'We've all done horrible things, James.'

'Not like this.' Before I could say anything else he stood up. 'Excuse me,' he said, his skin looked pale and clammy as he turned to run to the restroom, supposedly to vomit. He spent the remainder of Matt's set in the restroom or pacing back and forth the window outside, smoking cigarette after cigarette, trying to hide the fact he was crying.

That night, Jimmy opted for the spare bedroom over his usual choice of the sofa, and though I suspected it was because he would be closer to us, I didn't raise the question. It was easier not to. He would tell me what plagued him in his own time. He was, after all, the most dramatic person I had ever known, and I even bet myself it was nothing worse than an affair, a fling with a married man that went south when Jimmy caught feelings.

Before we went upstairs to bed, the three of us ate Melissa's lasagne at midnight, no plates, just three forks and alcohol induced hunger. It was damn delicious, so when Matt fell asleep I got my phone from the bedside table. I brought up the text conversation between Tyler and I, and I could no longer resist. I was tired, the fight was gone, and the extra bottle of champagne had loosened me up. It was only a text. I said, *Hey there. Sorry I'm only now replying, busy night. Your mum's lasagne was very tasty, she's a terrific cook. I hope you're okay.*

Tyler replied within thirty seconds. He was probably on his phone as the text came through, up late Snapchatting and WhatsApping his friends, talking about the latest FIFA game, or perhaps they were talking about school, silly little crushes and the latest teen drama. He said, *That's cool. I'm good thanks. I helped Mum make the lasagne, haha.*

I smiled to myself and made sure Matt was still asleep before I typed the next text.

—*Well no wonder it tasted so good. You're a chef in the making.*

—*I'm so not. But it's cool, haha.*

—*Practice makes perfect.*

—*Will you teach me how to make those burgers?*

—*Of course I will.*

—*Awesome!*

—*It's late, get some sleep, alright?*

—*Yeah, okay. Night Jules.*

—*Goodnight, you.*

In the morning I woke to the smell of pancakes. I could hear Jimmy talking, and remembered he stayed the night, so I walked into the kitchen wearily like I'd been invaded by aliens. I glanced at him and he had a wine glass in his hand, and inside was a dark grape colour liquid which he was gulping down like it was apple juice. Matt was making the pancakes, so I ran my fingers through his hair and turned my attention to Jimmy the Wine Thief.

'Is that my Caro?' I asked, praying it wasn't, knowing it was.

'*Yes*?' Jimmy said. 'Sorry, drowning my sorrows and that.'

'At ten in the morning?'

'*Yes.*'

'Care to elaborate on what those sorrows are?'

'It doesn't matter, nor does it concern *you.*'

'Correct me if I'm wrong, but you're drinking *my* wine. I'd say it most definitely *is* my concern.'

'*Christ.* Why are you *so* uptight over a bottle of wine? I can buy it back, Ju. *Chillax.*'

I looked at Matt, who stacked another pancake on the counter and said, 'Don't blame me.'

'I'm going to feed the fish,' I said, throwing my robe around me as I opened the back door. 'Call me when breakfast is ready?'

'Won't be long,' Matt said.

Jimmy added, 'Ju-Ju, I'll buy you another bottle for Christ sake.'

Outside, the pond water was so still I thought it had frozen over, until the fish recognised a presence and all swarmed to the surface with their mouths agape. Golds and oranges and whites swam around each other, blindly sucking at the surface, desperate for food. I tossed a handful of pellets into the water and watched them for a minute or so, as they all tried to be the quickest to catch the food, like hungry hippos. It was oddly peaceful, far more relaxing than the house, than my kitchen currently occupied with Brat 1 and Brat 2.

Something suddenly landed in the pond, splashing water everywhere and shocking the goldfish into retreating. My robe was soaked, my fish were in shock, Jimmy had selfishly opened one of my most prized bottles of wine which had been a gift from my father for the wedding, and there was a new kid in town whose football seemed to be attracted to my garden only. In fact, I had already established that as the case a couple days previously. I asked Tyler if his ball had landed in anyone else's garden, and he said no, no it hadn't. *Just yours.* I would have liked it if it was any other day, but my mood that morning was having none of it. My initial reaction was to put a knife through the ball, the urge bubbling away but kept at bay by my desire to be seen as the kind neighbour, to keep myself out of trouble. I picked the ball out of the pond, tucked it under my already damp arm, and headed for the back gate where I knew Tyler would be. I slid the lock open. The gate creaked as it swung open outwards, and I was miffed so I didn't bother trying to slow it down. It nearly knocked Tyler off of his feet, and I immediately felt like the worst person alive. I was happy he was there. I wondered if that was a good or bad thing, wondered if I even knew what those words meant anymore.

'Fuck, you scared me,' Tyler said. I blinked in surprise at the swear word, so filthy coming from someone so angelic looking. I sort of loved it. I sort of wanted him to say it again, and again, and never stop. The more secrets of his I kept, the more likely he was to keep mine.

'Sorry, kiddo,' I said. 'The gate's a little, uh, temperamental,' as was I. 'Do your parents know you use that language?'

'Please don't tell them.'

'Your secret is safe with me.'

'Cool, thanks. Sorry.'

'It's fine, I'm not going to say anything.'

'I'm super sorry about the ball again,' he said, and I realised I still had it. I tossed it to him and he caught it with small but fast hands. 'Did I break anything?'

'No. My fish had a fright, but they'll be just fine.'

'Shit, I'm sorry.'

'It's fine, Tyler.'

'Are you sure?'

The more he apologised the more it rattled my cage, and the more my cage rattled the more apologetic he became.

'Look, I don't have the time for this today. I have to go back inside now,' I said. 'Matt's cooking breakfast.'

'What's he making?'

'Pancakes.'

'Cool. Pancakes are my favourite.' Of course they bloody were. Like the Jaguar was his favourite car and my back garden was his favourite goal post.

I said, 'I'd invite you in, but we have a guest.' I was aware of how short I was being with him, but I refused to play the game with myself that morning. 'I'll see you tomorrow.'

Tyler looked really hurt, like a child on the other end of a scolding. I wanted to give him a hug, tell him the truth—I'm afraid of hurting you. I *will* hurt you, and I *will* enjoy it every step of the way.

'I am sorry,' he said. 'For scaring the fish. Are you upset with me? Are you going to tell my mums?'

I sighed, immediately feeling guilty. I was blaming him for my mood that morning but in truth, it was a mix of the hangover blues, mourning over my wine, being frustratingly aroused, and the unexpected encounter with him and that tormenting football.

'No, Tyler. I'm sorry for being blunt. Our friend stayed the night, I'm hungover, and I'm having a tantrum because he's currently drinking the wine my dad bought me as a wedding gift. Forgive me, won't you?' The word *tantrum* had the desired effect on Tyler, who chuckled and ducked his head in embarrassment for overthinking the situation. I smiled at him, couldn't help myself, and ruffled his hair again, as I had done in the kitchen the first time I met him, and as I had done with Matt not fifteen minutes before. As I would do to Tyler again and again. These were the touches that weren't quite touches. A quiver, a waver that was important not to ruin by taking my hand away too soon. I was holding my ground. Eye contact, short breaths, and then it was over before it happened.

'Go on, then. Best get home,' I said. 'I'll pick you up on Monday at 6.30pm, alright?'

'Will you still text me?'

'I did last night, did I not?' and his smile was so full of joy it was dizzying. I gave him an inch, wishing he would take ten miles.

Matt questioned why I'd been so long outside, and I considered telling him about Tyler and his football antics but decided against it. To bring him up would have been suicide, not to mention Jimmy was there too, drunk but present, nonetheless. I knew how it would go:

I'd say, 'Tyler and his ball again.'

Matt would say, 'I wish he'd kick it over his own garden.'

I'd say, 'He's aiming for us, every time.'

Matt would say, 'Not every young and beautiful boy is obsessed with you.'

I'd say, 'Perhaps not. But I'm obsessed with them.' So I didn't say anything at all.

# Four

Monday. Back to work and most importantly, football training day for Tyler. That morning I didn't say a word to Matt about my plans—he would make it a bigger deal than it needed to be, probably demand I call it off and disappoint the poor boy, which I would refuse to do, and arguing was not how I wanted to spend the morning together. I always left the house earlier than he did so I could get to work before lectures started, so I kissed him goodbye and drove to work, trying not to look at Tyler's house as I went past, miserably failing. I saw him there, playing football in his uniform, a gold logo on the front of his blazer. Immediately I knew what school he went to. Immediately I made myself forget about it. Tyler wasn't paying attention to anything but the ball, so I drove off without disturbing his morning. I would have plenty of time with him that night.

The topic of discussion in class that day was Hedonism. I liked the discussions best, getting them all involved on a topic. I found the students learned more that way. Not everything we learn has to be textbook, that's just half of the battle. You can read and absorb as much information as you damn well please, but you won't ever get the full picture if you don't consider the possibility of it being complete gibberish. History written is different than the history lived. The record of the past can have a great deal of significance, but the events themselves have significance only if you approach them from a philosophical standpoint and ask the right questions. I asked my students to tell me what they understood about the word *Hedonist*, and they threw various answers at me.

—*Well, it means pleasure, right?*

—*Not really. It's about avoiding pain. I think that's the main focus.*

—*It's about what's good for us.*

—*No it's not you idiot. It's about doing something that makes you feel good, even if it's not.*

—*But that's confusing. What about people who experience pleasure from pain?*

—*Exactly, it's a bullshit philosophy. It contradicts itself all the time.*

—*It's a paradox.*

—*Yeah but it's not a bad one, right? Even if the ethics contradict themselves, it's not wrong to do what makes you happy and feels good.*

—*Unless it hurts someone else.*

—*It's just another word for selfishness. It's ridiculous.*

—*You think being selfish is ridiculous?*

—*You don't?*

—*I think being selfish is the only way through living. One life is all we get.*

—*Oh, so you're gonna use 'YOLO' as an excuse to be a dick?*

—*No, I'm just saying that we only have one person truly looking out for us, and that's ourselves.*

—*Now* that's *a bullshit philosophy.*

I listened to them debating, and when they were done I cleared my throat. I said, 'All of you have great points, and I want to weigh in on something you said, Abby. That it's about doing things that make us feel good even when those things are often not good at all. That's an excellent way to put it. And Kyle, you said something interesting too—I believe your words were *bullshit philosophy*?' The room filled with laughter, I waited for them to stop before continuing with the lecture. I said how Candice's point about it being a paradox was also correct, because the philosophy did not take into account that human beings were impulsive, along with other things. We make decisions because in the moment it seems good for us, it's what we want, but someday those things can amount to a torrent of pain. So in the end we haven't maximised pleasure at all. All we've done is set ourselves up. Sometimes, the things we take pleasure from are not always what's best for us or others, and thus, hedonism is a bullshit philosophy. Still, it's good to have something to put the blame on.

I asked the class what they knew of its origin.

—*It's Greek. It comes from, um… what's the name…*

—*Hedone, the goddess.*

—*Yeah, the goddess of pleasure.*

—*Yeah but you're saying it well wrong. It's like He-Din.*

—*No, it's not. You say it like Jasper just said. She's a goddess, her name is Hedone, said like He-Doh-Nay.*

—*Whatever her name is, I can say it how I like. That's the freedom of speech right there.*

— *What?*

—*I can pronounce it how I want.*

—*Why can't you just admit you're wrong and get over yourself?*

—*Guys, we're veering way off topic.*

—*I have a legit question. How much sex do you think she had? Being a pleasure god and all.*

—*Why don't you ask your father? He's banged everyone else.*

—*You guys know she wasn't real, right? She's the personification of pleasure.*

—*You mean to tell me that Gods aren't real? Ludicrous!*

—*Real or not, Toby's dad totally banged her.*

I said, 'Alright, that's enough. The topic of conversation is hedonism itself, not whether Kyle can pronounce it properly, or if Toby's father participates in said topic or not.'

'Thanks, Prof,' Toby said, smug. They were bored by then and antsy to finish, their minds elsewhere, talking amongst themselves about who was going where for lunch, so I let them go early. I spent my lunch trying to get hold of Ashley, but she kept declining my calls and dodging my texts, until I eventually gave up and got ready for my next class.

My last lecture finished at 6.30pm so I had only 30 minutes to pick Tyler up and get him to the football club. I called Matt on the way—no better time to tell him I'd be home later than usual. He asked why, so I was honest. *I'm taking Tyler to football training, remember?*

'That's not a good idea,' he said on the other end of the phone. I couldn't tell if it was a threat or a fact. I didn't stay on the phone long enough to work it out.

When I arrived in the street there was no time for me to shower beforehand, so I parked the car right outside Tyler's house, saving him the fifty-yard walk. The car door clicked open and Tyler and his bag slid into the passenger seat. I almost made the joke, *What have you got in that bag? Are we going on holiday?* but I stopped myself. Or maybe it was him who stopped me, his excited expression and those ridiculously inviting black shorts. He was wearing a smoke-grey hoodie, Nike Air trainers, and he'd recently had his hair cut, the waves shorter, trimmed at the back and the neck, though I didn't mention I noticed. Nor did I mention how seeing the bare skin on his neck where hair once fell forced me into imagining my tongue there, my lips and teeth.

Tyler said, 'Hey! I didn't think you'd actually come,' as he clipped the seatbelt into place.

'What do you mean?' I said, pulling off and heading for the football club.

The boy shrugged. 'Don't know.'

'Of course I came.'

'Thanks.'

'How was school?'

'It was fine. Made a couple friends, so that's cool I guess.'

'Good, I'm glad of that.'

'How was work?'

'Work was great, thanks for asking,' I replied. 'Good group discussions. My students were actually engaged and learning, which is all I ask.'

It was only a short drive so Tyler and I were there before I knew it, ten minutes early.

I said, 'I'll be back here in an hour, okay? Enjoy yourself.' He looked scared all of a sudden, and he grabbed my arm.

'You're not going to stay here?'

'I can if you want me to. Just thought you might like to do your own thing, without annoying adults poking about.'

'You're not annoying,' he said. 'I wanted you to come watch me.'

'You want me to watch you?'

'Not in like, a creepy way—'

'Oh, of course not,' I said sarcastically, to turn the sudden awkwardness into something funny. He found me amusing. His amusement I found arousing. I instantly wanted to do something to silence that ridiculous giggle.

'So you'll come with me?' he said.

My head was spinning. I couldn't tell him no but I couldn't say yes either, so I just nodded, yes, I'll come with you. Yes, I'll come watch you and the rest of the youth team running and sweating and slippery with mud.

Yes, Matt was right—it wasn't my greatest idea.

Fortunately, Tyler wasn't the only new starter. Once we found the coach, he introduced Tyler to three other boys who were in the same position as him, and his anxiety eased a little.

'I'll go sit by the spectator benches,' I told him. 'Have fun, alright?'

I walked to the benches in a daze, took a seat that wasn't covered by the roof, and prayed it wouldn't rain on me.

I was watching, waiting. I was frustrated at how easily I was taken in, turned on, how I shamelessly devoured the juvenile charm. The gluttonous and charming moods of boys to men, the constant pushing of limits, always trying to prove something. Sometimes I found it exhilarating, sometimes I found it sickening. Sometimes the line between both of those things was blurred. It drove me up the wall either way. I shouldn't have wanted it, but it was a compelling view, shorts and taut thighs and the tender skin of youth. Muddy, free-flowing flesh. The distant odour of sweat and testosterone. Voices that had not yet fully broken. Their oblivion was their best attribute. There were twenty or so boys parading around in front of me and still my eyes tracked Tyler's every move.

Matt gave me grief when I got home that night, asking questions I wished he wouldn't. *How is the kid? How was training? Is he going to keep it up, maybe learn how to aim? He's sweet, don't you think? Did you enjoy yourself? Is this going to be an ongoing thing? Behave yourself, won't you?*

On Thursday it went the same. I said I'd stay in the car but Tyler insisted on me being there, so there I was, watching, imagining. Not to be ironic but I was like a kid in a candy shop. After that training session we sat in the car for a while.

'So what are you thinking?' I asked, referring to the training. 'Are you going to stick at it?'

'Yeah, I'm loving it. Thank you, Julian—'

'Stop thanking me, it's fine. Anything for you.' I wished I could take it back as soon as it was out. But Tyler didn't seem to notice, or if he did, he didn't see the strangeness of it, how inappropriate. But why would he? He was fourteen. I was the one overthinking my every move and word. Perhaps there was a part of me that wanted him to overthink, too. *Did he mean it that way? Is it true?*

Tyler said, 'I like that you watch me,' and my breath caught. I told myself not to react. *Stay cool, Jules.*

'Yes, it seems you like having a spectator.'

'Do you mind that I like it?'

'No, not at all. Why would I?'

'Dunno. Just in case you find it weird, or something.'

'Do you think it's weird?'

'Nah. It's cool.'

'Cool,' I said. 'I like watching you, too. Now, put your seatbelt on, please.' I started the car, and Tyler said, 'Yes sir, anything for you,' and I thought, *oh good god no*, like I was already sorry for the things I would do to him. I knew at that moment it was just a waiting game, and I always won. When I wanted to, I could conjure up the patience of a saint. Not much more was said as I drove us home, the radio humming quietly, replacing the silence. Out of the blue Tyler said, 'I wish you could take me everywhere.'

My ears ran hot. God, they truly are so sweet when they believe they can think for themselves. I was free-falling and powerless and I sighed nervously. I should have said, *Don't be so silly.* I should have asked why he would say such a thing, reassured him twice a week was more than enough. I probably should have told him we shouldn't talk that way around each other, *I wish,* and *take me everywhere,* and *come watch me.* But I didn't say or do any of that. I gave in to the inner hedonist in me, the contradictory pleasure seeker, knowing it could come back to ruin me in the future, going ahead with it regardless. I put my hand on his bare, muddy thigh, and gave it a squeeze. *I wish you could take me everywhere.*

'I do, too,' I said.

I completely forgot about Jimmy's birthday bash until Matt woke me up and urged me to please get out of bed, make us bagels for breakfast, listen to this piece of music he wrote last night, and pick which shirt he should wear to Jimmy's. I chose the navy one, and he set it aside to iron later on.

I sat beside him at the piano, both of us in our dressing gowns and nothing else. I was hanging off the stool and eating my bagel as I listened and tried not to fall off the edge, feeding him bits of the bagel as he played. We were going to be late to Jimmy's, forgetting time, focusing instead on not falling off the stool when he climbed on top of me, taking full advantage of the easy access our dressing gowns gave us. It was all clumsiness and laughter, his back hitting the piano keys, our melody, me balancing as he rode me, my hands on his lower back to keep him there, against me, on me, around me. I whispered sweet nothings in his ear until they became bitter truths. *I'm sorry for what I did to you, I'm nothing without you,* and Matt whispered back, *I know, I know.*

It was late afternoon when we arrived at Jimmy's bearing balloons and gifts. At first glance it seemed nobody was in—like it had been unoccupied for weeks. All of the curtains were shut, blinds closed. The house smelled like an ashtray. It was dark in every room apart from the lounge, where Jimmy was strewn across his sofa, passed out with a leaking bottle of whiskey staining the stark white fabric beneath him. It looked like the cat had pissed on it. There were two empty litre bottles of vodka on the glass table, an empty tumbler cup *next* to a coaster. A credit card, white powder, a curled up twenty-pound note.

'Is he dead?' Matt asked.

'Probably.'

'Now it's a party.'

'James, wake up.' The unconscious man didn't flinch, so I put the bottle of whiskey on the table, then shook him. 'Wake the fuck up, James.' Jimmy grumbled, groggy as a cranky child. *Fuck off* he said, lashing out at me with kicking legs, which Matt found hysterical. Then Jimmy passed out again.

'He pissed himself,' Matt said.

'It's spilled booze.'

'You sure?' Matt poked him in the stomach, then his leg, then he grabbed his arm and let it drop. 'That's amazing, he's out.'

'Behave,' I said.

'Can I slap him?'

'If he's not awake in five minutes, you can slap him.'

'Give him a line of coke.'

'We don't know if it's coke, Matt—' but before I could finish my sentence, Matt dipped his finger in the powder on the table and tasted it.

'Yeah,' he confirmed. 'Definitely coke.'

When Jimmy came around enough to realise who Matt and I were, he reached straight for the bottle of whiskey I'd put on the table, like it was a comfort blanket. I snatched it back off him, put it on the table again. Matt said he'd be back with a glass of water and went to the kitchen.

'What the fuck has gotten into you?' I asked.

Jimmy said, 'A whole lotta men. Drugs. *Booze*. Couple STDs. Want me to carry on?'

'Comical. What's wrong?'

'*Nothing*. Just leave me alone, Ju-Ju.'

'It's your birthday—'

'What's your point?'

'You have about four hours until everyone turns up. Pull yourself together for crying out loud.'

'I was going to cancel.'

'Well you didn't, did you?'

'I started drinking and just… didn't stop.'

'Why?'

Jimmy scoffed as he rubbed his eyes, then opened his arms out as if to say, *why do you think?*

He said, '*Look* at me.'

'Tell me what's wrong. You've been like this since last weekend, at least.' Jimmy's eyes filled with tears, threatening to spill out just like his secrets.

'If I told you,' he said, deciding to end his sentence halfway. Then it was too late. Matt came back with a pint of water, straw and all, which reminded me of the time I'd picked him up, drunk and clumsy and sixteen on my sofa as I fed him a straw. *Suck, please.* By the smirk on his face, I knew Matt remembered it too.

Back when I thought the worst thing he had done was sleep with a married man and threaten to tell his wife if he didn't let him leave. Back when Matt thought the worst thing I had ever done was hand him my email at fifteen. Before the dark truth, the bodies, the transgressions. Way before we realised we didn't need to hide from each other. I didn't know if that was better or worse, sick or healthy, but I suppose that's why our vows made sense. A lot of people who get married these days don't know what they're getting themselves into. They vow to love the person they have made themselves believe exists in you, not the real you. They promise to be there in sickness and in health, but flee at the first sign of hardship. Matt and I didn't flee, we never did. We both came for the innocence and stayed for the corruption.

Jimmy refused to cancel the party, despite my warnings that he was in no fit state to continue drinking and acting like everything was fine. It was like talking to a wall. Just before the guests were due to arrive, Jimmy decided to spring on me that he had invited my sister. *Sorry, Ju-Ju. I kinda forgot to tell you in all this drowning my sorrows business.* Yeah, I thought, you kinda did.

I couldn't believe it. There was no way Ashley would show up, she knew Matt and I would be there, and how could she come to my ex's birthday when she hadn't even shown up for me at my wedding? Either way, I asked Matt to be on his best behaviour. If she did come, I told him to stay away from her. Don't antagonise her. Please listen to me.

Matt smirked, said, 'Like you listened to me when I asked you not to get involved with the kid across the road?'

Fair enough.

'It's just football training, Matt.'

'Until it's *just* something else,' he said. He was right, just this and just that and just something else. Regardless, I refused to go down that road, not there in Jimmy's house. I forced the drunken idiot into the shower while Matt made jugs full of sangria and scrubbed the whiskey stains out of the sofa. He was good at that, excellent in fact. If you needed to get rid of evidence while drinking the best sangria you ever tasted, Matt was your man.

Abraham and Josh arrived together first, followed by

Harris, who was closely followed by two of Jimmy's younger friends from work. I had no idea of their names, and didn't care to learn them—I was thinking of other, more important issues. Jimmy's mental state, Ashley's arrival, her and Matt's rivalry, what I was going to do to stop them from clashing, Tyler—Tyler's smooth and clean chin, cheeks barely fuzzed, his too-snug shorts that bunched up at the crotch whenever he crouched down to pick up his football.

Ashley came late, full of apologies and kisses for Jimmy and not so much as an acknowledgement for me. *Happy Birthday, darling. I'm so sorry I'm late—traffic, you know. Will you forgive me?*

I said, 'Hey, sis,' giving her a hug she couldn't refuse. I didn't hear anyone coming up to us, just heard Matt suddenly next to me, as tipsy as a paddleboat in a storm.

He said, 'Hey, sis! Nice of you to show up.' A dig about the wedding, or being over an hour late, or both. I knew he was grinning without looking at him, I could hear the arrogance bellowing through his voice.

'Oh, Matthew, darling,' Ashley said, riddled with sarcasm. 'I can see that you're still just *horrid*.'

Matt laughed, said 'Have a drink, won't you? Hopefully you won't choke on the ice.'

It was uncanny, the two of them. Sometimes I wondered if the reason they hated each other was because they were so alike. They say you never like someone with the same personality as you.

I grabbed Matt by the arm to pull him away from her. I forgot where we were, what was happening, my mind focused on nothing but creating distance between the pair. When I yanked him I did it a little too roughly, and I know Ashley saw it, but she didn't say a thing. Matt didn't mind, though—we'd done a lot worse to each other, after all—and in retaliation he pressed his thumb on the scar he had given me two years before, making me hiss in pain. He knew exactly where it was, traced it with his fingers every night, kissed it when I was on top of him, dug into it when I was inside him. I could blind him and he would still find it. I could kill him and he could still ruin me.

After their mini standoff, Matt and Ashley ignored each other for most of the night. He was over by the conservatory smoking with Harris, Abe, and Josh, and my sister remained with Jimmy and his friends from work. I bounced between the two groups, keeping an eye on the tension, and when the night seemed to be getting on without incident, I sat down in Jimmy's swinging bubble chair. I realised only then how drunk I was. I was sitting on a cloud and the room was spinning, but not in a nauseating way, more peaceful, my body fluid and my mind begging to let it sleep. My eyes closed, but not to sleep, to rest, as I listened to everyone's conversations around me.

Matt laughed. Jimmy wasn't going to London Fashion Week that year, which truly meant he was suffering. Abraham wanted a different music channel but Josh wanted to keep to the same one. Harris told a joke and Matt laughed again. Ashley was going to Egypt in the summer. Jimmy's work friends weren't staying too much longer. Harris loved Matt's sangria. Abe and Josh were fighting over the music. Jimmy begged his work friends to stay for just a little longer. Matt told Harris about university and work. Abe got his way with the music, hip-hop filling the vast space of Jimmy's lounge. Josh needed a smoke. Harris was talking about an Arctic Monkeys concert he wanted to attend. Ashley hated Matt's sangria, of course, despite having swallowed two glasses already. Josh felt sick. Abe told him off for drinking too much too quickly. Matt was going to the bathroom before he pissed himself. Jimmy was going to die alone with fifty cats. His work friends were getting ready to leave. Ashley had a headache. The painkillers were upstairs in the cabinet under the bathroom sink, in a box labelled *The Goods*. Ashley was going to get them. Josh stole Abraham's cigarette. Jimmy needed more sangria (doubtful).

As I listened, I didn't realise until it was too late. Both Matt and Ashley had gone upstairs. To the bathroom. *Fuck*.

I stood up so fast it all hit me at once and I thought I was going to throw up. Someone asked where I was going but it didn't register, I was on the stairs and up, two steps at a time. Jimmy yelled out, 'Don't shit yourself!'

I got to the top of the stairs and stopped. Voices, vicious.

'What are you doing? You want to suck my dick?'

It took every ounce of strength I had in me not to run into the bathroom and snap Matt's pretty little neck.

Ashley said, 'You're disgusting. I hate you.'

'You're a broken record.'

I walked closer to the bathroom and the floor creaked, but neither of them noticed because they continued snarling at each other. Ashley was still going on, her voice berating and sharp as a knife, cutting through the air.

'You give me the fucking creeps. You're a murderer.'

The closer I got to the door the clearer their voices became.

'Do you have evidence to back your accusation up?' Matt asked.

'I know your type,' replied Ashley. 'Call it a gut feeling.'

'I hate to break it to you, Ash, but your gut feeling isn't proof of anything.'

'I'll find proof. If you don't leave Julian, I'll make sure you lose everything.'

Matt laughed, a bone chilling sound. 'You have no idea who your brother really is. You only see what he wants you to see.'

'You're a liar,' Ashley spat. 'Just leave. I don't care where you go, as long as it's out of Julian's life.'

'Tell you what, I'm leaving this conversation. But I'm sticking around, Ashley. Now, please move out of my fuckin' way.' There was a pause, silence, then Matt's footsteps thumped towards me before they abruptly stopped. 'Oh yeah,' he added. 'Say hello to your friend for me. I hope she's settling in well.'

What the fuck did that mean?

Jimmy called my name from downstairs as Matt threw the bathroom door open wearing the expression I knew so intimately—the one he'd get when he wanted to hurt someone. When he saw me he stopped for only a second, saw me give him the look that said, *I'm going to fucking kill you*, and went to walk back downstairs, smug. I grabbed him by the back of his shirt, and Jimmy called my name again, closer this time, on his way up the stairs.

Matt said, 'I'm not having your sister barge in and accuse me of being a murderer while I'm taking a piss.'

I wanted to say, *You are one!* but Jimmy was suddenly on the landing.

'What are you talking about?' he said. How much had he heard?

Matt smirked in my face and said '*His* fucking sister,' before I could intervene. The bigger the scene he could cause, the better. It was like I was floating out of body and mind. The words and the will to diffuse the situation were there, but nothing happened. I was a spectator, helplessly watching the show unravel all wrong from the audience. I was stuck. Whose line is it anyway?

Jimmy said, 'Ashley? *Why* would she say that?' not like he didn't believe him, but like he did. He'd heard it all, everything Matt had said to me at a minimum.

'Because she hates me. She's trying to get Julian to *see the light* and leave me.' Ashley came from the bathroom then, mascara under her eyes. Matt said, 'Isn't that right, Ashley, darling?'

Ashley didn't know what to do, much like myself. Matt and I looked at each other, prepared for a war.

Jimmy was on the verge of tears.

'What's going on!'

'Calm down,' Ashley said. 'It's not like it sounds—'

'So you didn't come into the bathroom and call me a murderer?' asked Matt.

'I don't expect you to understand, Jim. I know it must sound crazy and—'

'Get out!' The three of us stood in shock for a moment, two, staring at Jimmy in bewilderment. I thought he was talking to all of us at first, then he said, 'Ash, get the *fuck* out of my house you bitch!' He was sobbing, full body shudders rippling through him as he dropped to the floor, wailing into the carpet. I went to him, dropping to my knees and rubbing his back. He kept repeating under his breath, *get out, just get out, get out get out get out!*

Matt said, 'I think he wants you to go, Ashley.'

Ashley told him to go fuck himself and said that all three of us were insane, then stormed past us, down the stairs and out the door a minute later, slamming it shut. I told Matt to go downstairs and he crept quietly away, pleased with himself and the sudden drama he had conjured up. I still couldn't work out what had Jimmy so upset, but I knew it was something deeper than my sister merely calling Matt a name. I was upset too, profoundly so, but I was less devastated and more outraged at Matt's behaviour. If it wasn't for Jimmy's performance, I would have taken Matt out of there right then, drove him home and made him pay for it until he couldn't remember his own name.

At first Jimmy wouldn't tell me anything, couldn't even—he was barely able to breathe properly, like he was winded. I rubbed his back, spoke to him softly. When his eyes ran dry of tears and he stopped shaking, he just blurted it out.

He told me he killed someone. The little girl, the one all over the news that got killed in a hit-and-run at only eight years old. It was Jimmy's car, he was the one who hit her and ran. It was an accident, he said, a total fucking accident, and now a kid was dead, her family's life ruined, and he was dead too, on the inside, the outside, everywhere in between.

I said it was okay, 'I believe you, it was just an accident. I believe you, James.'

'*How* can I carry on? I can't go on living.'

'Yes you can.'

'But *how?*'

'You just do. Because you have to. You hold your head high and you swallow it down deep. You aren't the only person with heavy secrets, I promise you.'

'Not like mine,' he said. 'What have *you* ever done that's so fucking bad.'

I thought about offering up a confession of my own. *I slept with a pupil of mine at the first school I taught. Before you, before Matt. I knew it was wrong, and I went ahead with it anyway. Now I'm grooming the new boy in town. Just try and stop me.* I was amazed at my own ability to downplay things. *Slept with* was a cosy way of admitting to statutory rape. You see, we all have secrets, we all do bad things, sometimes by accident, sometimes intentionally, but it's how we carry those secrets that gets us through. I could have told Jimmy everything to make him feel less alone, but I sided with myself as I always did. I took a leaf out of Matt's tree instead, and stored Jimmy's confession in my mind for a rainy day. Better safe than sorry, after all.

Downstairs, it was excruciatingly obvious that the party was over. The living room was full of quiet goodbyes and awkward hugs and handshakes. Ashley had gone, and both of Jimmy's colleagues, too. Harris offered to stay with Jimmy for the night, who was out cold in bed upstairs. *Just keep an eye*. It was 10pm when Matt and I left in a taxi, both drunk, not saying a word to each other and tension between us was so obvious the driver turned the radio up.

The moment the front door closed I was overcome with rage.

'I don't want you in our bed tonight.' It was the only way I could think to diffuse the situation other than beating him to a bloody pulp.

'Why?' Matt asked. 'Did you not like my sangria, baby?'

'You know *why*,' I snarled. I was not in the mood for his little diversions.

'I mean, I know why, but something tells me you're going to have a pretty warped version. Let me guess... You're mad at me because I told your sister the *tiniest* bit of truth about you?'

'She's already suspicious, Matt! You gave her more ammunition tonight.'

'Nah, I'm not buying it. You didn't care when she

only suspected me—as long as it's not you, right?'

'I just don't want you to get in trouble, what is so hard to understand about that?'

'This isn't about me. It's never about me. You're mad because now, *you* might be in trouble. Well, newsflash asshole, it doesn't matter to me which one of us Ashley suspects is guilty of something. If I get caught, you do too. Everything you've done runs through me, Jules, and everything I've done runs through you.'

'What are you talking about? If you get caught, that's nothing to do with me.'

'Oh, no? My innocent husband. Tell me again how squeaky clean you are. Tell me again how you're not doing anything with the kid across the road—'

'I am *not* doing *anything* with the kid across the fucking road!'

'Tell me again how Will was asking for it—'

'You weren't there!'

'I was there when he came to find you for clarity. I saw the pain and torment in his eyes well before I stuck the knife in him.'

'Stop talking. Shut your mouth—'

'Or what? Are you going to break my wrist again?'

'I lost control that night. I said I'm sorry—'

'You're never in control. You're weak.'

'What about you? Stabbing me in the chest to prove a point you couldn't even make.'

'My *point* is that if I go down, I'm taking you all of the way with me. I don't give a shit if Ashley finds out.'

'You would take my life from me?'

'Nah, not your life. Don't be so dramatic, Jules.'

'My freedom then. It's the same thing.'

'Yes, I suppose it is for someone like you. I wonder how long you would last in prison. Do you think they go harder, or easier, on a statutory rapist, as opposed to a child molester?' It was a rhetorical question. No one cares about the differences of individual sex crimes. Once an offender always an offender. It doesn't matter whether your victim is fourteen or four, you're going to be tortured in prison by one criminal or another. As if a murderer is innocent, as if drug dealers are more worthy of life than a man with an uncontrollable hair trigger.

'Fuck you,' I said. 'I'd be out within 2 years. You? You're a fucking serial killer, Matt. You would never see the light of day again.' The urge to hit him tugged at me. Did he think I wouldn't make him cry again? Did he think I'd gone soft? Did he assume his place was above mine when I had only recently reminded him of the fact that I owned him entirely? Dance for me, monkey. He was mine. He would cry only for me. And if he wouldn't, I would make him. I would break his wrist again, and again.

'Pathetic,' Matt said. '*That's* what they would think of you. You'd be dead within a year.' He shoved me out of his way and I went flying back into the front door so hard it rattled in its frame. I caught up with him halfway down the hall, grabbed a fistful of his hair to bring him back to me, and he threw his head backwards. It hit my chin like a brick. I let go instinctively, checking my face for blood that wasn't there, then managed to grab his shoulder enough to push him against the wall. Our faces were inches apart, our stares fierce. Matt's teeth sank into my bottom lip, I tasted blood before I felt pain, and then I had my hands around his throat, squeezing as he tried to jerk and squirm his way out of my grip. When he was red in the face he brought his knee up and shoved it into my groin, kneeing me in the balls. My legs buckled underneath me, the pain soaring through my gut, hot and vicious. I tried grabbing Matt's leg through the banister as he ran upstairs, but it was too late, he won. I realised I was shouting.

'Fuck you! Get back down here. Matthew, I'm not joking! I'm going to fucking kill you! I want you out of this house! Now! Fuck!'

Matt yelled down the stairs, said, 'How about *you* get out of the house, Jules. Go stay with your sister. Or even better; go and knock on Melissa's door, ask her if Tyler can come for a sleepover. You can play with some Lego and build a den in the living room to fuck him in afterwards.'

I was on the floor in agony, filled with rage and no way to express it apart from shouting and holding my crotch like my balls would fall off if I didn't. I heard the bedroom door lock and resigned myself to the fact that Matt, a-fucking-gain, was right about the whole thing. It wasn't Ashley suspecting us both of terrible things that had me so angry, it was her suspecting *me*. As long as Ashley and everybody else thought I was a goody-goody, I was content. Perhaps I was selfish. Pathetic. Perhaps I wouldn't fare well in prison. Perhaps Matt was bluffing about the whole thing and perhaps he was not. One thing was for certain, though; we were bound together, and if it wasn't through love, it was through the atrocities we committed, together and apart. What we had was a brutal honesty we would never find anywhere else. Two monsters, a mountain of secrets, and the mutual knowledge that we would screw each other over if that's what it came to. We had done it before. We would do it again.

I stared at the ceiling in the hallway, a burning pain between my legs, and thought; if I'm going to get caught, if it's inevitable, I just might take Matt's advice, buy some Lego and build that den.

# Five

It was early morning when Matt woke me from the floor.
I must have drifted off before I could crawl to the sofa,
so there he was, kicking me awake with a gentleness
neither of us had shown the previous night. It was still
dark. The hallway was cold, as I imagined I was to touch.

He asked, 'Are you dead?'

'Yes.'

Matt giggled, and next thing I knew he was taking my
jeans and boxers off between my drifting in and out of
sleep. When I was naked from the waist down, he traced
his fingers up and down my thighs. I groaned, tired, a
dull yet painful ache between my legs from where his
knee had made contact.

I said, 'Leave me alone.'

'Don't be like that,' he replied, pouting as he climbed
on top of me. 'Do you think your willy still works?' I
laughed at that, the word *willy* was strange coming from
Matt's usually obscene potty-mouth, so... juvenile.

Intentional? I didn't know. It helped him get what he wanted regardless.

I said, 'I think you're going back to bed and leaving me alone.' He ignored me, as ever. Just chuckled, kissing me, rubbing against me until I was rubbing back.

'Definitely still works.'

'It would appear so, yes.'

'Come to bed?'

I laughed. 'Oh, I'm allowed now you're horny. No thanks. I think I'll stay on this wonderfully cold floor.'

'Come on—'

'No.'

'Fine. We'll do it here then.'

'We bloody well won't.'

I don't think I need to tell you that Matt got his own way, that he just did it anyway, used me while I laid there, unable to move. I didn't want to, in truth, I wanted to stay like that forever, Matt and I and nothing else. No outside threats, no distractions. Just us, the animals we were, fucking on the hallway floor. It was uncomplicated peace. I thought, *I'm getting too old for this*, and yet there I was, getting more perverse with age. People talk about ageing like fine wine, but no one mentions the parts of us that age like an open bottle of milk, those of us who let our rotting souls sit and fester. Sometimes I felt so much love for Matthew I wanted to crush him, sometimes he felt the same way, and then we would fight, like we had the night before, and afterwards we'd have amazing sex and all would be forgiven. Sometimes, we fought on purpose, for that very reason. We could do anything to each other, it was like the worse we hurt the better the sex, and neither of us wanted to do anything about it.

'This is rape,' I said, watching him on top of me, feeling him around me.

'You would know,' he said, knowing I was too weak to fight back, too fragile to show him what that word truly meant.

It wasn't early when Melissa knocked on the door, but Matt and I were back in bed, both groggy and exhausted, trying to decide which of us looked in good enough shape to answer the door. The answer was Matt—my lip was sore with an obvious bite mark and there was a bruise developing on my jaw. Matt looked no worse for wear, so off he went, dragging his feet. I laid there in bed with my eyes shut, playing a game of *Guess Who* with myself. The postman, Tyler with his football, one of Ashley's shock horror visits.

I heard Matt say, *Of course we will,* then something about a pizza. I couldn't tell what the hell was going on. The front door shut, Matt's footsteps ran up the stairs.

It was Tyler's mother, Melissa, who wanted to know if Matt and I would watch Tyler for a couple of hours that night—until midnight—the time Lara got home from work. The model citizens, the harmless, gay, married couple across the road. Who better to watch your teenage boy, right?

I didn't want to do it, start having Tyler over the house all of the time, but as Matt kindly pointed out to me; it was my doing. I had asked Tyler inside for burgers instead of sending him away. I had suggested taking him to football training. I was the one who offered to help anytime he or his parents needed. It had all been me. I was so subtle at making my first moves that sometimes I forgot they were moves at all. Breadcrumbs everywhere, just enough to bait the mouse.

Tyler came over at 7pm, preaching starvation as teenagers often are. Matt was in charge of ordering the pizzas, I was in charge of curing my hangover and improvising answers to the questions Tyler asked about my split lip. When did that happen? *Last night.* Are you okay? *Fine.* Did someone hurt you? *A fight broke out, that's all, and I got in the middle of it.* Did you win? *Call it a tie.* Matt laughed at that, and told Tyler that no, he was there, and I most definitely had not won.

'I'll win next time.'

'Sure you will,' Matt said.

Tyler found the tension between Matt and I amusing. Thank God someone did. Tyler asked me question after question that night. I wondered if Matt noticed how much attention he paid me, or if it was all in my head. I wondered if I seemed as nervous and edgy as I felt. When the pizzas arrived, the three of us sat in the lounge watching reruns of *Friends*. Matt was on the opposite end of the sofa to me, our feet touching, while Tyler sat on the floor in front of the coffee table rather than the armchair. While we ate, I noticed Tyler inching closer to my legs. With one slice of pizza he was in the middle of Matt and I, and by the next slice he was a little further to the right, to me. I pretended I needed to re-adjust my posture, stretch my legs. I hung them off the sofa and crossed one over the other, glancing over at Matt to see if he noticed the sudden change. He didn't, why would he? I was the only one in the room over analysing my every thought and movement, Tyler's too. In truth, it was exhausting sometimes, being me. To be so wrapped up in yourself and what is going on around you is a personal hell, but the pay-off is worth it, ten, twenty, a million times over. And I would get my dues.

It only took a couple of minutes. Tyler was pressed as far against my legs as he could be, and I tried not to react, smiled tightly as my stomach dropped when his hand slid up the back of my calf. I couldn't eat any more pizza, my guts were doing somersaults, and when Matt stood up to take his plate to the kitchen Tyler moved so fast I'm surprised he didn't give himself whiplash. Matt took my plate from me too, and then Tyler's, and left the room.

'What are you doing?' I whispered. The boy craned his neck to look at me like I just asked him to translate a Latin poem.

'What? I'm watching TV…' I thought I was going mad. Perhaps I made it all up, perhaps if you want something to happen so badly you can force yourself into believing it has.

'Never mind,' I said. Matt came back into the room and sat down, next to me this time. I put my arm around him, and Matt told Tyler to sit next to him on the sofa.

'It's cool, I like it on the floor.'

'That's what he said,' Matt mused. Tyler laughed, and

I shook my head at the absurdity of it all.

It was around 9pm when Matt said he had to go get his car from Jimmy's, where he had left it the night before. Tyler had the option of keeping Matt company on the taxi journey to Jimmy's, or staying with me. He chose the latter, but I didn't want to be alone with him in the house. Shock, I know, but we weren't *there* yet, and by *we* I mean Tyler and I, and by *there* I mean close enough for me to trick him into my bed under the guise of love. The way Tyler looked that night with his windswept brown curls, dusted cocoa freckles, and a laugh as innocent and beautiful as it was painful, if I'd been left alone with him I knew I could not trust myself. Something told me Tyler was relying on that, but I pushed it to the back of my mind. Ignorance always was my best friend.

'Why don't we all go?' I suggested. 'I can drive us over in my car. I don't really want you getting a taxi there alone, Matt.'

'I'm a big boy,' he grinned, and I couldn't help myself.

'That's what he said.'

In the car Tyler sat in the back and Matt rode passenger, turning up the radio and screaming along to a song that was playing, I believe it was *Tainted Love,* by one of the various artists who covered it. When we got to Jimmy's I kept the car running, and Tyler said he wanted to ride with me on the way home. Matt got out, I told Tyler to get in the front, and once he'd climbed in, all lanky limbs and messy hair, I drove home, Matt following in his yellow Mini. It didn't take long for the boy to speak.

'Jules, can I ask you something?'

'Of course.'

'What was that about? Before, at your house.'

'What do you mean?' I asked. I thought it was going to be about my calling him out, when he crawled to my legs inconspicuous as a spider and then had the nerve to deny it all the way.

'You didn't want to stay with me, did you?'

My eyes drifted from the road to Tyler, and then from him to the rear-view mirror, at Matt, as if he could hear us. What was I supposed to say? Tell him not to be so silly, that I just thought it would be nice to get out for a drive, that I didn't want Matt to walk or get a taxi alone at night despite having done so many times before?

I decided on the truest form of a lie. 'No, I didn't.'

'Why?'

I shook my head. 'It doesn't matter, Tyler.'

'Why?'

'Because it's complicated.'

'Do I annoy you? Did I do something?'

'It's nothing like that.' I swallowed nervously. I really did not want to be having this conversation, but something told me he wasn't going to drop it. Not until he understood *why*. How do you explain something that not even you understand?

'So what's wrong?' he asked.

'Nothing.'

'I thought you liked spending time with me.'

'I do. That's the problem.'

'That doesn't make sense at all—'

'I told you it was complicated.'

'Well it shouldn't be—'

'Precisely.'

'Just tell me!' It was the first time I'd heard him raise his voice apart from when he was on the football pitch. 'Stop acting so weird. Stop it.' He was clearly upset, and so was I. I sighed, relenting, giving in to his persistence.

'If I tell you, you can't tell anyone. Not a soul,' I said, hating myself for how it sounded, like every cliche deviant: *You have to keep it a secret, don't say a word or bad things will happen. I can trust you, can't I? Don't let me down...*

'I won't.'

'I mean it, Ty—'

'I promise. Cross my heart.'

I took a deep breath, felt the guilt rise like bile at the back of my throat. My insides were twisting, and the more they twisted the more I thrived from it. I was all crossed wires and broken hard drives, sparks that threatened to blow the fuse.

'I like spending time with you,' I said. 'The problem is that I like it too much.'

I looked at him, taking my eyes off the road for longer than I should have, which only proved my point. Too much, far too much. It was dangerous. The only thing it led to was blood and tears and both of our lives in ruins. Tyler didn't say anything for a moment, long enough for me to look back at the road, contemplate crashing into an oncoming car.

'You mean, like…' He stopped, not needing to elaborate. He knew.

'I think you know what I mean.'

Tyler gave me a slight nod. We remained awkwardly silent for a while. I was driving, he was watching me drive, and it was too quiet, so quiet I could hear my own thoughts louder than ever before, two voices that belonged to the same animal brain, battling it out between themselves. Right and wrong, or perhaps they were just wrong and more wrong.

#1—*You stupid idiot. Why would you tell him that? He's just a child.*

#2— *Oh, shut up. Quit being such a queen about it. It's not like you hurt him, not yet.*

#1—*You're sick.*

#2—*If I'm sick, you are too. We're part of the same brain, remember?*

#1—*Stop, just stop. He's a kid.*

#2—*That's why we're here…*

#1—*Fuck you. I'm trying to keep us out of trouble.*

#2—*But you feel it, do you not? The exhilaration.*

#1—*Yes. Yes I feel it.*

#2—*And you love it, don't you?*

Yes, yes I did.

When Tyler and I got close to our street I said that I was sorry, for being weird earlier, and for making him uncomfortable.

He replied, 'It's okay, I like weird. And you don't make me uncomfortable.' He was casual, confident, and

#2 wanted to stroke his face and make him mine while #1 wanted to say, *You're fourteen. You don't yet know what you want or what you like.* I did neither. Instead I offered an ultimatum, thus tricking him into compliance. The choice was entirely his.

'If you don't want me to take you to football training anymore, I completely understand.' Whatever his answer, it was his to make. He could take up my offer to stop the weekly training sessions, which in turn meant we would not continue to see one another; or we could carry on as usual, which meant he was fine with my confession, even if he was not.

Like a working charm, Tyler said, 'I want you to. It's cool, I like that you take me.'

'Are you sure?'

'Yeah!'

'Alright, then.' I smiled at the boy and he smiled back, bashful and blushing. 'As long as you're okay with it, so am I.'

Tyler thanked me, and in a moment of utter surprise he ran his fingers down my arm. A shiver forced its way down my spine. I checked for Matt's wolf eyes in the rear-view mirror—he never missed a beat, that one. Fortunately, he was a couple of minutes behind us. I'd been driving fast, perhaps over the limit, I couldn't remember. I wondered if Tyler knew what a risky game he was playing. Perhaps he did, perhaps he was like me and the thrill mattered more to him than right or wrong. Perhaps I was projecting my own feelings on him and perhaps I didn't care that I was. I looked at it like this—

Tyler noticed I was off that day, he knew I didn't want to be alone with him, and perhaps I'm deluded for thinking this, but why would he have noticed if he didn't feel the same way about me? Was he waiting for the moment to strike, to get me alone in a private location? Did we have the same expectations? Whatever the answers to these questions were, I only knew one thing for certain: I could not have gotten this far already without a helping hand from Tyler. It was usually such a challenge, these hunts for pliant prey, but he made it oh so very easy. We were making quick progress. I couldn't slow down now.

Tyler's hand slipped away just as Matt pulled up on the drive next to us. It was like none of it happened; like he hadn't slyly touched me on the leg back at the house; like I hadn't just admitted to some pretty severe stuff. The three of us went back into the house, no one saying anything. I told myself nothing had changed, but when Melissa turned up for Tyler, it was obvious that everything had.

'You're both absolute life savers,' she said. 'Jules, will you be picking Tyler up for training tomorrow?'

#1—*It's not too late to stop this.*

#2—*It's already too late.*

'Absolutely,' I replied, and the word felt like the filthiest thing I had ever let pass my wayward lips.

Later on, when we were settling down for the night, Matt told me that Jimmy's cat was dead. The way he announced it was like an afterthought.

'Oh yeah, I totally forgot to tell you, Jules. Jimmy's cat is dead by the way. She got run over, flat as a pancake.'

'What? Taffy?'

'Does he have another one?'

'How could you *forget* to tell me?' I said, mildly upset. 'She was my cat for years.'

'Well you sped away with the kid so fast, and she wasn't *my* cat, so by the time we got home it just slipped my mind.'

'How did she get out of the house? I saw her just yesterday. Jimmy doesn't let her out anymore.'

'She went missing last night, someone must've forgotten and just opened the door for her. She was found this morning, flat as—'

'As a pancake, yes, I get it.'

'Just saying,' Matt said, a sparkle in his empty eyes.

The next day I couldn't get the cat out of my head. Flashing images of roadkill, flat as a pancake on the side of the road, a road she wasn't meant to be on in the first place, flesh and blood and bone and fur, tyre marks and concrete. I informed Matt I was going to see Jimmy with a card and some chocolate. I knew he would be torn up about it, he adored Taffy.

'It was just a cat,' Matt said, expressionless while peeling a tangerine.

'Yes, you're correct. Well done.'

'You know what I mean. What's the big deal?'

'Be careful, Matthew. Don't let your mask slip.'

Matt glared at me. He hated when I demonstrated how much I knew the true him. He liked to think he had me blind like everyone else, but that ship sailed long ago. His eyes darkened, two oceans at night.

'At least I still have mine,' he said, absently chewing on a segment of his tangerine. He swallowed it, smiled. 'You lost yours a while back. You're transparent.'

'Oh, I'm transparent? I see through *everything* you do.'

'Yeah? You think?'

'Yes, I do.'

'So I suppose you know I'm the one who let the cat outside, then?'

'What?'

Matt rolled his eyes, nonchalant as a sloth. 'Are you going deaf?'

I was momentarily shocked to the core. 'Why would you do that?' I asked. 'Why, Matt?'

He shrugged, smiled. 'I was bored. Wanted to see what would happen.'

At Jimmy's house I sat on the sofa while Jimmy cried into my lap. *It's my fault, Ju-Ju, I hit the kid and now someone's hit Taffy. It's my karma, I'm being punished, Ju-Ju, she's dead and it's all my fault.* All I was hearing was *me me me*.

'*Who* let her out?' he asked. '*Someone* must have left the door open. I should have been keeping an eye on her, it's *my* fault. I'm the *worst* person to ever exist. It should be *me*, Ju-Ju, *I* should be run over and killed.'

Jimmy threw himself on the floor, so I rubbed his back, coaching him through his grief. It was dramatic, to say the least, and Matt's words repeated in my head, *she was just a cat*. Granted, Jimmy was drunk out of his mind, again, heightened feelings swimming in a cocktail of liquor and cocaine. I imagined his liver would fail by the time he was my age. He kept repeating, *Who let her out, who was it, who could it be?* I had the answer and yet I could not tell him. When Matt had said it was him who let Taffy out I made the responsible decision of leaving the house right away. God only knows the harm I would do to him if I stayed. He got a beloved cat killed for no other reason than to cause chaos. Matt could not stand it when life was going too smoothly for him and those around him, he enjoyed putting a curve in the road and watching people trip over the traps he so thoughtfully set. He was spiteful, still very much a child in that sense. But a cat, for Christ sake?

There I was, gathering the pieces of Matt's spite as Jimmy cried them into the rug. I ran out of words to say to him, there are only so many times you can repeat *It'll be alright,* and *It's not your fault.* It became a mantra I eventually grew tired of. Add to that the tension rope I was walking with Tyler, and my utter contempt for Matt's cruel games, I was a cocktail of ferocious lust. Because of this, I did not object when Jimmy kissed me, nor when he climbed into my lap. I would have done anything to get him to quit blubbering like a toddler, in truth, and if I remembered one thing from our brief whirlwind of a relationship, it was how sex never failed to brighten Jimmy's mood. I suppose I was killing two birds with one stone. I provided Jimmy with a little slice of heaven during his tour of hell, and at the same time, got back at Matt in my own way. Not that I would tell Matt what I did when I got home, that would be stupid of me, but I would be self-satisfied, less enraged, and less likely to beat him to a pulp when I saw his face.

When I left Jimmy's later that night, the smell of sex clung to me, and on the drive back, with the windows down in an attempt to air out, I prayed for a miraculous intervention of some kind. Perhaps Matt went out with Josh, or Luca called him in to work, perhaps he was getting a cold and wouldn't notice that I reeked of Jimmy. Imagine my surprise to find my prayers answered.

Matt's car was not on the drive, and the house was bathed in darkness. It was difficult to ignore the eerie feeling that sometimes crept up when I was there alone and guilty as sin. So much had happened in that house over the years; blood was spilled in nearly every room, stained into the wooden floors which I had to cover with rugs, and those rugs quickly got replaced too, when Matt felt artsy or one or both of us were heady with blood-lust. In truth, I was expecting a bloodbath that night, or a row at the very least. I imagined Matt would tease me over the cat, ask me how Jimmy was doing and revel in his heartbreak, and I would lose patience, grab him by the throat and threaten to throttle him then and there, and Matt would fight back because he always did, claw at my arms and face, bite and spit and kick. But he wasn't home, just like I hoped, and I found myself surprisingly disheartened. Where was he?

By the time I showered that evening's evidence away, Matt was still nowhere to be seen, so I called his phone. No answer. I started getting agitated and paranoid, my possessive streak was waking up, and I was about to go out looking for him when he waltzed into the house.

'Where have you been?' I asked, and I bit my tongue, stopping myself from saying anything else. An hour before that I was balls deep in my ex-boyfriend and I had the nerve to question his whereabouts.

'Out,' replied Matt, smiling but vague as ever. 'Did you enjoy yourself at Jimmy's?' It was an innocuous enough question, yet it sent an ice-cold chill through me. What was I supposed to say? Yes, I enjoyed seeing Jimmy in such emotional despair? Yes, I enjoyed fucking him on his sheepskin rug while he cried and laughed and told me he loved me, he's always loved me, and he's been waiting for this for years? Yes, I enjoyed taking back control in my own way after Matt rubbed it in my face that it was him who got the cat killed?

The satisfaction I felt with Jimmy was already wavering. You can't truly get revenge on someone if they don't know about it, and Matt knowing about it was a deathly scenario. All he needed was one reason to get rid of someone, and he would do it. Poor Jimmy had been through enough. So although yes, I did enjoy myself at Jimmy's, it soon became clear I made an irrational decision in the midst of losing control.

I said, 'Not really, Matt, considering the circumstances.'

'Oh, that's a shame.'

'You're a real piece of work.'

'A masterpiece,' he said agreeingly.

# Six

Jimmy didn't give himself more than a day of pining before he started calling my phone at least once every couple of hours. The texts were even more frequent. *I loved the other night. Was it good for you? Whatcha doing? I need to talk to you. Ju-Ju, answer me! Are you ignoring me? Why aren't you answering your phone? Text me back! Please answer me, Ju-Ju. Should I come over? I'll come over. Be there tonight around 7.* All of that in one day. The last one got my attention, so I called him on my way home from work. He picked up on the second ring.

'*There* he is,' he said.

'Yes, hello, James.'

'I've been trying to get hold of you for *weeks*.'

'It's been two days.'

'*Where* have you been?'

'Working, James. I can't text you back every five minutes.'

'You haven't text me back *once*.'

'James—'

'You're a fucking asshole, *Christ*.'

'Yes, as are you. It's why we broke up, or have you taken so many drugs since then that you don't remember?'

'Fuck *you*.'

'What do you want, James?'

'You know, I read *somewhere* that narcissists repeat people's names over and over as a way to seem more *powerful,* or some bollocks.'

An involuntary laugh escaped my lips. 'Is that why you wanted to talk to me?'

'No,' Jimmy sighed on the other end. 'I just... I *miss* you. Can I see you? *Please*?'

'I'm busy, I don't have the time.'

'I'm not asking you to leave Matt for me, Ju-Ju. I'm *asking* to see you, that's all.'

'And I do not have the time, *James*.' I hung up the phone, continued driving home. I couldn't believe how idiotic I was. I fell into bed with Jimmy, of all people, Jimmy the clingy, neurotic, gossip queen. I suppose I should have seen it coming, but I did have other, more *pressing* things on the mind between my legs, things such as keeping Matt in the dark about my comings and goings, and keeping up a regular routine with my new plaything. Once again, I had failed to foresee the consequences of my own actions.

With Tyler, it was like I was on fire. He was the fuel keeping my desire burning. The only way to extinguish it was to touch him, but I restrained myself, held my ground, contained the blaze and let it spread. But you know how it is with fires, the longer you leave it the bigger it gets, the more it destroys. I don't know at what point I started to live my life around seeing the boy, but I suppose it always works that way—you don't know how deep you're in until you try to get out. It was quicksand, and I bathed in it, lurking beneath the surface waiting to strike at the naive little mouse following my breadcrumbs and devouring them on the way. My night with Jimmy helped tame the urges for a brief period of time, but I was still seeing Tyler on a regular basis. Pretty soon the reins wore down, and all I began thinking about were ways to speed the process along. It was not enough, the fruit of an extramarital affair. I wanted the ripest, the sweetest, the pick of the patch. I wanted the forbidden, the poisonous, the undeveloped.

Tyler and I naturally grew closer, weeks went by where all I thought of was him and his football training, counting down the days until I got to pick him up again. The best part was that I had a reason to be seeing him at least twice a week. It was a free pass, and left no one wanting for an explanation. As far as everyone was concerned, I was the good, kind-natured neighbour helping a kid out, all out of the kindness of my hidden, decaying heart. Even Matt left me alone about it, which was what I had been the most concerned about when Tyler first came into our lives. I couldn't have Matt kill the kid in a jealous rage, especially not before I had a little fun with him.

Our nights together gradually extended, only by increments, mind you; fifteen minutes here and there. It was an easy enough lie to Matt and Tyler's parents—training ran on; the coach was late; there was an accident and one of the boys twisted their ankle. We both made sure to be in on the same lie on any given night in case we ever got suspicious questions, but none came. In truth, all we were doing was sitting in the car after he finished training and talking to each other. After the night Matt and I had him over for a couple hours; the one where I confessed to liking him too much, neither of us had taken another step forward, both too frightened of tipping the scales of comfort we had found in knowing-but-not-knowing. On one particular day, however, I didn't have a choice in the matter.

It was a weekend morning and I was outside, under Matt's car, giving it an inspection after he complained of a loud scraping noise while he drove. I was half under, blind to my surroundings, but a strange feeling crept its way through me, the feeling of being watched, observed. I heard footsteps, and then someone playfully kicked my leg.

'Hello, Tyler.'

'How do you know it's me?'

'Call it a wild guess.'

'Cool,' Tyler said. 'Whatcha doing?'

'Fixing Matt's car.'

'What's wrong with it?'

'I'm not sure yet, I'm looking for the source. He's probably hit something on the road. He drives like a lunatic.'

'Need any help?'

'Actually, yes,' I answered. 'I need a torch, I can't see shit under here. There should be one in my toolbox, can you see it?'

'Will the torch on your phone work?'

'I don't have my phone on me—'

'It's in your pocket,' Tyler said. 'I'll get it for you.'

All of a sudden his agile little hand was in the pocket of my shorts, and I froze. I couldn't see his face, couldn't move to get him off, all I had left was control of my own reaction. *Keep still, don't react. Perhaps if you play dead he'll leave you alone.* It had occurred to me that Tyler was also getting impatient, but impatience doesn't necessarily guarantee tenacity, so when I felt his hand squeeze my crotch it blindsided me. All I wanted was a torch, a little bit of light, so how come everything seemed much darker? I didn't know whether to yell in glee or anger, joy or panic. And then it was over, faster than it started. The nerves on that boy—his sheer confidence was astounding, mesmerising, and quite frankly, I wanted to destroy it, slowly, tenderly, like one would a baby bird. I would pluck his feathers one by one, clip his wings and forbid him to fly. Feed him my seed from the palm of my hand. I know how I sound, but the term "Necessary Evil" came from somewhere, right?

'See ya,' Tyler said, and I listened to his footsteps fade away. I remained under the car, stuck there, trapped from shock, and hard as the dickens. I couldn't believe he left me there so exposed. When I eventually pulled myself together enough to slide out from Matt's car, I had no diagnosis for him, no idea what was wrong with it. I told him he would need to take it to a garage, a mechanic. Someone not so easily distracted, so easily taken advantage of.

'Why are you flushed?' Matt asked me, referring to the reddening of my cheeks.

'Oh, it's warm outside,' I replied. 'Warmer than it looks, anyway.'

Matt took his car to the only garage that was open on a Sunday afternoon and I went upstairs to shower, to wash the filthiness away, sweat and grease and carnivorous need. Despite the vigour in which I scrubbed, the memory of Tyler touching me had permanently stained itself into my skin. Sleeping with Jimmy was supposed to take the edge off but I was as sharp as I'd ever been, brimming with tension and arousal.

Thirty hours later I was back at the football club, sitting on a sheltered bench in the spectator stand. The pitch was boggy from a recent downpour of rain, and slippery because of it. The team of youths all followed the orders of their coach, sprinting around in the mud and doing various exercises with a football. As you can imagine, it was my favourite sight. I never was a football guy, but I was willing to pretend to be anything Tyler wanted me to be. I could adopt the hobbies of any beautiful boy, like I did with Matt when we first met. When I lied, telling him I used to run in the hopes he would ask me to join him, it had worked like a spell. The difference was that Matt was clever, far from naive, and he had cast an invisible spell of his own. With Tyler, I didn't need to worry about that—he was younger, innocent, and as much of a gullible fool as William once was. Obsession can be oh so exhausting.

On the drive to the football club I was a bag of nerves, and neither of us brought up what had happened the day before. I didn't know if it was for better or worse, but ignoring it was welcome to me. Why bother facing your problems if you don't have to?

While he was on the pitch I didn't take my eyes away from Tyler. After a while of interchanging and intense workouts the coach called *warm ups*, he made the boys work even harder. They were already covered head to toe in mud and skidding across the pitch like new-born deer on ice, and I couldn't shift the burgeoning feeling in my gut that something bad was going to happen, someone was going to get hurt. Not that the coach cared. Every time one of them slipped he would yell at them to get back up and quit their whining, but I wasn't watching, not really. I was there for Tyler, the boy I was looking directly at as he collided with another boy and dropped to the floor. The coach treated him no differently, told him to get up, power through it, but the boy didn't listen. I couldn't work out what happened despite having been watching his every move, increment by increment. I had heard the thud from where I was in the football stand, like two hollow boulders smashing together. It was just a split second, he was there running and then he was on the floor. I thought he was unconscious for a moment, my heart racing as I stood up, and then I heard him call my name. A couple of his teammates gave him a hand up as I tried not to rush onto the pitch, hold out my arms and then never let him from my grasp again. Tyler limped toward me and he was clearly hiding a lot of pain, his eyes wet when I tucked my arm around his waist. I sat him down on one of the benches where I had been sitting, watching, gawking, whatever you want to call it, and wiped a stray tear from his cheek with my thumb. He was holding his thighs together, wincing every time he moved slightly. I kneeled down in front of him. The training session continued on behind me.

'Are you alright? What happened?' I asked. 'It's okay to cry.'

'I don't want to. I'm fine.' He blinked away from me, so I brought my hand to his knee.

'Show me.' Tyler hit my hand away with a sound of discord, a puppy's growl, trying to bite back the tears that balanced on his waterline. I touched his calf instead and he jerked away from that, too. It became a game, him swatting my hand away and me pretending the blow hurt more than the last, until he was smiling and so was I, until he let me draw lines up his shin and over his knee. A sharp slap stung my hand and I looked up at him from where I was kneeling before him and focused on his mischievous, bright eyes. 'Come on. Let me see, please,' I said, before moving my hand gingerly, the way you might approach an animal when you test the waters to see if it will bite. He didn't bite. He didn't move. My hand settled on his knee and I eased his leg open so I could see his inner thigh and assess the damage done. He didn't hit me that time. It wasn't so bad, but it was not exactly pleasant either. The wound looked like a severe type of carpet burn, a couple layers of skin missing, blood and mud and skin all mangled together. I got a bottle of water out of Tyler's bag and some paper towels from my coat pocket that I stashed from work now and then, and I tried to clean around it but he wouldn't let me, not really, so I ended up just folding the towels and pressing the wad against his thigh. I held it there until it stopped bleeding, and though the boy resisted a little, he let me clean it as best I could.

'Thank you,' Tyler said, then he bit his lip, looking down at me with a look that said a whole lot more than a simple thanks.

'You're most welcome,' I replied, staring back, and out of no control of my own I touched his calf, the way he had done mine in the house, in front of Matt, and then denied it straight after. I slid my hand up his calf and to the baby-soft skin of the back of his thigh, which soon erupted with goosebumps when I tickled there lightly and a shiver possessed his body. He started to shift on the bench, inching forwards as if his body was begging for my touch. I brushed the back of my fingers against the red-hot skin surrounding the graze, and he slid his hips forward, to the edge of the bench, as my hand got further and further into the danger zone. I said nothing, nor did he. We just looked at each other, frozen in time and space and ignorant to the team still training behind me, the coach yelling, the thud of the ball being kicked about. It was dark, the flood lights beaming across the pitch which afforded us the most privacy, just two silhouettes in the football stand, not doing anything untoward at all.

Tyler opened his legs wider, shameless in his sudden arousal at my hands teasing his exposed nerves, and in a moment of complete loss of control I slid my hand up his shorts, my fingers dancing over the wiry dark hairs on his inner thigh, thicker the higher I got. I stopped at the hem of his boxers, already too far, not allowing myself more than that, but before I could draw my hand away Tyler grabbed it, keeping me there. I looked up at him and his cheeks were flushed, he was biting his lip, breathing unsteadily. He was just a teenage boy in the midst of heady testosterone and an anything-goes sex-drive, and unfortunately, I was a man more than happy to indulge him.

I also happened to have an anything-goes sex-drive.

So I kept my hand there, wandering, and other stuff started to happen fast, things I hadn't expected at all—touching, kneading, squeezing over his boxers where I could feel him hard against the restricting fabric, his arousal trapped and pulsing in my palm. I could smell him, sweat and mud and musk, sweet as honey to my deluded brain. Then I was really touching him, skin on skin, my hand trapped in the confines of his boxers as I tugged hard and slow. Tyler closed his eyes, put his head back and quietly moaned with it, a sound so perfect I could have taken him there and then. I would have, if it wasn't for my realising the football training had come to an end, the team all swarming off the pitch, all farewells and exhausted sighs. It was over as soon as it started, I pulled my hand out from his shorts and stood up, clearing my throat as he adjusted his shorts to compliment his current situation. I could see in his eyes that he was still in another world, one made of pleasure, a world where consequence was no more than a trivial idea.

'Why did you stop—'

'I had to.'

'Why?'

I didn't say a thing, just nodded in the direction of the stairs behind him, where the football coach was standing, staring at me like he knew. Then, as if it didn't look shady enough, Tyler turned around to see who had intruded, then turned back to me with eyes wider than an owl's. I casually offered him his bag, to which he looked totally bewildered. I usually carried it back to the car for him.

'To help with your, uh, situation,' I said quietly, looking down at his tented shorts, and we both laughed as he took it from me and covered himself as we walked out of the football stand, me almost sprinting like a suspect caught in the act and Tyler limping, pretending his leg wasn't killing him. Tyler said bye to the coach, I smiled and nodded, and the coach did the same back. It meant one of two things: Either he hadn't seen anything; or he had seen everything, and he was just like me. The coach asked Tyler, 'Alright, champ? How's the leg?' And Tyler answered, 'Fine, thanks coach!' as he ran after me, following me but not quite catching up—I didn't slow down, couldn't if I tried, my heart telling me to flee and my head telling me nothing happened, *you're exaggerating, Jules, you didn't really do that.* I forced myself to believe it was just a fantasy, my crooked mind filling in the blanks, but the harder I tried to convince myself the worse the lie felt, the heavier it sat on my chest. It *had* happened. It fucking happened, and it would happen again, worse next time. Like it had with Will, the first time I put my hand on his thigh in class and it inevitably led to that night in my car, heady kisses and hushed moans, so full of life and ambition and innocence that I couldn't help but be a thief. I swore never to do it again and I didn't. Until Matt. The one who changed it all... or at least that's what I told myself. Fifteen and the most capricious little thing I'd ever stumbled upon, far more beautiful than you could imagine, taunting enough to make a statue blush and confident enough to know how to use it against any man he wanted. And boy did I want him to use it on me.

But that was different, was it not? Matt and Will had nothing in common apart from my company. I slept with Matt when he was sixteen—sure I'd given him my email address the year before, refreshed my emails daily to look for any sign of him—but it was legal. Here in the UK the age of consent is sixteen, so what had I done wrong there? With Will, I knew better: I was his teacher; he was underage, but with Matthew? He was absolutely nothing at all, if not willing. And then there was Tyler. An enigma, Will reincarnated. *He* touched me first. I only repaid the attention he gave me.

I saw a pattern emerging, wondered how many more boys there would be despite promising myself there would be none. What constitutes a pattern, when does it become one? Does the pattern ever break? Was it them, or—God forbid—was it me? Did Matthew count in all this madness, or had I been fooling myself all along into thinking he was as ferocious in his pursuit as I had been? He married me, after all. Which was it: Victim, willing participant, husband, or all of the above? Think about it carefully before you decide—don't forget that when Will came to find me to confront me for what I'd done to him years before, Matt killed him Hannibal Lecter style. Bowels in or bowels out.

I slammed the car door shut behind me, waiting for Tyler to join me in the passenger seat. All of these thoughts ran through my head and I couldn't make sense of any of them. Was I good or bad? A bad man who did good things, or a good man who did bad things? Are those two things the same either way? I went to speak but I had nothing, no words that could possibly make the situation any less unpleasant. It's funny how you can be so intimate with someone and then feel further apart than you ever have before. I had just had my hands all over him and now I couldn't look him in the eye. I suppose that's what shame does to you. But shame isn't all bad, it's not always the worst thing to feel. A heightened self-consciousness, a deep self-loathing—those feelings were the making of me, they were my angels in hell, and without them I would have been nothing.

Tyler asked, 'Are you okay, Jules?' and I nodded, told

him to put his seatbelt on while I turned the key in the ignition. I had just had him moaning on a bench in the middle of the football stand and he asked if *I* was okay. If he was trying to turn me into a villain he was succeeding. 'You look really spooked. What's wrong with you?'

'I'm… I'm really sorry,' I said. I put my hands over my face, shook my head.

'For what?'

'For back there, just now. I shouldn't have touched you like that.'

'But I liked when you touched me.'

'Please don't say that.'

'But I did. You did, too, I know you did—'

'Tyler, please, just—'

'Please *what*?'

'Please just give me a fucking second to think.'

'Jules, chill—'

'Tyler!'

The boy jumped out of his skin. I'd frightened him. I snapped at him because I was frustrated with myself, and I was unable to channel it in any other way. What a nightmare of an evening. A delicious, devilish nightmare.

'Don't shout at me,' Tyler muttered. 'You have no right to shout at me.'

'You're right,' I replied. I realised I was driving with no recollection of pulling off. 'I'm sorry, Ty, I'm not mad at you. I'm angry at myself, alright? Listen to me, please hear me out.' The boy nodded, and the look of terror replaced his usually relaxed expression. 'We can't do this. We can't.'

'What? What do you mean we can't do this?'

'Listen to me. Taking you to football training, having you over the house… It's too much. It has to stop *now*. I'm so sorry, I just—'

'But I don't get it! Why? What changed?'

'Please don't be upset—'

'Explain it to me then!'

'That's what I'm doing. You aren't listening to me.' I panicked, closer to our street than ever. I knew it had to be my last moment with him, then and there in the car. It had to be. *Had to*. 'I can't be around you anymore. I can't control myself around you. I'm only going to end up hurting you, and I don't want to be that guy.'

'But… But I don't care—'

'That's not the point.'

'So what is? You can't hurt me, what does that even mean? I don't care about any of that, I just… I like you, I think you're cool.'

'Look, right now you don't care. You think you know what you want and what you like, but that could change at any point. It *will* change. I bet you don't even know if you're straight, or gay, or if you want to get married, if you want kids, what you want to do for a living. And here I am, confusing you when I know better.'

Tyler was staring straight at me the whole time while I dodged his gaze. I'd parked up at the end of the street to give us more privacy. He didn't respond straight away, and I was worried he'd burst into tears, right there on our street. He did not.

He said, '*You* don't know what I want, but that

doesn't mean I don't. You don't get to decide for me, cos you ain't me. You say that I'll change my mind cos I'm young or whatever, and I don't know what I like, but *you* change too. Everyone changes. Being young doesn't have anything to do with it. It's already changed for you, cos you want me and you didn't think you'd want me.'

Touché. Which means *touched* in French, by the way.

I replied, 'It's wrong, this is all just so wrong—'

'I don't think it's wrong. Don't feel wrong, anyway. It's cool—'

'It's not *cool*, Ty. What I just did is unacceptable.'

'So why do it then?'

*Exactly.* I don't have an answer for you. I don't know why I do the things that I do. I just know I do them, and I've tried to stop but I never do, and because of that, I need to stay away from you.' What beautiful poetry, the confessions of a mad man.

Tyler scoffed, hastily grabbing his bag from the floor between his feet and hissing in pain, having forgotten about his injury. I wanted to ask if he was okay, stroke his hair and calm him down, but he must have sensed it, shutting me up by raising his hand in my face.

'Fine, whatever, get rid of me. We'll see how long it lasts, I guess.'

'Meaning?'

'You just said it yourself. You never stop.'

'Tyler—'

'I'll see you on Thursday,' he said, and he was slamming the car door and storming towards his house quicker than I could stop him. Perhaps I was frozen there, stuck in thought, drowning in an ocean of guilt and confusion and anger, trying to ignore the voice inside me that overpowered everything else, the one that told me to just do it, give in, you know you will eventually. He had started it, after all, so there was no one to blame but him.

Despite what you may think of me, I did have some self-control, some will—no pun intended of course. Or perhaps willpower had nothing to do with it, it could've been defiance, or delusion. It could have been the part of me that craved the back and forth; the chase; the cat and mouse games; the thrill of it all; the build-up and the ecstasy when it all came to a climax. If I was a predator, then surely my impulses and actions were born from instinct: fixed patterns that took me to my source of nourishment, my mates, and, ultimately, my death.

Matt was in the shower when I arrived home, and I of course took it upon myself to intrude, taking him as I pleased—which pleased him too—stealing away the innocence and peace the white-noise of the water afforded him. I tended to do that, lose control when he looked so pure. My Matthew, my devil shed in an angel's halo, the halo I would tear apart again and again because I couldn't bear to be the only one with so much darkness running through my veins. Pleasure; power; the ability to capture innocence and hold it in my heart forever. Butterfly in a jar. A collector never quits, and nor would I, not until I caught them all. Sometimes, though, if you aren't careful enough, you catch the wrong one; a pest disguised as a wonder, one that devours the rest of your collection if you don't get rid of it quick enough.

That night Matt told me that we had a visitor while I was out with Tyler.

'Who was it?'

'Who do you think?'

'I have no idea,' I said, but really I knew, I could feel it in my bones.

'Jimmy.'

'Oh, really? He didn't call.'

'He said he did, said you're ignoring him. Why are you ignoring him?'

'He's been calling me nonstop since his birthday. He's a mess. I think he needs help.'

Matt looked at me with an expression I knew all too well. 'What kind of help?'

'Not the kind you can assist with.'

# Seven

*Stop showing up at the house, stop calling me.* Trying to get through to Jimmy was like picking a fight with a brick wall, and the more he kept imposing on my life the more treacherous sneaking around with Tyler got. It was hard enough with Matt around. But people will risk everything they have for a little bit of something beautiful, and I was no different—instead of cutting contact with Tyler as all signs told me to, I persuaded myself I had it under control.

It should go without saying that the more you risk, the riskier it gets, but what if the opposite is true? What if it gets easier, what if you enjoy the risk? With me, it became like playing Russian roulette with someone with Parkinson's—addicting, thrilling, and completely chaotic. When you're balanced closer to ruin than ever before and you get away with it, it's almost like there's a god giving you the green light. Thumbs up, go for it, shoot for the stars. *You do you,* as the youth of today so casually throw around. *You only live once.* There are only so many times a man like me can try to stop and fail miserably before succumbing to the beauty that taunts us. And it did taunt me, it tortured my every inch, crept into the back of my mind when I tried to delete it, latched onto my skin like a leech and sucked my morality dry.

Every second I was not with Tyler after the night he hurt himself and I took advantage of his loose shorts and his spiked hormones, I counted the seconds left until I got to see him again. Days passed, days filled with reminders of what I had done. Nights of nightmares; or dreams—I did not know the difference. Nights of looking across the street into Tyler's bedroom window; drinking wine after wine while Matt was sound asleep upstairs, trying to pluck up the courage to text Tyler, tell him to meet me outside, that I wanted to talk to him. *Wanted* isn't the right word, though; I *needed* to talk to him, to see him, touch him even more. Days of teaching the philosophy of what seemed like my entire life— controversial, pederastic, scandalous; how the ancient Grecians could explain away their illicit behaviour and get praised for it even, because the gods and the philosophers and everyone in between said so at the time. I suppose when you think about it, it was another religion in the list of religions, and the Greeks were just another group of worshippers willing to use that religion or the opinions of those they deemed as Gods for bad as well as good. God forgives all, does he not? *Bless me Father for I have sinned*, and I will again, and again, and again. Like the people after me, like the ones before me. People often say that it was a different time, they didn't know better back then. Yes, they did. I assure you. Human beings have always known what is right and what is wrong. It's why wars are fought, why riots and movements happen all around us, why we have rights and laws and legislation. We have always known exactly what we are doing. And yet we excuse it, still to this day. I mean, there I was, standing in my lecture hall full of impressionable young students, teaching them about a moral code not even I understood, that no one ever would. It was like teaching them how to rationalise their worst selves and dressing it up as an important lesson, calling it history. 'Let us not judge our predecessors, but learn from them.' The thing is, we do learn from them. We learn how to better conceal our inner desires, and we learn how to fool society into thinking we're a better generation than the ones before us. If no one knows, you can't get caught. A philosophy all on its own. You are what you teach, I suppose.

Thursday's last class was about the Greek Stoic philosopher, Chrysippus, and his work 'On Passions', where he demonstrated by theory that passion and temptation are neither natural nor necessary, and claimed people can be trained to reject and resist them. I hated how everything could be flipped on myself, how I could relate to it so clearly and because of that give an excellent and insightful lecture. I was like a priest, preaching to the church goers about innocence and evil and resisting temptation while harbouring my own dark desires; anticipating the end of service so I could give in, let the devil inside of me out to play with the altar boys after service.

In my office, I dithered over texting Tyler to ask if he was still expecting me to pick him up for football training. The last time we spoke I told him I needed to stay away from him, which he refused to accept. But things could have changed, he might have been angry at me, disgusted. Perhaps his testosterone came to a crash at the same time the adrenaline from his injury did, and he was suddenly hit with a shockwave of realisation—*Julian is not a good man after all, I should have listened to him when he said we have to stop.*

I expected his parents to show up, in truth. Every knock on the door sent my heart racing and my mind spinning, but it was always the postman. I decided to just show up outside the kid's house, hope and pray and beg for the best, and at 6.30pm I drove home and waited for Tyler to climb into the car.

'How's the leg?'

'I knew you'd show up.' I pulled off and headed for the football club while Tyler clipped his seatbelt into place. 'My leg is better, thanks. Wanna touch it?'

I said 'no, thank you for the offer,' and he giggled in the way that said *you know you want to. You know you will.* I parked up outside the football club and we were right on time. I was pleased, it meant we didn't have time to talk about anything, but behold Tyler, the teenager. What did he care if he was late?

'Can I tell you something?'

'Can you wait? You're going to be late.'

'Don't care.'

'Well, you should.'

'Cool. So can I tell you now?'

'Sure,' I sighed. 'Go ahead.'

There was silence, dread inducing. I thought he would never speak again.

'I want to… umm…' Tyler trailed off, stopped talking. My heart thumped like I'd thrown myself off the top of a skyscraper. 'I want to—'

'Too slow,' I said, partly teasing, mostly petrified. I didn't want to know. 'Go, you're really late—'

'I want to touch you. For real.'

The confession, despite not being entirely out of character for where we were in our courtship, struck me like lightning. I wanted it to kill me. I welcomed the bolt with open arms but nothing came, nothing but a silence I was expected to fill with a response other than the uncomfortable hardness in my trousers. Boy, I wanted him to touch me, too.

'No,' I whispered. 'Tyler, please don't say that.'

'Why not? You touched me. I want to feel you now. Not like before when you were fixing Matt's car. Properly.'

It was as if he had told me his favourite colour. He wasn't embarrassed, he was the embodiment of brutal honesty.

'We can't, we just can't.'

'Pretty please?'

'No. It's not right.'

'Why not?'

*I ask myself that all the time*, I thought. *I still do not know the answer.*

'It just… It's not. It's wrong, and it's… Do you know how long I'd go to prison if anyone found out?'

'I'm not gonna tell anyone, Jules.'

'That's not what I'm talking about—'

'Then what *are* you talking about?' Tyler asked, rolling his eyes. I hesitated, realising he had a point. What the fuck *was* I talking about?

'Ty, you have to understand that you and I can never happen.'

'But it already has happened.'

I scoffed, shook my head and stopped myself from saying, *You're fourteen. You shouldn't be thinking about these things. Shouldn't be thinking about me. It's wrong, it's dangerous, and if you keep pushing me, there will be no turning back for either of us.* A natural reaction for any adult in my situation, apart from mine. I had no right, not a single leg to stand on, because to tell him he could not do or say something wrong would be hypocritical. After all, is that not the reason I was there with Tyler in the first place? To do something wrong. Something so ill-intended that if I was to wear a cross around my neck, it would burn and embed itself into my skin.

Instead of speaking my mind, I resorted to ignorance because it really would have been foolish to do the wise thing.

'You're late,' I said. 'Go.'

Tyler looked surprised. 'You aren't coming to watch me?'

'No, I'm not.'

'You're angry.'

'No, I'm not,' I repeated, which was a barefaced lie. Though I suppose angry wasn't the right word; frustrated perhaps. Emotionally, sexually. Who was he, this courageous lion cub, who did he think he was? He was the one who sent me back into this world, and I resented his intrusion.

'But... You always watch.'

'Well, not this time. I'll be right here waiting until you finish.' Tyler huffed and puffed, aggressively snatching his water bottle from the cup holder between us. 'You have to get used to attending things alone, at some point. I won't always be able to take you places.'

'Whatever,' he said. 'You're so full of shit. Why don't you just go? I'll walk home. I know the way now, I don't need you or your stupid car.'

'Tyler, calm down—'

'*You* started this. When you told me you liked me, and when you touched me.'

'Oh, when *I* touched *you*? How about when you rubbed me up in broad daylight while I was trying to fix my husband's car? You were begging for it then, and you're begging for it now. You're lucky we aren't inside somewhere alone right now. You're nothing but a silly little boy.' I heard the words come from my mouth, felt the fire behind them, the threat looming in the distance. I bit my tongue, but it was too late. I'd already said it, already meant it. Tyler saw a glimpse of the monster.

He got out of the car, slamming the door so hard it

rattled. I was surprised the windows didn't shatter. I watched him from inside the car, and when he caught my gaze he made a face at me, scrunched it up in frustration, and then he kicked the door to my Jag, hard, and then again for good measure. I could have screamed, but I kept it inside and let it simmer. Tyler walked away, not once looking back at me as he did, through the football club grounds and onto the pitch until he disappeared from my view. I stayed there for ten minutes, gave it time for the anger to subside to the point I no longer wanted to drag him back to the car by his curly hair, force his face into the dent on my door like a puppy who needs to learn right from wrong.

By the time the monster was tamed, I missed the boy. I wanted to apologise, soak him in with my eyes and store the memories there forever. It didn't take long for me to join the other spectators, which I suppose won't come as a surprise to you, but it did to me. I continually impressed myself with how ridiculous my decisions were. How blindly selfish. Nothing else happened that night, we just drove home in silence, both of us too embarrassed and resentful to say anything else to one another.

Matt asked me about the car that night. Why the scraped paint? Is that a dent? It was all easily explained away with a story about Tyler and his goofy football skills.

'You would think he'd be a better aim by now, with all the training you've been taking him to.'

'Yes, you would think so.'

'Oh, I spoke with him the other day, now that I think of it,' Matt said. 'I just remembered.' I had tunnel vision. I had to sit down before I fell down. *Act normal, don't react.*

'You did?' I said, feigning a headache.

'Yeah, we had a pretty good chat.'

'What did you guys talk about?'

'Oh, it was nothing,' Matt smiled. 'Doesn't matter.'

I had the dent repaired that weekend, just in time for Tyler's first official football match. I told him if his team won, I would take him out for lunch afterwards. Perhaps it was guilt for how things had gone the last time I saw him. Of course, I would have taken him out anyway, but an incentive is always good. I knew he would put his entire heart into the game if it meant me taking him out; he had asked me again and again for a secret date and I was beginning to give in.

That morning I woke up early and quietly got myself showered and dressed, making as little noise as possible so as not to disturb Matt, who was still out cold, dead to the world. It was better that way. The plan was to slip out of the house before he woke up, but he must have heard me putting my jeans and belt on because he said, 'Where are you sneaking off to?' from the bed. He had eyes on the back of his head, I'm telling you, and ears everywhere else. I told him the truth. 'I'm picking Tyler up for his first football match.' Then I told a lie, 'I did tell you, it was a couple days ago.'

'Ah. Of course you are,' he said, mocking me in an obvious way. *Where else would you be going, eh?* These little remarks, they put fear in me, but not enough to constitute any genuine worry. I thought he was onto me, once again, and my heart froze.

'What's the tone for?' I asked. Matt looked at me like I was a lunatic.

'No tone… You just said it yourself—you told me already. A couple of days ago. So, *of course* that's where you're going.'

'Oh, right…' I said, because that's all I could say. My mind was spinning. Matt used my own lie against me and I could no longer figure out if it was a lie at all. Had I told him about it a couple of days before and just forgotten, only to pluck it back up in self-defence, hoping to fool him? It didn't make sense. Had I imagined the sarcasm in Matt's words? Perhaps I allowed my guilty conscience to take hold of the room. Perhaps everything transpired exactly as I thought it did and Matt was playing with me. Either way, I had a teenager to pick up, so I gave Matt a kiss and told him I'd be a couple hours. I was still uneased, looking for any signs he was messing with me; his tell-tale smirk or his mischief-ridden stare, but I found none. I told myself to stop being so paranoid and left the house.

Tyler's team won the match, but I wasn't keeping count of the score, not exactly. It's difficult to focus on one thing when you're giving something else your all. True to my word, I took him out for something to eat after the game.

'So what's for lunch?' he asked. I knew just the place.

It was a little cafe just outside Oxford I'd taken Matt to the first time I allowed myself to see him on a weekend, out of work. Just like I had back then, I told myself I would stop, and just like back then, I knew I would not.

Tyler ordered a pint of Pepsi, a cheeseburger, and chips, while I opted for an omelette and a latte. I'd subconsciously ordered the same thing Matt did, six years ago. A mushroom omelette. The only difference was that I actually ate my side salad, rather than shoving it around my plate.

The food there was as good as I remembered, (despite the cafe being as run down as I remembered), and the same people from nearly seven years ago still worked there, just as warm and welcoming as before. It was as if they hadn't aged a day since, and I wondered if they thought the same about me, if they noticed the grey hairs starting to show, if they wondered why I was there with another boy old enough to be my son—that is if they recognised me at all. It was like groundhog day. Something needed to give.

'I'd like to ask you something,' I said. Tyler nodded, mouthful of food. 'Have you spoken to Matt recently?' Another nod. 'What about?' He looked at me, swallowed his food.

'Nothing really. He just got my ball for me.'

'Where was I?'

'Dunno,' he shrugged. 'Working, or something.'

'Why didn't you tell me?'

'It wasn't a big deal, Jules.'

'Was he nice to you?'

'Yeah, I guess. He's cool. Why? Do you think he knows something's going on?'

'No. I don't know. Did he say anything to indicate that he knows?'

'No, he just got my ball like I said.'

Speaking of the devil, Matt was calling my phone. I thought it was Jimmy at first; I already had four missed calls off him that day. I looked at Tyler, put a finger to my lips. *Shhh, be quiet, don't make a peep...*

I said, 'Hey, Matty. Everything okay?'

'Yeah. Where are you?'

'The game, it's still going on,' I replied, which caught Tyler's attention, his eyes darting from his glass of Pepsi to me. 'I'll be home in around an hour, don't worry.'

'It's still going on?'

'Yes, it is—'

'What are you up to, Jules?'

'I'm not up to anything, Christ.'

'You've been gone for hours.'

'Yes, because the game has run on.'

'Sure it has.'

'Look, I better go.'

'What's the score?'

'Ty's team is winning by miles.'

'Great, but what's the score?'

'Uhh...'

'The score, Jules. What is the score?'

'Fifteen - Nil.'

'Oh, really?'

'Yes, I told you—they're winning by a mile.'

'Great. See you later.' Matt hung up without saying anything else, and I thought to myself, *fuck*. I gave Tyler a smile and tucked my phone away in my jacket pocket. I forked at another bit of omelette while Tyler finished chewing his current mouthful of food.

'You know Fifteen - Nil is almost impossible, right?' he said.

'So it's not impossible, then?'

'Why lie anyway? Why not just say we're having food?'

I sighed, looking down at my plate, focusing on the colours of my salad, anywhere was better than getting caught in his gaze.

'Does it matter?' Tyler shrugged, pushing his plate to the end of the table, signalling he was finished.

'I just wanna know. I'm nosey.'

'Yes, I'm aware of that.'

'If he doesn't know about us, what's the point in lying to him? Aren't you allowed to have lunch with someone?'

The waitress came to take away our plates, so I asked her for the bill. 'Ready to go?' I asked the boy.

'Not yet.'

'Why not? You want dessert or something?'

'No, thanks. Tell me why you lied. You didn't need to lie.'

'Tyler, come on, we're leaving.'

'You can go if you want to, but then you'll have to tell Matt and my parents why you abandoned me in a cafe miles away.' He put his hands up in the air as if to say, *totally up to you*. Take it or leave it. And there was a feeling, deep down in the belly of the beast—do I crush him or care for him. He could be a different person every day. I suppose that's what teenagers are about, figuring out their way through the world and where they could possibly fit in. What do they bring to the table, how can they be better, smarter, faster, how can they be the prettiest or the most handsome in the room, what can they get away with, how hard can they push.

'Fine,' I said, forcing the irritation away, the impulse to lunge across the table at him and show him exactly who he was talking to. He was a kid, after all. He was an invasive, cheeky, enticing young man. 'Have I told you about how Matt and I met?'

Tyler shook his head. In truth, I didn't know what to tell him. How much of Matt and I's story could I realistically reveal without him fleeing my presence? Would Tyler be jealous to know he was not my first, my one and only, the special boy who changed it all? Or would he find it promising, use it to push me over the edge?

'The reason I lied to him boils down to this—I have a history, you could say. I met Matt when he was only a year older than you.'

It was simple, yet effective, and I watched as Tyler absorbed it. His face switched from cocky to confused, and I saw the moment the realisation hit him. From Tyler's point of view, Matt and I were both adult men. Matt was self-assured and confident, almost as tall as me, and at twenty-two he had a job, a degree, a house, a car, and a husband, all of the responsibilities teenagers find so tediously frightening. But Matt had once been a kid, a genius perhaps, but still a kid, and the very reason I was there eating lunch with Tyler was because I missed that part of him. Matt had grown cold, calculated, whereas Tyler was warm and naive.

'So, he does know?'

'He knows I have a soft spot for your age. Hence my earlier question about what he may have said to you when you spoke to him.' The waitress returned to the table, so I smiled at her, paid the bill, imagined burning the place down with me and Tyler still in it.

'How many others?' he asked.

'Two.'

'So all that stuff you said about wanting to stop was just bullshit?'

'No, you don't understand. I want to stop.'

'But you can't?'

'But I can't.' To my surprise, the boy put his hoodie on and stood up, leading the way out of there without another word. Perhaps it was because he had been such an antagonist, or perhaps it was just him, the way he made me feel, and perhaps I would have done it regardless, but when we were outside on the cold and grey street I grabbed the front of his hoodie, pushed him hard into a brick wall, and held him there for a beat, two. Then I kissed him. I'd acted on total impulse, yet a-fucking-gain, indifferent to the environment around us and the fact there could have been someone watching. The coach had nearly caught us once, my hand up Tyler's shorts like I was making sure his boyhood was still intact.

I hadn't cared then, nor did I care now, there with my tongue in his mouth in the cold street in the middle of the day. I was not thinking about anything except for my primal need to taint Tyler's innocence with something dark disguised as light. It was all silence and rhythm, breathy moans and wet lips. My pulse was through the roof, I felt as if something exploded inside me and it hurt in an exquisite way. All my longings, my desires, my total anguish, the secrets that slept deep within me came to life. I pulled away first, afraid of letting it get too far out of control too quickly. Thirty seconds in a busy street in London was enough to get me arrested. We ran back to the car like two teenagers out at night when they shouldn't have been, and on the way home Tyler blushed like he'd just been asked to the ball by Prince Charming, and I wondered if he knew that he was the prince and I was a dragon, disguised as his knight in shining armour. I was waiting patiently for my moment to strike, get him at the right time, bathe him in my fiery breath and devour his every cry for help.

# Eight

I was terrified of being hasty, acting too fast and making him hate me. I would be stabbing myself in the back, setting myself up for the future when he suddenly realised I was not the answer to his problems, but the cause of them.

I took it slow, made sure Tyler was the one who craved me rather than the opposite way around. I picked him up for football, and afterwards when he was caked in mud and exhausted, we would wait for the car park to be empty, and one of us would make the first move depending on who was feeling brave enough. It was always needy, desperate, aching for one another to take it even further. I never did, but Tyler tried again and again, and I would deny him each and every time, remove his hand from my crotch when he was feeling particularly audacious, tell him that we couldn't, that it was wrong, that being able to kiss him was more than I could have hoped for.

He would say, 'But what if I hoped for more?' and I would shut him up with more kissing, intensified, the kind you never want to end but have to because you can't breathe. I had him moaning from just kissing more times than I could count. He would be shaking with need, begging for me to touch him again, just once, just one more time, but I never did. I learned a lot about myself at that time; a lot of dark truths I find difficult to admit, even now. I learned everything I had forced myself to believe was a lie. I had self-control, I knew exactly what it was and how to hold it over someone else, how to drip-feed that control and hold back just enough to fool everyone around me. Like I fooled Will, and Matt in a sense, and then Tyler. Catherine, Graham, Ashley, Jimmy… the list goes on, I'm sure. The point is, I knew exactly how to make Tyler feel as if the whole thing was his idea. That is until the night he demanded more from me, refusing to leave the car until I did what he wanted. I loved when he begged.

We had been making out for a while when he started to get frustrated. Every time he put his hand somewhere he shouldn't I batted him away, held his hands together tightly while kissing him as he struggled to get free of my grip. I'd never seen him so full of lust, writhing like a snake in the passenger seat.

'Please touch me,' he said, on the verge of tears. 'If you don't touch me, I'll die.' There it was. I saw my own pattern, saw how easily I switched our roles with the intention of using it to my advantage down the line. If he ever tried to use that moment against me he would need to rationalise his behaviour toward me, too. So I touched, let him guide my hand to his shorts and took the hint, sliding beneath the waistband of his boxers, tugging them down slightly to make it easier, and then got to work. The car park was empty around us, silent, but inside the car it was anything but as Tyler tried and failed to quiet his ecstasy as I coaxed it out of him. Afterwards, he was covered in himself and shaking from the intensity. He caught his breath as I tasted him from my fingers and then he went to repay me, but I shook my head and grabbed his hand, gazed into his eyes and kissed him. I thought of Matt's words, how not every young and beautiful boy was obsessed with me. He was right, they weren't, but I knew exactly how to make them think they were. Take Jimmy, for example. I slept with him on a whim, I was angry with Matt and upset over Taffy's death, and now I couldn't shake him off.

Tyler said, 'I want to do that to you, too.'

'I know. I'm just being careful,' I replied. 'I don't want to do anything you're uncomfortable with.' Drip feeding, planting seeds, shifting blame and building trust. I asked myself when I became such a monster, but I did not have an answer. It could have been when I met Matt, or the day I decided to become a teacher, or when I first saw Will. Perhaps I'd always been that way and there was no trigger, just an accelerator caused by Tyler being the reincarnation of the first time I let my corrupt libido act as it pleased. Isn't that the foundation in which we're all built? If you're stubborn with pride we call it healthy self-esteem, if you're a narcissist we accept it as self-love and improvement, if you're an adulterer we say you're following your heart, and if you're greedy and gluttonous we brush it off as ambition. They're all sins we justify in every way we can.

After that I was like catnip to him. I'd given him a taste to make him crave more. I drove him to the brink of hate every time he saw me, saw how desperately he demanded to touch or be touched. It would all happen in due time, not that I ever told him that. I was stretching his resistance band, so to speak; setting him up for when the time was right for me to snap it. If I were to click my fingers and demand him to kneel before me, obey my every command and grant my every wish, he would do so without hesitation or regret. That's how I wanted him. Compliant, flexible. I wanted him to be incapable of stopping me. You can't pursue someone with the vigour Tyler had and then change your mind, say no. He'd had plenty of chances to heed my warnings that I'd ruin him, and the clock was tick-tock-ticking away; his opportunities to leave getting less and less frequent each time I offered one up. *We can stop this, you know? I don't want to hurt you.* But he never wanted to stop it, and in the end, just like in my dreams, he couldn't.

It all fell together quite smoothly in truth. Matt was going out one Saturday night with Josh, he even cancelled his shift at the Keysmith's to dance the night away in London. It was a widely anticipated event in the gay scene, a nightclub called Luxe, and though I'd been begged to go on more than one occasion, I declined. I would rather spend the night in the house, get some work done for once; perhaps I'd do some gardening in the daytime, tend to the much-neglected rose bushes, brush the stray stones on the drive back to their rightful place, and in the evening perhaps I'd have Tyler over, cook dinner for him, watch something funny on the tv, take him to bed and give him what he'd dreamed of for months. Wine, dine, and... well, you know.

Matt was due to leave that afternoon, and when he came downstairs he was dressed in black shorts that were far too short and a rainbow striped T-shirt, silver glitter on his cheek bones and his eyelids, Doc Martens on his feet.

'What ya think?'

'I think I'm regretting my decision not to come with you.'

'It's not too late,' he said, musing.

Five minutes before pick-up was certainly too late. 'No, you go and enjoy yourself, be free. If I was with you I'd have you on a leash.' Matt smiled, said that it wasn't the worst idea. I asked him to refrain from murder, only half joking.

'Oh, Jules, I almost forgot,' Matt said. 'My laptop is upstairs but it's taking *forever* to update, so I've left it plugged in and open to just do its business. Don't close it, okay? I need it to be working by tomorrow, I've got to submit my music to Camille on Monday.' Camille was his professor, and I told him not to worry, I wouldn't touch his laptop. When he was gone and his taxi had disappeared from the street, the first thing I did was hoover up the glitter spilled over the bedroom floor, and the second was text Tyler updating him on my current status—home alone, lonely, bored, and missing him. The entire night to myself.

Tyler was there within half an hour of my first message, and I locked the front door behind us as he skipped into the lounge. I wasn't about to make the same mistake thrice, after all. Ashley, Catherine, neither would have ended up hating me if I'd just locked the damn doors. Hell, Cath would probably still be alive, all over a split-second decision, a single moment of rationality amongst the absurdity. *Want me to get her?* I followed Tyler, turning off the main light in the lounge to take the edge off. No one likes to be fucked in the stark reality of day.

'What time do your parents get home from work?' I asked, watching as he took his shoes off and put them neatly next to Matt's piano. It was the first question I asked because it was the only one that mattered to me right then.

'Midnight,' he replied, chewing his lip, standing there like he didn't know how to break the ice. Luckily for him, I did. I'd bought myself enough time to prepare, to plan, and I knew how to execute it without it looking like my idea. I knew him, his every trigger, and every button I needed to press to have him smash that ice with a hammer. A teenager in an arcade playing whack-a-mole. I put the TV on, paying no attention to what channel, unimportant to me for obvious reasons. It was to steer the atmosphere away from awkward silence, a little background noise to allow for the fumbling moments where neither of us knew what to say. Only one thing was relevant to me: how I could achieve my twisted fantasy. By the expression on the boy's face, I was deeply concerned my plans for him needed to be postponed.

'What's wrong?' I asked.

'I… Something weird happened earlier.'

'What was it?'

'Nothing, nothing really. It doesn't matter, it's cool.'

I didn't know whether to coax it out of him or take advantage of his vague response. I did know, however, that I was running out of time to decide. I chose the latter because it was easier. Besides, he was already there, under my roof, and we were alone with no threat of interruptions, so why wait? Why send him home now when I was so close to getting what I wanted? It would have been foolish, self-torture. It would be weeks until I got the house to myself again, and you know what they say—you should always finish what you started.

'Come here,' I said, and when I held my arms out Tyler practically ran to me, wrapping himself around my chest like a snake. I kissed his forehead, he kissed my neck, on the tip of his odd-socked toes to reach. I could almost smell the lust emulating from him, tangible in the space surrounding us. I needed to make him work for it, needed him to look back on this night and see himself as the instigator. 'I'm not expecting anything from you, you know? We can watch a film, I'll order a pizza in. We can even go for a drive, okay? And you can leave anytime you wish.'

'I know. I want to stay here with you. I want…' Tyler stopped and buried his head in my chest in embarrassment. I held him tight against me, swaying for a moment, two.

'You can talk to me. You're safe with me.'

'I know. I'm not afraid.'

'I know you're not. You aren't afraid of anything.' Tyler smiled up at me, his eyes like dazzling diamonds. One hand settled on the small of his back and another in his hair, pushing him closer to me, tugging his head back slightly in a moment of weakness. He drove me crazy. The sound he made was bliss, but I couldn't act out of line, not yet. 'What do you want? Tell me.'

'I don't know,' Tyler whispered.

'Are you hungry?' He shook his head. 'Do you want to go for a drive?' No. 'Watch a film?' No. 'Go home?' Another shake of the head. No. Definitely not home.

'Tell me, come on.'

'I want you.'

Tyler's lips met mine and I closed my eyes with it, allowing the ground to fall from beneath my feet. The boy was trying to climb me like a koala in a tree, and the weight of him on me sent me falling backwards onto the sofa. The ice was broken. Both of us burst into laughter, then he was on my lap, straddling me the way he had weeks ago on the driveway. The urge to pin him down on his back and loom over him was fierce, but I couldn't do it, not yet. It was important to me he didn't feel forced, but that's not the same thing as being in charge. The TV hummed low in the background while two voices rang dissonant between my ears. Start and stop, begin and end. I did nothing, left Tyler in control to press himself down against me until we were both hard and restrained only by our clothes. I put my hands around his slim waist, rolled my hips upwards and pressed him down hard, whispering that I wanted him right then more than I ever had. It was the truth, and nothing but.

'Me too.'

'Are you sure?'

'Yeah. Please.' How could I deny him, this curly-haired ghost from my past? Dorian Gray, my mirror of sins.

I lifted his t-shirt over his head to expose his warm, pale skin, pressed my lips there and grazed his nipples with soft fingers until they stiffened. Replacing fingers with my tongue, Tyler moaned, a quiet little sound he tried to hide by burying his face in my chest, so I grabbed his chin, made him look at me and told him not to hide—I would have him moaning louder than that. I would pull noises from him he did not know he could make. I brought his lips to mine in a deep kiss, and the boy didn't weigh a lot so I stood up with him, his arms looped around my neck as I carried him upstairs where he wanted to be. Not that I didn't, but that night was about Tyler and only him, not me, not my seedy desire. So why could I feel the possessiveness building? Why could I not quiet the voice inside my head that screamed for control?

Upstairs, I kept my underwear on to keep the shock of it from hitting him at once. I didn't want him getting second thoughts. Tyler copied me, kept his boxers on but stripped from everything else, though our mutual arousal was evident to anyone with sight. I took his hand, leading him to the bed, and he took the hint, climbed on in, waited for me to shuffle next to him and then jumped on top of me, rutting against me, desperate for more, more, more. He was not scared, he was far from it. He was confident and persistent, his hips grinding down against me on their own, until he was almost vibrating above me from the new sensations that must have been intoxicating for a boy of fourteen. I settled my hands on his waist and gently moved him from above me to below me. I slipped my boxer shorts off and asked him to roll over, lie on his belly for me, which he did. Once more with feeling, I asked Tyler if he was sure he wanted this. *It's not too late to change your mind.* I thought of all the times I told him I wanted to ruin him, and that I would. I wondered if he remembered too. Not that it mattered if he had forgotten because I would make him recall it soon enough. In truth, if he had said no and tried backing out at the last minute, I doubt I could have let him go. Perhaps the deal was sealed before we even got upstairs. Silly boy. Foolish boy. I couldn't wait to be at the centre of him.

Tyler said yes, I don't wanna change my mind, I won't, I want you, Jules, please, so I yanked his boxer shorts down. My adrenaline was at a peak high and my heart drummed fast and hard, the thrill of it all consuming my every cell and forcing me into action. The sight of him belly-down in my bed, his face buried in the pillows, it's a sight I'll never forget. It's an image burned into the hard drive of my mind, where I kept my memories with Will. There really was no going back, not now, and I couldn't wait a second more.

In one quick move I brought Tyler's arms behind his back, and I paid no attention when he struggled against me. I couldn't risk letting him go now. Better to have and hold than lose and chase. His face was buried in the sheets below us, but I heard him clear as day. *Jules, stop, you're hurting me.*

There were tears, a scream, and then silence. The kind of muddled up pain and pleasure that renders you speechless, takes your mind elsewhere to focus on something else, until snap, you're back in the room, and it's the best feeling you could have imagined. Worth the pain and more. These are the things I told myself, reasons that justified actions. Tyler was no longer trying to escape me, he was pliant and flexible as I held him there and took what I visualised taking from him since day one. The longer you get away with something, the more reckless you become, the more inhuman and untethered. From the beginning humans have used God to justify the unjustifiable. My God was Pleasure. Hedone, goddess of all things that satisfy. Please me, and if you don't I'll make you. Cry for me, and if you don't I'll force the tears from your bright blue eyes. If there aren't meant to be people like me who seek the greatest thrills of life, take it up with the ones who created these personifications to justify the actions of others. So call me Hedone, call me Julian, call me a monster and beg me to stop. Make me. I am the personification of corruption, and once something has rotted away to nothing but dust, that's it, you can't get it back. My core, my soul, expired.

I wanted it over quickly, the less pain for Tyler the better, but there was also the part of me that never wanted it to end. But it would end, sooner rather than later, the sound of my name on his tongue, Jools, no, don't, stop, or did he say no don't stop? Things get jumbled up in the throes of ecstasy; broken boys, satisfied men, we're all the same, different sides of a single coin. I left my mark on him, stained the walls of his temple of youth, and when it was over, Tyler didn't move an inch. I could hear him whimpering slightly, could feel the guilt, the vomit threatening to burn my oesophagus. It is maddening what being aroused does to a human being, you can justify anything when you're aching with need. But once that desire is released, I'd say it's the closest you get to tasting a slice of hell. So I avoided it, slung my arm over Tyler and fell into a nightmarish sleep.

I dreamed I was standing in a pool that was slowly filling with water, and Tyler was there, sitting on the edge, legs dangling over the side. He was dressed head to toe in white, staring down at me with black eyes, his hair wild. Another Tyler appeared and sat down in exactly the same way as the other, and the pool started filling faster. I realised the double wasn't Tyler at all, it was Will, even though they were identical. I was swimming, trying to keep my head above water, and that's when Matt appeared, hair golden as the sun, wearing my favourite Cheshire grin. My saviour. He would rescue me, he would take my hand and pull me out, I was sure of it. Only he didn't, he stood there between Tyler/Will, laughing like the stereotypical villain as I swam and swam and never got close enough to the edge, my lungs filling with water as exhaustion took its hold.

I woke up, naked and covered in a sheen of sweat. I was breathless, so I figured I must have been shouting into the darkness that surrounded me, damp bed sheets stuck to my back, and I was alone. Tyler was not where he was supposed to be. I shot up out of bed in a panic, a thousand thoughts hitting me at once, a downpour of torrential rain. What time was it? Where was Tyler? I tapped my phone screen—01:56 am. His parents were due home two hours ago. Shit. I imagined myself out cold, his parents banging the door down as he climbed out from beside me and hurriedly put his clothes on, opening the door all red-eyed and bushy tailed, pretending he wasn't slick between the legs with a man when he was still a boy. They would know. The moment he opened the door they would have known, but it was 2am, so no, that didn't make sense. Two hours. Melissa and Lara would have had me lynched in less. I searched upstairs, called his name over and over, then downstairs, the hallway, the kitchen, the study, back through the kitchen, into the lounge. It was obvious pretty soon Tyler had left, but why without telling me? I opened the front door and stepped outside in a daze, stark naked, perplexed and still groggy from feverish sleep, and looked up at Tyler's bedroom window to spot any signs of life. The cars were on the drive, but there were no lights on in the house. In fact, the entire neighbourhood was like a ghost town. I got my phone out, clicked the name 'Ty' in my recent calls list, and listened as it rang. No answer. I began to doubt that any of it had even happened, perhaps I'd dreamed it all and fallen asleep as soon as Matt left, or imagined the whole thing. I went back inside, closed the door, and checked my text messages. Sure enough, there was my conversation with the boy from the previous afternoon.

Me: *Hey, kiddo.*

Ty: *Hi!*

Me: *You alright?*

Ty: *Yeah, all cool. What's up?*

Me: *I'm all alone.*

Ty: *Oh, really?*

Me: *Yes.*

Ty: *In yours?*

Me: *No, on the moon, darling.*

Ty: *Hahaha*

Me: *No, really. I'm on the moon.*

Ty: *You're losing your mind.*

Me: *Yes, I suppose I am.*

Ty: *Cool.*

Me: *Wanna come over?*

Ty: *I dunno. I don't feel good.*

Me: *What's up? Cone on. I'll make you laugh and you'll feel better.*

Ty: *I want to but I dunno.*

Me: *Okay. I'm here all night if you decide you want to see me.*

Ty: *I do want to. I promised Mum I'd stay home and keep the door locked.*

Me: *So just tell your mums you're with Matt and I.*

Ty: *Ok.*

Me: *I miss you.*

Ty: *Me too.*

Me: *Coming?*

Ty: *On way, there in 30 secs.*


If one thing was for certain, Tyler had been in the house. And if he was in my house, it meant that I indeed took him to bed with me, made him weep, hurt him in the way I was afraid of. No wonder he left my side the second he had a chance. I couldn't sleep the rest of the night, tossing and turning and getting myself tangled in the sheets, a part of me praying I would get stuck and suffocate by morning. I kept checking my phone, my heart lurched every time I heard the slightest of sounds, and when the sun began to dawn I scrolled through our texts again. *I promised Mum I'd stay home and keep the door locked.*

The door. Keep it locked. I shot out of bed again, fumbled through my jeans, and there was the house key, exactly where I'd put it. I locked the door. I *knew* I locked the damn door. Tyler couldn't have used the key to get out because he had no idea I even locked us in. No, the door was open before Tyler left, right? It had to be. Either someone unlocked it before we woke up, Tyler was a locksmith, or I really was losing my damn mind.

# Nine

Seven times I called Tyler's phone that morning, and I probably texted him at least double that, all before 9am. He answered me on the eighth try, his voice thick with sleep and deeper than usual.

'Hi.'

I tensed my jaw to stave off the frustration. Hi? Fucking *hi*?

'Hey, good morning. What happened last night, Ty?'

'Are you really asking me?'

'Yes.'

'I came over, and you—'

'Yes, no—not that. After. What happened after? Where did you go?'

'Where do you think? I had to come home, it was nearly midnight, so—'

'Why didn't you wake me?'

'Uh, I tried. You were out cold, so I just came home to bed.'

'Oh, alright. Are you okay?'

Tyler sighed on the other end. 'What's going on, Jules? What do you want?'

'How did you get out?'

'What?'

'How did you get out of the house?'

'I shimmied down the drain pipe. Why are you asking me these stupid questions?'

'Never mind, don't worry about it.'

'You're such a weirdo, you know? Just leave me alone.'

'I'm…' I paused, struggling with Tyler's tone, his words. Leave him alone. How was I supposed to do that? 'Ty, I'm so sorry about what happened last night.'

'I don't wanna talk about it.'

'Ty—'

'I don't wanna talk about it, okay?'

'Okay, that's alright.'

'Cool.'

'Listen… Have you, uh… Did anyone… Are you sure you're okay?'

'I haven't told anyone, is that what you want to hear? Can I go back to sleep now?'

'Yes, sorry, of course you can. Can I ask you one more question, before you go?'

'What?'

'Was the front door open when you left? Was it unlocked?'

A pause. 'Yeah.'

'Alright. I'll pick you up tomorrow for football

147

training.'

'No. I don't wanna go. I'm skipping tomorrow.'

'What? Why?'

'Are you really asking me why? Jules, you know why.'

'Because of me?'

'It's not all about you!' I held my phone away from my ear instinctively, shocked at the anger radiating through it. 'You hurt me last night, Jules. I ache all over—'

'Okay, lower your voice, Ty, please. I'm sorry, I—'

'Whatever. I hate you.'

That was the last thing I heard him say before the line went dead. He hung up on me, which I deserved, I knew that, but it didn't stop me from throwing my phone across the room in a fit of rage. Had I really been that rough with him, lost control? Flashes in my memory; the words *stop, no, don't, please*; the pillow beneath him damp with tears; my hands tight around his wrists to hold them against his back. I also recalled his moans of pleasure; his hips bucking back against me as mine thrust forward; the stains he left on my sheets. I hoped it was all enough to keep Tyler from tattling, at least until I could see him again to make him forget all about the hurt and focus on the good bits, and remind him the evil he witnessed was only a small part of the Julian he knew. Besides, he couldn't say I didn't warn him. I had, again and again, and still he came back for more. He had bigger eyes for desire than he could stomach, how was that my fault?

Keep busy, it's all I could do. Don't think about it, don't

dwell. It was a minor glitch in my matrix. I had a couple hours before Matt would get home, so I went around the house, paranoia-cleaning every room from top to bottom, trying my best not to be sick with guilt. I washed and dried the same bed sheets to put them back on the bed, fresh for Matt, to keep any suspicions at bay. I hoovered the floors; sprayed fabric and air freshener in copious amounts over all of the furniture; lit every candle we had, which was a lot thanks to Matt's scent addiction; locked the front door, unlocked it, locked it again. The key definitely worked. My key. Did Matt take his with him? I checked the sideboard drawer, bingo—it wasn't there, which meant... But wait, no. It couldn't have been Matt who unlocked the door. He sent me photos of his night, and even if he hadn't, they were posted all over his social media accounts for the world to view. But we were the only two people with a key—I took Jimmy's off him and Ashley gave hers back long ago. Unless Matt orchestrated the entire thing; lied about going to London; fabricated the whole story; faked the photos. He would have had to call a cab, leave the house, come back an hour later and then wait for Tyler to get there, all while keeping himself hidden. And then let himself back into the house to what, exactly? Watch me fuck Tyler in our bed and then just leave again, post his photos as if he's been out partying all night?

Matt was dramatic, cunning, and elaborate even more so, but all that seemed a tad too complicated, even for him. All that waiting around, he would have grown bored, and with boredom came his appetite for destruction. He would have killed me and the kid there and then, bored, destructive, jealous little psychopath. My mind was spinning, dizzy, and the only thing that really made any sense was I hadn't locked the front door after all. Why make such insane assumptions when the most obvious answer was right there in front of me the whole time? I was in overdrive mode, fight or flight. My plan had fallen apart and instead of satisfaction with a splash of guilt all I felt was dread. Pure, existential dread. Tyler could hate me as much as he wanted to, but no one would beat how much I hated myself. Every creak of the floorboards and groan of the pipes had me flinching that day. The wind flapped at the letterbox and whistled through the gaps in the windows, the boiler gurgled and mumbled as if it had something to say. I was on high alert, like a man most wanted, and every sound that entered my ears made the hair stand up on the back of my neck. I went out back to feed the Koi, and the rustling of leaves being blown up the path in the breeze sounded like someone dragging their feet behind me.

When Matt was home it provided me with some small dose of relief. I watched his videos of him dancing, drunk and giddy and sparkling with glitter as he laughed with his friends and swallowed shot after shot. He showed me more photos, neon lights making his hair a different colour in each one. Blue, red, green, purple, silver, back to blonde, the glitter on his cheekbones fading as the night went on. He was as beautiful in the last photo as he was the first; as he was right then, next to me and giggling when I would chuckle wholeheartedly at a funny photo or video in particular. He told me about a celebrity that was there, an English actor rumoured to be into younger boys.

Then there was the golden question: 'How was your night?'

'Uneventful,' I replied, bringing him close and squeezing, seeking comfort. 'I cleaned the glitter you left scattered all over the bedroom floor, and then I marked some assignments. But mostly, I missed you.'

Tyler avoided me as much as he could after that night. He didn't respond to any of my texts or calls, didn't kick his football in my garden once, and if I saw him in the morning before work he would turn away, pretending not to see me. Jimmy, on the other hand, wouldn't quit. The texts and calls seemed to go on forever. Matt asked why I wasn't taking Tyler to football training but was otherwise oblivious to the sudden stop of routine and my new stalker. I suppose it didn't affect Matt in the way it did me; a gaping wound in my gut, desperate for attention and reassurance. I needed Jimmy to leave me alone and for Tyler to forgive me, to tell me it was going to be okay and he was over his tantrum now and he's sorry, so sorry, he did like it, maybe he liked it too much, and that's why he got scared and left, but he's totally fine, it's cool, he hasn't told anyone, he was just mad at me, but he misses me, and he wants to do it again. Let the wolf blow your puppy-dog mind. I started to get antsy, embarrassingly so, and I decided one morning before work that week I wasn't letting him get away with it. Who did he think he was, taunting me, making me fall for him, and then ignoring me once he had what he wanted from me, pretending I was the one in the wrong? Perhaps I was the pretender, I didn't know anymore. I just knew I craved the very sight of him, that I'd never stop until I had him again, and I was not a very patient man. I knew I was being stupid, but it didn't stop me, it never did. At seven-thirty I heard the football being kicked across the street, so I decided to leave early, hoping to catch Tyler before his parents were up. I couldn't for the life of me understand what it was I thought I was doing. You know the drill. Same song and dance on a different groundhog day.

He saw me coming and tried to go inside, but I caught up to him, grabbed him by the arm and pushed him against Lara's car, making him look at me. I suppose you could say I had completely lost it at that point.

'Let me go,' he said, red in the cheeks and vibrating with fear, so I let his arm go. I didn't want to cause a scene first thing in the morning and have the police show up at work while I was mid-lecture.

'Why are you ignoring me, Tyler?'

The boy was glaring at me. 'Because you hurt me. Because you're a bad person, and a hypocrite, and you only care about yourself—'

'That's not true. I care about you.'

'No, you care about what you want from me.'

'Where the hell are you getting all of this? Where's this attitude come from?'

'You locked me in,' he said. I heard a car drive down

the road behind me, a bird cooed from Tyler's rooftop.

'What?'

'You *locked* me in your house, Jules.'

'Is that what you're so worked up over? Ty, I locked the door because I didn't want anyone walking in unannounced. If you wanted to leave I would have let you, at any point—'

'You're a liar. You're lying. I asked you to let me go, I asked you to stop! You locked me in so I couldn't leave, and you hurt me.' Tears formed in his eyes, balancing on his waterline. I wanted to hold him close and whisper apologies in his ear, but I couldn't touch him, not there, not then.

'Tyler, I'm sorry, I am. Please, just… Hang on a second. How did you get out? You told me the door was open.'

'Is that all you care about? Oh, big deal, I *lied* to you. How many times have you lied to me?'

'Just answer my question.'

'No,' he muttered, shaking his head. He looked down at the ground, anywhere but me. 'I don't wanna talk to you. Go away.'

'Stop acting like a child—'

'I *am* a child.'

'Oh, fuck you,' I said. 'Look how the tables have turned. I *told* you I didn't want to see you anymore, but no, you persisted, you wore me down. Practically threw yourself at me, and now what? You get what you want and you just toss me to the side, then blame me for it?'

'You're twisting my words. I know what you're

doing.' The boy was smarter than I'd given him credit for.

'All I'm doing is trying to find out how you got out of my house.'

'And *I* am not telling you.'

'Tyler—'

'Get out of my garden,' he demanded. 'I have school soon. Get out before I scream.' My hands throbbed to grab him by the throat, my brain struggled to find the catalyst of this seemingly sudden loss of power and control. Where had I gone wrong? I realised being there on this teenage boy's front garden while we argued about how he got out and whose fault it was he got hurt certainly wasn't helping the situation. I took a step back, swallowing down the rage rising like the sun. And then it was too late. I dug a hole and threw myself in.

Melissa opened the front door, and she seemed as surprised to see me as I was her. Imagine that, being shocked to see someone open their own front door. I suppose I was selfish, but isn't everybody? Thank God I stepped away from Tyler just moments before she came outside. What's the best you can act? There were a few star moments in my life but this one had to be my best performance yet.

'Melissa!' I said, like she was the answer to my problems. 'Just the person I wanted to see.'

'How are you, Jules?' she asked, offering a warm smile. 'I wanted to see you too, as it goes.' My stomach felt like it was full of feral cats clawing to get out.

'Oh, really?'

'Yes. Lara and I wanted to invite you and Matt over this Friday night for some drinks. What do you think? You've both been absolute saviours since we moved in, so think of it as a thank you piss-up.' Melissa and I both laughed, and I took a breath to steady myself as Tyler looked at me like the whole situation was the funniest thing he had ever witnessed.

'Of course, we'd love to,' I replied, an automatic response. I wasn't exactly thinking straight. In reality, it was a disaster waiting to happen, but what excuse could I possibly give to get out of attending? I was blank. 'Consider it a date.'

'Fabulous. A date it is, then.'

'Or a gang-bang,' Tyler muttered.

'Tyler! What the hell?' Melissa was clearly dismayed. 'Be polite, please. Where did you learn that term?'

Tyler rolled his eyes, 'I'm fourteen, Mum.'

'I'm sorry about his language, Jules,' she said, eyeing her son to behave. 'He's been acting out lately.'

'Oh, no need to apologise at all. Matthew has a potty-mouth. You'll see on Friday, he's outrageous.'

'I can't wait. So, what can we do for you?'

I looked at her blankly. It stumped me. 'Sorry?'

'You were here looking for me, right?'

'Oh, of course. Yes, right. I was coming over to ask you and Lara over for drinks, as it goes.'

'What a coincidence,' Tyler smirked.

'A coincidence indeed,' Melissa added. 'Well, great minds think alike. I best get back inside but I'll see you on Friday. Nice talking to you.'

'Ditto, I look forward to it,' and when she was gone Tyler and I stared at one another in silence. Then he started laughing.

'That was embarrassing to watch,' he said.

'I'm leaving.'

'Oh *now* you're leaving. You're no fun at all.' I turned around, deciding to let him have the last word because it was the only way I was getting out of there without killing him with my bare hands in the middle of our street. 'Oh, Jules?'

'What?'

'One day I'm gonna hurt you like you hurt me,' he said, and I pretended it didn't make my blood run cold as I crossed the street.

At work my life still followed me everywhere, twisting through the sentences I spoke and the lessons I taught. Forbidden love, sex, vengeance, and the rest of the obscenities of the Greco-Roman world. The tragedies and the romanticism of some of the worst acts of humanity. It was like I was teaching a class about my world, young boys and controversy and revenge; the war between power and weakness, love and hate, good vs evil. Historians often say those who do not know history are destined to repeat it, but I think what we learn from history is that we never learn *from* it. History is full of lies and exaggerations about events that supposedly happened, written by people who weren't there, and then we go ahead and repeat those events anyway. In fact, I think if history teaches us one thing, it's to be smarter than our predecessors, to hide things better, to pretend and blend in like a wolf among sheep. Kings, emperors, gods, rulers. It's no different to society today, really. The only thing separating them from us is freedom. Does something suddenly become wrongful because the person in charge says so? Yes. That's the way it works. But do people suddenly become model citizens, ditch their depravities and brush them under the carpet as if they were never really there? No. We conform, and by conform I mean we adapt. Those of us who desire darkness just evolve into creatures of the night and become better predators, silently hunting our prey without getting caught, in and out like a devil's whisper. But what happens if we aren't good enough and get exposed? We're just another example, another headline in a quarry of headlines, another one to add to the never-ending list of us. Another demand by society for *NO MORE,* knowing there will be more. Perhaps if humanity was wiped out entirely and nothing remained of the past, nothing to influence our actions, no historical references, it would restore our innocence and create a better generation. Perhaps it would all go to shit anyway. Who knows? There's nothing you can do to stop it either way. Human beings are corrupt the moment we are born, some are aware of the deviant inside while others remain closed off from the innate part of themselves that screams for more, take, take, take. We're often reminded to live life to the fullest—*you only get one life* they say, so do what you want to, nobody is going to remember you when you're gone—and yet when we listen we're selfish and narcissistic; hedonists and criminals and pederasts; and the very people who jump into uproar at the slightest mishap are often the most selfish and hypocritical of all.

It was lunch time when Jimmy turned up at the office. I was with a student, Grace, going over some key points for an upcoming assignment, and there he was, storming through the door without knocking.

'Oh, *sorry*, I didn't realise you had *company*.'

I looked at him, then at Grace who was as disturbed as I was. 'You do know this is my *office*, right? Where I work?' Jimmy rolled his eyes and sat down next to Grace like she wasn't there. 'Grace, I'm terribly sorry about this. I'll catch up with you later, alright?' She put her notebook away in her bag and left the room, closing the door behind her. 'What the fuck, James? What are you doing?'

'You won't answer your *phone*. What *else* am I supposed to do?'

'Not show up at my work, that's for sure. You could get me fired for Christ sake—'

'Please, Ju-Ju. Just *talk* to me.' Tears formed in his eyes and I sighed.

'Fine. You've got ten minutes. What do you want to talk about?'

Jimmy looked away from me, his head down like a guilty dog. 'Has Matt passed on my messages?'

I paused, my teeth clenched tight. 'You've been talking to Matt?'

'I guess that's a no, then.'

'What have you been saying to him?'

'*Nothing*, Christ. I just asked him to tell you to *call* me.'

I rubbed my hand over my face to hide my anger. 'Do not bring him into this again, James. I'm warning you.'

'I didn't know what else to do, I—'

'I don't care. You leave him out of it.'

'You don't give a *shit* about Matt anyway! You don't care about *anyone* but yourself.'

A flicker of rage ignited inside me and I slammed my fists on my desk. Jimmy jumped along with my pens. 'Don't ever underestimate my feelings for Matthew,' I said. 'The other night between you and I meant nothing, James. It was a quick fuck in a moment of weakness, I couldn't bear listening to you whine and whine. Woe is fucking me.'

Jimmy was stuck, a deer in headlights, and when he spoke he stumbled over his words. 'No… You… You… You're… You're a monster.'

I laughed, couldn't stop myself. '*I'm* a monster? I wonder what that little girl's parents would think of you, their daughters murderer—'

'Stop it! Stop it, Ju-Ju—'

'You're a murderer, Jimmy. Whether I say it out loud or not.' I was angry with him, and quite frankly terrified. Badgering me was one thing, Matt not so much. If Jimmy knew the damage he would bring himself by becoming a burden to Matt, he wouldn't dare. He would run as far away as he could get and never look back. Perhaps I was being a monster, but it was only to protect Jimmy. The further he was from us the safer. Perhaps that's what I told myself to feel better. Perhaps deep down it was a thrill to be able to speak my mind with no consequences. All of the above, yes, no, perhaps. It gets so murky, lying to yourself.

'I *hate* you,' Jimmy said, crying into his hands. 'I thought you loved me.'

'Love hurts.' I checked my watch, it was 1.20pm. 'You have to leave now, James.'

Still sobbing, Jimmy stood up. 'I'm going!' he said, hysterical. 'You *changed* when you met Matt. I love the kid, but he's made you a selfish, *selfish* piece of shit.'

'Stop calling, stop texting. Get a grip of yourself before you contact me or Matt again.'

'Fuck you. You don't have to see me anymore, but you can't stop me and Matt being friends—'

'And what a wonderfully faithful friend you are, fucking his husband.'

'I really do hate you,' he replied, then he slammed the office door behind him. That really got to me. Tyler slammed doors. *Children* slammed doors. I wanted to scream at Jimmy, tell him that he was wrong about me, wrong about Matt. I was always a selfish piece of shit, it just got more difficult to hide the more someone coaxed it from me. Will, Matt, Tyler, Jimmy. They pushed and pushed and pushed. I was at a loss, so I told myself to continue on, power through, keep lying, and pretend like nothing had happened. If you can't climb out of the hole then keep digging, there's an end somewhere. There has to be.

# Ten

I couldn't say I was excited. Matt and I stepped into Melissa and Lara's house—Tyler's home—Friday evening and I was on the defensive. It was my first time meeting Lara, which did strike me as a little bit odd initially, but was easily put down to people, parents particularly, making utterly ridiculous choices. There I was, a middle-aged man watching her son for her, and she was so preoccupied with her own life she had failed to give me a single screening herself.

'It's nice to finally meet you,' I said. 'It's been a long time coming.' *Massive fan of your son.*

'Yes, lovely,' Lara half-heartedly replied. 'You're obviously Julian.'

'You've met Matt already, I hear?'

'Once or twice.' When she said this she glanced toward Matt, who was talking with Melissa, and he raised his bottle of beer to her with a wink.

'Well, I'm sorry about not coming over here sooner

to introduce myself,' I continued. 'Work keeps me pretty busy, as I'm sure you understand. Tyler says you're both nurses?'

It was clear to me from the start she didn't want us there, and for some reason unknown to me there was a tangible tension between her and Matt, as if they had a mutual dislike of one another. Melissa, on the other hand, was none the wiser, and Lara was pleasant enough to me, so I put it down to paranoia again. I was looking for signs my jig was up, creating more guilt just for the hell of it. Perhaps Lara was like me, kept herself to herself. There was a twisted hopefulness in me that perhaps she, too, harboured secrets. Wishful thinking is one thing, reality another.

The more I told myself to calm down the more impossible it seemed, and the mere idea of the presence of others was distressing. Melissa's welcoming voice made me shudder, Lara's curtness made me want to flee, and every time Matt smirked, it bruised me. I couldn't look anyone in the eye, couldn't face reality, and the only distraction from the hell inside my mind was the booze. An entire four bottles of champagne and a box of beer were on the dining table, along with various plates of snack foods. Music was playing quietly from the TV, Matt and Melissa were getting along like the best of friends, and Lara busied herself in the kitchen, so I sat down on one of the sofas, willing myself to blend in.

The champagne was opened, glasses filled, and Melissa asked how Matt and I met. I told the false version of the story, of course; the one where Matt turned up at my lectures in his aggressive pursuit for knowledge, and I fell head over heels in love with him. And I was lucky he was not my student and thankful he was the age of consent, or else I would have been in a world of trouble. If you can sell yourself as a good person, even the bad things you do have a polished finish. Tell your story just right and instead of vilifying you, your audience will relate to you, because we're all looking to relate to someone over something or other. Matt and I were love at first sight, the way we told the story, just controversial enough to be comfortable. It was romance, it was love, it was boundless. Age is just a worthless number.

Matt headed for the kitchen to get a bottle opener after having misplaced one already, but Lara abruptly sent him to sit back down.

'I'll get it for you, Matthew. And don't lose this one.'

'Yes, Miss,' Matt said.

'How about you, Melissa?' I asked. 'How did you two meet?'

'Actually, our relationship sparked its own kind of controversy,' she replied. They met at the John Radcliffe hospital where they both worked as nurses, and Lara was engaged to a man at the time. They started an affair that lasted two years before Lara's engagement came to an inevitable demise, and they had been together ever since then. They had a child together through donor insemination, and along came Tyler.

At the mention of his name, I noticed his scent, swirling all around me. It clung to the walls, the fabric, my skin, theirs. He was not in the room with us but I could feel his presence regardless, he was like static, electrifying. I didn't know if it was him or the booze or the hunger but I was desperate for something, anything, and as I finished my first glass of champagne I blurted out, 'Where is the kiddo, anyway?'

'Upstairs,' answered Lara, returning with another bottle opener for Matt.

'With enough pizza and chocolate to kill a dog,' added Melissa.

'Yes. He won't be bothering us.'

'Oh, he wouldn't be bothering us,' I said.

'Yeah, of course not,' started Matt. 'It's his home. Go get him, let's get him drunk.'

'Matt you are a *riot*,' Melissa said, while Lara added, 'Don't be so absurd. He's a child.'

'I was joking, Lara, darling.'

'Were you really?' she asked, but before Matt could respond, Melissa stepped in. Perhaps it was only me who noticed the tension, but I was certain I saw the look of hatred pass between Matt and Lara.

Melissa asked, 'Is that the kind of stuff you were getting up to when you were Ty's age, Matt?'

'Oh, God forbid I told you everything I used to get up to,' he answered, laughing. I thought, *Please do not open your mouth.*

'Come on, enlighten us,' said Lara.

'Well, let's just say I was a virgin to nothing by the time I was fourteen.' He said nothing and yet it was everything. I half expected him to add manipulation and blackmail to the list, throw murder in for good measure. Needless to say, both women were shocked, but in different ways. It seemed to irritate Lara, as did everything else Matt said and did, whereas Melissa was worried.

'I have to be honest,' she said, sighing. 'I've been a little concerned about Tyler lately. He doesn't really seem like himself.'

'He's fine, babe,' Lara said. 'Teenagers are like that.'

'But he's been so distant for the last couple weeks. And he won't talk to us. It's not like him at all. Has he said anything to you, Matt? Anything at all?'

'Not really, but he's with Julian a lot more than he's with me.' All of a sudden, all eyes on me. Fuck. *Fuck you, Matthew.*

'Oh… I mean, I'm not with him *all* of the time. I don't think he's mentioned anything, not that I've heard, anyway. He seems just fine to me. What has you concerned?'

'He's lost interest in the things he once loved. He's stopped enjoying school, stopped playing games. He says he doesn't want to play football anymore. Has he told you why?'

I hesitated, collected my thoughts and analysed every word before I spoke. 'He didn't give me a reason, no. He just said he doesn't want to do it anymore. Perhaps it's not for him. I'm terribly sorry.'

'That's alright,' Melissa replied, her hope drained. 'Keep an eye on him, won't you?'

'Of course.'

'We would tell you straight away if we thought there was something wrong,' added Matt, and I felt like the worst man on the planet.

Lara said, 'Mel, Tyler is absolutely fine. You worry too much.' In truth it was Lara, the one in the wrong. Neither of the mothers were worried *enough* about Tyler. If *they* had kept an eye on him instead of leaving it to the neighbours, perhaps Tyler would have been fine. Perhaps I never would have sank my teeth into him, perhaps things wouldn't be so fucked up. Blame the parents, blame anyone but me. It was getting a little too hot under the collar, so I excused myself, asked for directions to the bathroom. Melissa said it was upstairs and to the right, but Lara said no, it was to the left. I suppose it was an easy mistake to make, they had only lived there for a couple months. Matt knew, but he couldn't chime in, not without having to explain Graham and the sordid past. In truth, I didn't know if it was the bathroom I was headed to or Tyler's bedroom, but thanks to his parents, if I got caught in the wrong room, I had a valid explanation for it. Some things will work out even when you think they won't.

In the bathroom, it hit me how much I had to drink since I got there. I was at the point where another glass of champagne would send me over the edge, but the thought of stopping depressed me. I stared at my blurry reflection in the mirror, my overgrown stubble, and noticed Tyler's football kit at the bottom of the laundry basket. The alcohol had me confident, nonchalant, and I knew I could justify any of my actions no matter how terrible or idiotic. I left the bathroom and crept down the hall, stopping right outside a door with a plaque that said *Tyler's room*. Tyler would probably think of me what I thought about Jimmy: Stalked, exhausted, at the end of his tether; but I had no desire to stop it. I knocked on his door, two quiet little taps just to get his attention, and a soft voice on the other side of the door said to come inside, so I did. He rolled his eyes when he saw it was me and dropped his phone next to him on the bed, full of attitude and sass. For a teenage boy, his room was surprisingly immaculate, which made sense after finally meeting Lara. Tyler followed her in terms of neatness, and Melissa in terms of naivety.

'Why are you here?' he asked me. I shut his door behind me, sat on a black beanbag in the centre of the room.

'Well, hello to you too, handsome.'

'Seriously. Why?'

'I'm here with Matt to socialise with your parents, as you know—'

'I mean up here with me. You shouldn't be here.'

'I shouldn't do a lot of things. I still do them.'

'Yeah, don't I know it.'

I laughed, lazy, like a humming drunkard. 'What's the point of life if you always do as you're told, eh?'

'Are you, like, drunk?'

'Don't be silly.' I laughed again, hiccupped. 'Alright, I'm pretty hammered.'

'Cool! I've never seen you drunk before.' This surprised me, considering the amount of wine I consumed in the few months I knew him. Alcohol is sipped during the evenings, after all, when the kids are sound asleep in bed.

I opened my arms, saying, 'Well, you're seeing it,' and Tyler presented his first smile.

'You know, you're not as funny as you think,' he said.

'No? Then why are you just *desperate* to laugh?'

'Because you look like an idiot.'

'Ouch,' I said, like his insult physically hurt, and that time Tyler couldn't help it. He grinned, wide, and for a brief, tender moment, it was just like before: easy and fun to be together, before I muddled it all up. Looking at him, lying on his side in bed, propped up on one arm, I wanted to reach out and touch his pink cheeks, rewind time and control myself. Memories of him swarmed me, belly down on my satin sheets, the way he writhed and begged me to stop, the scream when I ignored him. He was all innocence and angelic beauty, a curly haired siren tempting me from the waves, and a sudden jolt of guilt electrified my heart.

'Listen, Ty,' I said, my words catching in my throat. 'I'm so sorry.'

'It's cool.'

'No, it's not. What I did to you was—'

'I don't want to talk about it. It's cool. I'm over it. I was just angry before, okay? And I'm sorry too, for being a dick to you.'

I felt my heart shatter. The mere thought of the boy apologising to *me* was incomprehensible. It was only days before that he said he wanted to hurt me, that he hated me. There, in his bedroom, in my drunken state, I found myself being honest for once, even to myself. A thought hit me: the only reason he hurled abuse at me that day was because I had abused him. That's when the tears started. I had tainted our every interaction with betrayal, and I was crying before I had the chance to stop it. At least I wasn't a complete monster.

'Please, Tyler, never apologise to me. You haven't done anything wrong. *I'm* sorry. I... I don't know what's wrong with me.' I rubbed my shirt sleeve over my face to dry it, but it was no use. Tyler didn't know what to do. He stood up from his bed and walked wearily over to me, saying my name and telling me to calm down.

'Don't cry. Why are you crying, Jules?'

'Because I'm a monster. I wish I was different, I wish I didn't like doing the things I do. I wish more than anything I hadn't hurt you.' And William. And Matt. And the others to come. 'If I could take it back, I would. I just... I lose control, sometimes, and I can't—'

'I know, I know. It's okay—'

'Don't you hate me? Don't you want to tell everyone what I did?'

'Nah.'

'What's happened since you saw me the other day?'

Tyler shrugged, stepped closer. 'Like I said, I was just... angry before, I guess. We're cool.' All of a sudden there were only a couple of inches between us, and he wrapped his arms around my middle and nuzzled himself against my chest. I was speechless, confused, and felt like a total fool. Blubbering like an idiot to a fourteen-year-

169

old schoolboy. I held him there, breathing him in, his hair tickling my chin. He was morphine through an IV line, capable of rendering me useless in thirty seconds flat, and mixed with the booze and the added thrill of being caught, I was a cocktail of heady desire. I kissed him, or perhaps he kissed me, and we were edging closer to his bed when he pulled away from me.

'Don't,' he whispered, breathless. 'Not here. It's too risky.'

I nodded, pressing my forehead against his. 'I know. You're right. I know.' I kissed him again, took a step back. 'Thank you.'

'For what?'

'For everything.' For giving himself to me. For not telling a soul. For accepting my apology. For being the level-headed one in *another* moment of weakness, the, dare I say it, *mature* one.

'I'll see you soon, yeah?' Tyler said.

'Yes. Bye, Ty.'

Downstairs, I walked into a discussion about the house. Melissa was saying something about the house being unusually cheap, Matt was playing the part of attentive listener, and Lara was eyeing them up with disdain. She averted her eyes when I walked in the room, and Matt looked at me then, said, 'What took you so long?'

'I uh, felt sick. I'm fine now.'

'Oh goodie,' Matt grinned. 'I was just about to tell Melissa about the people who used to live here.' I shook my head subtly, pleaded with him using only my eyes not to say another word. Too late. I was always too late.

'Did you know them?' Melissa asked.

'Well, not really, but Jules and I know what happened. Town gossip, you know. And it was in the news, only for a couple days.'

'The news? What the hell happened?'

'It was years ago now. Jules knows more about it than I do, to be honest.'

'Oh, no, definitely not,' I said. 'You're the storyteller, darling.' Matt smiled and it sent rage through me. Games, always playing games.

'It'll be far better coming from you.'

'Jules, you must tell us,' said Melissa, and Lara rolled her eyes. Perhaps it was my desire to be liked, but I gave in to Matt's whims and told the story. The lie.

Graham and Charlotte, mutually, happily married to denial. They kept to themselves most of the time, but I spoke to Graham now and then in passing. One day, Graham moved out, and we heard afterwards Charlotte wanted a divorce; something about an affair. Graham was gone perhaps a month when someone broke into his new place and killed him. After that, Charlotte wanted more than anything to get out of town, which was why she continued lowering the asking price until someone snatched it up.

'He was *killed*? As in, murdered?'

'What else does *killed* mean, Mel?' Lara said.

'That's not even the best part,' Matt added. 'Tell them, Jules.'

'I don't think they need to know this—'

'Oh, come on. It's the juiciest bit.'

I took a deep breath, preparing myself. It felt like Matt was punishing me, but I knew it was my guilty conscience telling me its own stories. 'When he was discovered dead, the police uncovered some disturbing things about Graham. Apparently, he had a thing for boys. Young boys, teenagers. Charlotte was devastated, of course. She had no idea. She found receipts for hotels and restaurants and assumed the affair was with another woman. She was too ashamed to stay in Oxford once the news outlets got a hold of the details.'

I tried to act indifferent, not like a man riddled head to toe with sin, but I could feel my heart pounding. Lara and Melissa couldn't believe their ears, firing questions at me I didn't want to answer.

*How many boys?* No idea. *How old were they?* I think between the ages of thirteen to sixteen. *Did they catch the person who killed him?* No, they never did. *Good riddance, I say, but did the wife really not know what her husband was up to?* Apparently not. *How can you live with someone like that and not know?* You never truly know a person, not a single one.

'How come we're only now hearing about this?' Lara asked, sounding sceptical, accusing.

Matt shrugged, sensing her tone. 'Like I said, the news moves on with everyone else.'

'That's not what you said—'

'Google it, if you don't believe us. His name was Graham Bradley.'

Graham Bradley: husband; predator; cheat; liar. Once

172

Lara was satisfied, after having actually searched the name, the night sort of fizzled out. Tyler came downstairs at around midnight for a glass of water, and he wouldn't look at me or Matt. Shortly after he went back to his bedroom, Matt and I said our goodbyes to Lara and Melissa and went home.

That should have been it, go home, go to sleep next to my lover, wake up. Instead my mind was racing. It was like Matt and I buried any mention of Graham shortly after the night we killed him, and being forced to relive it again set my nerves blazing. Back when I first met Matt, I refused to admit I was a wolf just like Graham, but after leaving Tyler's house that night, I couldn't deny it anymore. I was no different, no better than him. I was Julian Blake: husband; predator; cheat; liar, and I would do anything in my power to keep it that way.

# Eleven

I could feel a burgeoning shift in the air. My heart beat itself against my ribs in a constant rhythm; I was nauseous; my skull felt like it was trapped in an ever-tightening vice; and the only thing that eased me was the glimpse of Tyler I got every morning before work. Other than that, I heard nothing from him or his parents, and ever since I saw Jimmy the day he came to my office, I hadn't heard a peep from him either. I thought that would at least provide me with some relief, one less nose poking around my business, but it was actually the contrary. Jimmy was not the type of person who gave up, but I suppose threatening someone with turning them in for manslaughter is a hell of a deterrent. I thought of calling him, or asking Matt if he'd heard from him, but I knew that would be asking for trouble, and I needed to stay as far away from trouble as I could get. Matt was unusually snarky, which usually meant he was up to something, but I couldn't put my finger on it.

I started having frequent panic attacks, unable to handle the unravelling of my life, so I took a day off work to see a doctor. She asked me what happened to trigger the attacks, but what was I supposed to tell her? Where would I start?

*Alright, Doc, I kind of have a thing inside me, this thing I can't control. This irritating and depraved little worm bedded beneath my skin that tugs me the wrong way and ignores the right. I can't seem to keep it in my pants. I'm a hedonist, Doc, what's wrong with that, right? Well, the walls are closing in. I can feel it, it's crushing me, I can't breathe.*

No. I couldn't say that, not any of it. I would be signing my life away. So I did what anyone else would do in my situation: I lied. Pretended I was fine, that it was just work related, that I couldn't sleep, which caused a vicious cycle. The doctor prescribed me lorazepam when I insisted a referral to the mental health clinic was a waste of time. *You'll sleep on these beauties,* she told me.

*Beauties* was the right word: I felt like someone had taken my brain out of my aching skull and put it in a warm, soapy bath. Everything was a lot more bearable. I felt buoyant, like I was drifting through time rather than fighting through it. It all blended together to form one murky puddle where memories should be kept. I would catch myself drifting off halfway through a sentence during classes, but none of my students ever noticed or cared, and though I can't recall any of those classes, I must have been sufficient enough because I never heard a complaint. Unless I did, and blanked those out, too.

A fog clouded my every move, and in the end I didn't

know what time of day it was, or the date, in truth. I relied on Matt to wake me up for work, and that was about it. When I was home I either slept or drank, or both, and on my days off I stayed in bed all day while Matt forced me to eat chicken soup, and even that seemed to make me dizzy.

I misplaced mine and Matt's things more than once, but I never remembered when he told me about it. Apparently I was dropping his candles and breaking them all of the time, or I ruined his favourite clothes in the wash. One day when I was looking for a tie for work I realised Matt had moved all of his shoes, because they weren't in their usual spot in the wardrobe. As it goes with drugs, my body started to get used to the lorazepam, so the haze began to clear from my vision enough for me to question Matt on where his things kept disappearing to. He made me realise it was all in my head—he'd told me about his plans to sort through his clothes when summer was approaching, more than once, and did he have to keep repeating himself? Were those pills doing me any favours? And why was I back on them, anyway? I could tell him anything, I knew that, right? Share the burden. See also: Problem halved. See also: Another body added to the list. So I said nothing, which was what I did best. Blend into the wallpaper, be still and silent. Don't question anything odd if you can't explain your own oddities. People in flammable clothes shouldn't throw matches, or something to that effect.

# Twelve

It had been nine days since Jimmy came to my office and I threatened him with the police. Nine days of dreading calls, anticipating texts, worrying about him showing up at work, all for nothing. You could say I was slightly disappointed, but worried more so. I expressed my concerns to Matt, who said I should just go see him.

When I pulled up on Jimmy's drive, I noticed the house was pitch black, so assumed he wasn't in. I had a key, though, so I thought it best to check it out, if only for my own peace of mind. I put my key in the door but it wouldn't turn, which meant it was already unlocked. I opened the door, instinctively watching the floor for the cat, but then remembered she was dead, and the smell hit me. Rotting meat and old flowers filled my nostrils and I gagged behind the back of my hand. An immediate sense of dread balled itself up inside my gut, but I forced myself further into the house, turning on the lights as I went. When I got to the living room it was all I could do not to vomit. The smell was worse, and the sight even more so. The room flooded with light and on the sofa was a bloated red form, barely recognisable as Jimmy. I couldn't believe my eyes at first. Everything slowed to a halt as I tried to make sense of what I was seeing. There was white and brown powder on the coffee table along with a rusted spoon; a needle and syringe next to Jimmy on the sofa; a lighter on the floor; and a belt around his arm, which was triple the size it should have been.

I don't remember leaving, but I know I did, because the next thing I knew I was home, spilling my guts out to Matt. He was as shocked as I was, but made sure to ask the important questions. *Are you sure he's dead? Did you call an ambulance? The police? Anybody? Did anyone see you? Did you touch anything?* It reminded me of the reason I loved him—he always had my back, always had my best interests at heart. When I was useless he gave me strength. When I was scared he gave me a dark corner to crawl into. *I'll take care of it,* he said, *I'll call the police as a concerned neighbour, tell them there's a smell coming from next door.*

I cried for three days straight. I had to take the rest of the week off work because I could barely function. Matt made me coffee and tea and gave me pill after pill but I didn't mind because it made me feel better. All I could think about was Jimmy, all I could see in my mind was his swollen body and bulging eyes, and I couldn't help but blame myself. I caused so much hurt to so many people in my life, all in the name of selfish desire, and I knew I would never stop.

It was the weekend, and I woke up feeling groggier than usual, even on the near tranquilisers the doctor prescribed me. I was so drowsy, in fact, Matt suggested I give his set that night a miss, which told me I was in far worse shape than I thought. I spent most of the day lazing about, staring into space or at the TV despite having no idea what was playing. Suddenly it was late afternoon, and Matt was dressed ready for work. He came into the room wearing a white shirt with a blue blazer and matching trousers, and he had a silver and blue striped tie on.

'How do I look?' he asked, also wearing my favourite Cheshire grin. 'Like the greatest showman ever?'

Beautiful. He looked beautiful. At the same time he was both the innocent boy I met in the library and a complete stranger. When did he start wearing ties? When did he start looking so mature? And when did he start caring about my health? Since the day I broke his wrist he was indifferent towards me, cold, and I didn't blame him, not one bit. But there he was, expressing concern, feeding me chicken soup and coffee and giving me the day off from watching him play. It was out of character, but Matt had no singular character, not really. He could be anyone he wanted at any given time, so I let it go, had to—I didn't have the energy or the wherewithal to question the sudden switch.

Matt told me to get some rest, to sleep it off and relax, then he left. I didn't think I would be able to sleep, but I didn't have the energy for much else either. The TV was still humming in the background, some kind of soap opera full of school kids in their comprehensive uniforms, and I found myself with a sickening craving for the schoolboy across the road.

I must have dozed off on the sofa, because I woke up with a metallic taste on my tongue and a desert-dry mouth. I drifted upstairs to brush my teeth, back downstairs and into the kitchen for a pint of water, and the clock on the wall told me only fifteen minutes had passed.

Knock-knock-knock. Little hands, knuckles tapping against glass. I wasn't expecting anyone, or was I? Was it Jimmy? What did he want now? Too many questions filled my head. I couldn't think straight. Stumbling my way to the front of the house, I opened the door and there stood Tyler, brazen and beautiful, smiling up at me with a bottle of wine in his hand. Not just any wine either, and perhaps it was the drugs I was brimming at the seams with but he looked more like Will than he ever had.

'Is that Caro?' I asked, without saying hello.

'Uh… Yeah. You said before that your friend stole yours, or something, I dunno.' I nodded, remembering the conversation I had with him, which felt like a lifetime ago. How did he remember that?

'And why are you holding a bottle of it?'

'It's for you, duh.'

'Oh, uh, thanks. Thank you.'

'You're welcome.' We looked at each other for an awkward ten seconds or so, then he said, 'You look like shit, by the way.'

I chuckled. 'You sure know how to make a guy feel good.'

'Cool. Can I come in?'

'No, you can't. We can't.'

'But it's cold out here.'

'No, Tyler. It's not cold.'

'But I miss you.'

Every memory of when I first met him months ago swarmed me at once, my mind was like a wasp's nest, painful images stinging through the flesh of my brain. He had always been a bold, audacious boy. That shameless courage that comes only with his particular age group. 'What are you doing here, Ty?'

Tyler shrugged. 'Wanted to see you.'

'You *can't* be here.'

'I waited for Matt to leave,' he said, as if that was the only problem. 'You said we would see each other soon. Why can't it be now?'

'You know why, Tyler. I don't want to let you in. I don't want things to end up like they did, and—'

'It won't be like last time. Come on, I brought your favourite drink—'

I laughed, cutting him off. 'Oh, because that automatically gives you an invite, does it?'

'Yeah.'

'No.'

'Do I have to huff and puff and blow the door down?' he said, grinning, clearly finding himself hilarious. So did I, I'll admit, trying to control the smile that nagged my lips. It was good to see him. Oh so deliciously good.

'The *door* is already open, so that doesn't make sense. Try again.'

I didn't have time to ask him to leave again, or close the door on him. He did it himself, from the inside, and then I pressed him hard against it in a carnivorous embrace. He nearly dropped the bottle of wine, so I took it from him and put it on the coffee table in the lounge, then sat down on the sofa next to where Tyler had settled, shoes already off, feet curled under him.

'Are you gonna drink it?' he asked, nodding towards the bottle on the coffee table.

'Are you joining me?'

'I'm too young, remember.' His eyes were full of mischief, and I couldn't stop the grin that rose on my face. Oh so good, being so bad. Too young. Too young and yet I could have him at any moment I chose.

'Just one won't hurt,' I said.

'Fine. But do you have, like, a beer? I hate wine.'

'It's your lucky day, kiddo.'

'Cool.'

In the kitchen, I was giddy. I felt like a child, defiant and indifferent to the rules of the game because their parents will let them win regardless. Matt was out of the house, and I didn't even have to summon Tyler, despite how badly I wanted to. He just showed up for me, stars aligned. I got a beer from the fridge and a wine glass from the cabinet, and walked to the study to find some pills I had hidden. I was planning on crushing them and putting them in Tyler's beer. I lifted the lid of the globe bar where I kept them, but they weren't there, and neither was my money. I was baffled, confusedly looking at the empty space, but I didn't have much time to think about it, not with the boy waiting for me in the living room. I put it down to having misplaced them in my daze, like Matt kept telling me I was doing, and hoped to god I remembered where I put everything, sooner rather than later. I was disheartened about not being able to drug Tyler, it would have saved the screams and the tears of last time, but not all was lost.

I returned to Tyler, all freckles and brown curls and orange fluffy pillows. Before I gave him the beer I leaned over the back of the sofa, kissing him deeply, claiming him back after what felt like an eternity without him. The drugs and the endorphins mixed together made me feel like I was flying, and I forgot the reason I was taking them in the first place was because I was climbing the walls with need for him. And it wasn't necessarily the need for sex. It was ownership, power. It was knowing I held him in the palm of my hand. I *needed* to be in control, I *needed* to watch his every move. How else was I going to know if he decided to spill the rotten beans; tell his parents; the police; or a teacher at school; hell, even Matt. Especially Matt. I couldn't be the cause of another sudden death. I couldn't watch Melissa and Lara in the aftermath. Granted, my visit from the police was what tipped me over the edge, but Tyler was the catalyst of it all.

Tyler sipped his bottle of lager, and I sipped a hefty glass of wine. We talked for quite some time on either end of the sofa, playing footsie when he wasn't resting his legs on mine.

'Why do you look like that?' he asked. 'Did someone die?'

'Actually, yes. My friend died a couple of days ago. I don't want to talk about it.'

'Oh, shit. Sorry—'

'No apology necessary,' I said. 'Humour me, what *do* I look like?'

'Like one of those shaggy homeless guys outside Tesco.'

'Wow.' I supposed he was right. I hadn't shaved in days, my hair was untamed and long enough to be in its afro phase, and I had bags under my eyes, as if I'd been sleeping rough. 'To tell you the truth, I haven't had the best week. My friend dying was just the icing on the cake.'

'Why? Are you and Matt like, breaking up?'

'No, nothing like that. Did you tell him anything?'

No, no way. I swear down.'

'You *can't* tell him, Tyler. I'm serious—'

'I won't tell him. I'm not, like, stupid.'

'I know, I know you're not. I'm sorry, I... I haven't been able to breathe without seeing you, you know? It's been so difficult. My thoughts have been running wild.'

'Well, I'm here now.'

'It's not that,' I said. 'I hurt you, and I want to keep hurting you. I want to ruin you completely, and I want to hang myself because of it. I want to make you scream my name in hate and at the same time I want you to love me.

I want what no fourteen-year-old should be forced to give.' I couldn't control the words as they spilled from me. The concoction of pills and wine made me brutally honest, even to myself. 'It's like there's two people inside me, and neither of them are good guys, but one is better than the other. I want to be the better one.' I wondered if any of what I was saying made sense, feeling the words twist lazily from my mouth. Was I slurring? Had he noticed?

Tyler said, 'You can be really intense, you know that?'

'I'm sorry,' I replied, then swallowed the rest of my glass in one before pouring another.

'It's cool.' We stared at the murmuring TV in silence, pretending to watch it as we sipped our drinks. After a couple of uncomfortable minutes, Tyler broke the silence. 'How's the wine?'

'It's delightful,' I replied, realising how lightheaded I was all of a sudden. 'Where did you get it, anyway?'

'I saved up to get it for you. I've had it for a while, but I didn't give it to you because I was angry after... uh... you know.'

'I understand. Well, I think that's very sweet of you. Thank you.' Tyler shrugged, apparently unaware of what a generous act it was. 'Tell me why you're here,' I asked. 'What do you want, Ty?'

The boy swallowed another mouthful of beer, only halfway through his bottle, as was I. Granted, my bottle in question was four times the volume of his. 'I wanted to give you your gift—'

'You could have left after that,' I said. 'But you were

determined to come inside. Why?'

Tyler sighed. 'I told you. I miss you. I miss your hands on me. You're all I think about.' My stomach dropped, and I blinked languidly at him in disbelief. Why was he not afraid I would hurt him again? It didn't make sense to me, but it wasn't inconceivable, either. He was naive, it was one of my favourite traits of his. Besides, it was like a dream come true, the opportunity to do it again.

'You're all I think about too,' I said. 'But you're so young... so young, so beautiful...' I trailed off, fighting now to stay awake. My eyelids were like lead.

'But that's why you like me so much, right?'

'Yes. Right. You're so right.' It was beginning to be a mountain of effort to speak the simplest of words, and it didn't go unnoticed by present company.

'Jules, are you cool?'

'Yes, fine,' I replied, then I yawned uncontrollably. 'I'm cool. I'm cool.' I felt like I was submerged in thick, hot tar. 'Listen, would you mind going home? I really need to sleep, I'm exhausted.'

'I'll come to bed with you,' he offered.

'No, that's not a good idea. Matt won't be gone for long.'

'I'll tuck you in, then.' I didn't have the ability or the energy to stop him when he crawled across the sofa and climbed aboard my lap. My eyes screamed for me to close them, to wade into the quiet and pretend everything was fine, block out the same desire the mere scent of him ignited. Anything was better than having to confront my demons head-on. I wasn't even sure I could get it up, if you catch my drift.

Tyler told me to stay awake, grinding himself down against my unresponsive cock. I wanted him, I really, truly did, but I was so tired, so comfortable, so enveloped in the promise of sleep. The pills were supposed to take the edge off, not get rid of it entirely, but there was no edge in sight. I had not a single care in the world, I was free from remorse and guilt and everything in between. I was numb as Tyler kissed me, and his soft lips were the last thing I felt before I waded into the quiet and let darkness cloak me.

# Thirteen

I dreamed I was being dragged up a never-ending staircase. Matt was there, and so was Tyler, and they were whispering between each other, tugging at my arms and lifting my legs. I couldn't do anything about it, I was paralysed, watching myself from above as I was mercilessly shoved this way and that by two boys-to-men. I couldn't distinguish their voices from one another but I knew it was them, that strange dream logic that makes everything fit together. *Don't drop him,* one said. *I'm trying not to, he's heavier than he looks,* said the other.

*I can't believe you couldn't get him upstairs yourself.*

*Sorry, I tried, I swear. He just, like, totally passed out. Are you sure he isn't dead?*

Matt laughed. I could tell his laugh from worlds away. I wanted to get a look at him but my eyes were glued shut, and the more I tried to pry them open the tighter they seemed. Time came to me in flashes: one minute I was at the bottom of the stairs with a step painfully digging into my back, the next I was halfway up, held there by hands on my hips, then I was on the landing with an aching shoulder. It was shown no mercy as I was yanked into the bedroom. I couldn't talk to express the pain, but for a dream the pain was excruciatingly real. I tried to move but I remained out of control of my body while Matt and Tyler finally got me into a room. My bedroom. Or was it? It was too dark to tell. My eyes were too heavy. My mind was soup, senses backwards. I could taste danger, it was hidden in the black somewhere, crouched like a hungry tiger waiting to strike.

*How do you want him?* one of them said. *Face down,* said the other.

\* \* \*

My headache woke me up first. I was face down, which struck me as odd as I never slept that way, and my muscles were screaming with tension, especially my arms. I tried to move them but they were no use to me. I couldn't remember if or why I lost consciousness, and I was disoriented. When I regained the ability to think, I discovered I was lying naked on my bed, my wrists zip tied to the bedpost and my legs spread painfully apart. I tried to get to my knees but my legs wouldn't stretch far enough, and then I was thrashing, yelling, and a sharp, ice-cold pain returned to my hands. The room around me was dark, silent, but I knew there was someone else in there with me, I could feel it; eyes like daggers skinning me alive. The tiger from my dream. Was it a dream?

I lifted my head up, whispered, 'Matthew?'

The floorboards next to the bed creaked, and then I heard a nervous sigh, loud enough to scare the shit out of me. Then someone spoke, and it wasn't Matt.

'Matt isn't here. It's just me.'

They were the same words I'd said to Tyler, more than once. Now they were being spoken back to me by that same boy.

'Tyler?'

'*Surprise*, Jules,' he said.

'What the f—'

'If you scream, I'll gag you.'

Had he lost his mind, or had I lost mine? Was this really happening?

'Ty, I have no idea what's going on but would you please just untie me—'

'Why should I?'

'This isn't funny.'

'I know.'

'Wha… what's happening? This is fucking insane!' My head split in half when I raised my voice, I thought for a moment Tyler had taken an axe to it.

'Crazy, right?' he said. 'Kinda cool, though.' Cool. Of all things, it was *cool*.

'My arms hurt—'

'*My* arms were hurting when *you* pinned *me* down and I told you to stop.'

'Tyler, come on—'

190

'Did you stop? Did you let me go?'

'Ty—'

'Another rule. If you don't answer when I ask a question, I'll gag you. Understand?'

'Jesus, kid—'

Tyler screamed in my ear. 'Do you understand me?!'

'Yeah, *fuck*. Yes. *Yes* I understand.'

'Cool. So… Did. You. Stop?'

'No,' I replied, trying to free my hands again, but it was futile. Panic kicked in.

'No *what*?'

'I didn't stop! Look, Ty, if that's what this is about we can talk about it, alright? I know you're angry, but what do you think you're doing? Do you realise how much trouble you'll be in when I tell your parents?'

Tyler's high-pitched laugh scared me half to death. Let me tell you something: there's nothing more terrifying than a teenager in the midst of revenge. They're all selfish Neanderthals up to the age of eighteen, so add a little rage in the mix, you have a problem on your hands. I thought of every consequence under the sun for my seedy behaviour, every consequence but one, and the realisation of my corruption hit me like a volcano. I felt like Pompeii, waiting to be wiped out. The kid was hell-bent. He was the hungry tiger.

'Tell them, that's cool,' he said. 'We'll see who gets in the most trouble.'

'Fuck!' I said as loud as I could, thrashing at my restraints. 'Untie me you little shit! Help! Someone!'

Tyler was suddenly sitting on my back, shoving

something in my mouth to shut me up. I didn't see what it was, but I knew it was fabric from the way it absorbed every bit of moisture in my mouth and throat. What time was it? Was it even still Saturday? How did the boy get me upstairs on his own? I didn't have the chance to ask, not that the boy would have told me. I gagged as he pushed the cloth as far back as he could, and said, 'I told you not to shout.'

I blinked the tears from my eyes, tried coughing the gag out to no avail. It was stuck there, and no amount of pushing or wiggling my tongue was going to dislodge it. Talking was out of the question. It was all I could do to remain calm as possible, taking deep, steady breaths through my nose so as not to suffocate. He was heavy on my back, his knees digging into my lungs as he took a deep breath, as if he was preparing himself for something.

'I'm gonna make you bleed,' Tyler said, tracing something metal over my bare skin. My shoulder blade twitched from the unexpected cold. 'You made me bleed, did you know that?'

I tried to scream, begging him to please reconsider this for a moment, but all that came out were muffled words and choked moans. His answer was yes, I did know that I made him bleed. I washed it off my skin in the shower, boiled it out of my bed sheets.

'Sorry, I know you can't talk. I don't really want an answer anyway. It was a, um… a rhetorical question. That's the one.' A shiver quaked through my body when I felt the tool again, and I realised it was sharp. It nicked my skin, stung like a paper cut. 'This will probably hurt, so try not to bite your tongue off,' he said. Like I could have with the fucking gag anyway. I wanted to thrash and jerk but I couldn't move, with his weight on my back, my strained muscles, and the pill and wine concoction still in my system, I was completely powerless. My worst nightmare.

Tyler shuffled down my back until he was straddling my hips, and with one hand splayed on my shoulder to hold me still, the other brought the sharp implement to my skin. It cut deep, or at least it felt like it did. I couldn't think, couldn't do anything apart from focus on the searing hot pain. Tyler paused for a moment, and I heard him gasp. I imagined it was at the sight of my blood being drawn. No one ever truly understands that blood does get everywhere, not until they're swimming in it. Regardless, it didn't deter the boy, right back at it. I wondered as I lay there how I could be so wrong about nearly everything in my life. My best decisions always caused the worst problems. But Tyler, of all people? That shameless cheek; his endless curiosity; the smile that took me back seventeen years—I knew it must have been too good to be true. So it goes.

I flinched as I felt my skin splitting, tried to scream but ended up choking. Another line, a curve, then another line. Horizontally, vertically, one line crossed through another to make a join. He was writing something. *Carving* something. There was a third letter, and a fourth, which hurt more than any of the others because it was directly on my spine, in the middle of my upper back. I bit down on the rag in my mouth hard, so hard I felt like my jaw would break, but despite my groans of anguish Tyler didn't stop. Another letter, or was it two? I was numb by then, I lost count. I could feel the blood oozing from me, hot and wet, and every now and then Tyler put the blade down to wipe his hands in the bed sheets. I thought it was never going to end. I could feel tingling, blood drying, more white heat as the implement dragged another line into my flesh. It was agonising, insufferable, and yet I had no option but to suffer through it. I felt the curves of an 'S', begging any god that would listen to please make it stop. I had been cut and kicked in the nuts and even stabbed by Matt, but nothing compared to the twisting torture of having my skin slashed open by poorly practiced fingers. Some parts were deeper than others, but I couldn't tell the difference after a while. The only reason I knew was because Tyler would utter, 'Shit,' and then wipe his hands, start again, like a kid colouring outside the lines. It all started to feel the same to me, my exhausted body desperately trying to keep me numb, but it would wear off when I thought too hard about it. It was like scorching oil had been poured over my back and then set on fire. At one point Tyler stopped to take a breather, gagging from the urge to be sick. I imagined the copious amounts of blood pooling around each slice, could still feel it running down my side. I could smell it, too, that warm and rusty iron odour. I thought I might pass out, hyperventilating and fighting the urge not to vomit myself. He had worked his way from my left shoulder blade across to the right, and I hoped with every ounce of capacity possibly remaining that he was finished. Just one word; left to right; no more; please just fucking stop; I'll die if you don't stop.

The blade left my skin, and then there was a brief sample of relief as Tyler slid off my back and his weight disappeared. I didn't know my own name. My mind wanted me to block the entire thing out, sleep it off, but I couldn't. I couldn't stay there, like that, bleeding out and suffocating. I tried to tug at the restraints again, shook the bed frame a couple of times which caused more damage than good. I had no voice but I needed to scream. I had no movement and I needed to move.

Tyler said, 'I'm sorry,' and if I was capable of it, I would have laughed. I didn't know what kind of lesson he thought he was teaching me, but I'd never wanted to destroy him more. I wanted to put my throbbing hands around his neck, squeeze my fingers until they broke if I had to. I wanted to tear him apart, bite by bite, rip his flesh into shreds with my claws and consume his every last drop. I was an animal amidst a frenzy. In that moment I became the predator he made me out to be, and I knew there was no going back. He was lucky I was tied up.

Nothing felt real, but the pain I was in disobeyed my mind into shutting off. I didn't move an inch. Perhaps I was in shock. Perhaps I was trying to make sense of the nonsensical. What happened? It all transpired so quickly I hadn't thought about how I got there in the first place. I wondered how much blood I'd lost, and something triggered in my mind: the wine. The little prick spiked me.

I heard Tyler's footsteps fading further away from the bed, and it was only then I truly understood I was in the clear. I didn't try moving until I knew he was gone, and when the front door clicked shut downstairs I blanked the pain and lost myself to fury, struggling against the zip ties and the steel bed frame, attempting to force my hands through a non-existent gap between them. No such luck, not unless I wanted two broken wrists. I took a deep breath, as deep as I could, the gag still there for me to bite down on, and I thought of Tyler; going behind my back; planning all of this. It was almost too cleverly orchestrated, familiar even; the wine; the drugs; dragging me upstairs; the zip-ties; the tool he used to slice me open. Almost too... Matt. It hit me: my dream wasn't a dream at all. It was real. It had happened. Matt and Tyler dragged me upstairs like I was a rag doll. But where was Matt now?

The betrayal of it all swarmed me, I was in shock and denial and there were too many pieces to put together. I thrashed my arms and threw myself forward, pulling and pushing the frame in a state of hysteria. Something made a ringing noise, metal clanging, and I had never felt hope quite like it in my life. I kept shoving against the bar that was giving way, shaking it vigorously, and it detached from the bolt that was keeping it in place. I just had to bend it and I could slip my hand free. I pulled the bar toward me and lifted my hand and the zip tie off it, wincing in fear of my hand falling off, and I gasped in relief: I was free. Well, sort of.

The first thing I did was remove the soaking wet gag jammed in my mouth. I took the fullest breath, spluttered and fought greedily for any air I could get. The second thing I did was to get the scissors from the bedside cabinet, cutting my other hand free. I turned the bedside lamp on, the first light I'd seen since I woke up, and it stung my eyes as I blinked to get used to the brightness. I gasped when my vision came back to me. For a moment I thought I was still dreaming, swimming in the reddest of seas.

The blood was unreal. The bed was drenched in it. Next there was the issue of freeing my feet—I would need to arch my back and stretch my split skin further. I screamed as I got on my knees, stifled a sob when I leaned back at an awkward angle to cut the plastic ties from around my ankles. Everything hurt as I cried into the bloody mattress and forced my body to comply with me, and I got on my knees, stretched my sore muscles, and slowly crawled to the edge of the mattress before attempting to use my legs. With my feet lowered to the floor, I willed myself to get it together, but stumbled when I tried to stand, like I was stepping on a skateboard. Determined not to let myself fall on my back, I held my breath and caught myself just in time, then tried again. I could have cried in relief when I gained use of my legs again, and I wasted no time before stumbling towards the full-length mirror on the wardrobe, craning my neck to see what my back said. It was such a bloody mess that I couldn't tell, so I staggered into the shower, put it on cold, and forced myself under it, shaking, sobbing, and stripped of everything except for boundless rage as I watched the stream of red water disappear down the shower drain. I stepped out of the shower dripping wet, thinking twice about getting a towel to rub myself dry, so I walked stark naked and bleeding back into the bedroom. The blood on the bed was almost black where it had soaked into the white sheets. It looked like something out of a gore movie, worse than any scene Matt and I had caused, be it through sex or war. I picked up a small mirror on the cabinet, and when I was at the wardrobe again, I held it up to finally see what my back was permanently scarred with. Eight letters, jagged edges cut into my flesh. Perhaps it hurt so much because it was true. I didn't make it to the wicker bin before I threw up everywhere, wine and bile all over the place.

Scribed in raw, bloody letters across my back was one simple word: PEDERAST.

# MATT

# One

Home sweet home. Days as dark as night, high buildings and low morals. Fog everywhere. Fog up the river, flowing around green islands and meadows and marshes; fog down the river, rolling discreetly into the city streets, as if the city itself were suspended in misty clouds. Always an edge; a chill; the wild voice of wind roaring through alleys and open windows. A far cry from the closeness of Greek air, the tropical clinginess, the unforgiving heat, the clean white buildings and the azure blue skies.

London, baby. On the drive home from Heathrow Airport, I took it all in, soaked up the fog, revelled in the greyness, the mist, the clouds, the cold. Darkness was everywhere. It was in the night, the day, the streets, the people, the car. It was inside me and inside Julian. It was all I looked forward to on the flight home. A good place to disappear.

It was supposed to be my turn to drive, but after

having broken my wrist in Greece, Julian had to do it. He merged onto the M40, took the A40 exit to Oxford, and then we were home from our honeymoon. Home sweet home. It was there in the car back from Heathrow that I realised just how fond of the place I was. Not a whole lot of things gave me joy, but the symphonic shriek of an entire city in desolation, the cry of the 9-5 working humdrum, police sirens, road ragers, riches and rags; it was enough for me. It was my muse. It was the place I refined my craft. It was a place so populated, so hungry for crime, so full of dark corners and tight crevices, rivers that ran deeper and longer than the city's unsolved murder cases. It was home. Sweet and sour and perfectly home.

Since I took Graham's last breath from him and his wife subsequently moved out of town, the house across the road had remained empty. The day after we got back to Oxford, it was a pleasant surprise to learn we had new neighbours. But Julian couldn't wait a day longer before going to confront his bitch of a sister, Ashley. She didn't come to our wedding, whatever, but Julian's ego couldn't let something like that go. It was all I heard him talk about in Greece, all day, every day, and honestly, I was looking forward to having a couple hours of peace. He wanted me to go with him but I told him no, which was not a word Julian liked to hear, but a word I loved to tell him, nonetheless. There's nothing more entertaining than watching a control freak lose his reins, and after what he did to me, it's safe to say my usual contempt for the man was tenfold. Sometimes I wondered why I sought him out all those years ago, why I stuck around for so long, but the reason I hated him was the same reason I loved him: he, too, was possessed by a darkness, albeit a little different to mine. Truth is that if you've made a deal with the devil, it's because you're yet to find more favourable terms. There's nothing you can do to make someone love you, nothing you can do to make yourself love someone else, but you want it, search for it, and make every effort to sustain it.

Julian left the house that morning to see his sister, but not before bringing me a mug of coffee, some painkillers, and a kiss so riddled with guilt it was palpable. Not an hour after, I heard a commotion outside, and I got out of bed to look out the window and check it out. I saw a Jeep and a moving van parked across the street at the house that once belonged to Graham and his wife, Charlotte; and more people going in and out than the house had seen since I left her a widow. Curiosity got the better of me, so I adjusted the bandage around my wrist, put on my friendliest expression, lit a cigarette up as I locked the front door, and casually strolled across the road in the direction of two women who were also smoking cigarettes.

The first rule of blending in, as I had to learn growing up, is to observe. The second to mimic. I could read every word of a soul, become deeply engrossed in the study of it and not stop until I'd comprehended every detail. My desire to know a person's every layer and nuance was uncontrollable; I was just doing what I did best.

The moving-van employees were carrying bulky items of furniture inside the house: An American-style fridge; a crushed velvet sofa and armchair; a vintage shabby-chic sideboard and wardrobe; a gaming chair. There were boxes full of personal items scattered all over the garden: in one of them I saw blue hospital scrubs; in another there was an Xbox and a wooden plaque with the name *Tyler* and a bunch of footballs painted onto it. The two women stood among the chaos, quite obviously overwhelmed, dragging on their cigarettes like there was nothing better to be doing. Like I was reading from a script, I said 'Hey, I'm Matt. I live across the road with my husband, Julian. Would you like a hand with your stuff?' The irony of it almost made me break character. *A hand.* The stern looking one stared me up and down in a suspicious manner, while the friendly, hippy-looking one with blonde wavy hair replied.

'Hey, neighbour. I'm Melissa, and this is my wife, Lara. It's a pleasure to meet you.' She noticed the bandage around my wrist and hand. 'Thank you for offering your help, darling, but we couldn't possibly accept with your arm as it is. Are you okay? What happened?'

'Oh, this? I promise it's worse than it looks. I've just come back from my honeymoon. Got a little too drunk and tripped over.' I laughed, and so did Melissa. Lara didn't make a peep, she was far more cautious than her cheerful wife. She was figuring me out, and I wondered if she had come to any conclusions yet. Within minutes of being there I learned the following information: At least one of them was a nurse; they had a teenage son called Tyler; Melissa was naively trusting; Lara didn't trust me at all; and their taste in furniture was fantastic. I couldn't help but absorb, I was a slave to an intense, mechanical pull inside me to devour and abuse knowledge like it did something awful to me.

'Oh, dear. Is it broken?' Melissa asked concernedly.

'Yeah, but it's not too bad, honestly. I'm sure I can manage a couple boxes for you.' Just then a young boy came bounding out of his new home, nearly bumping into one of the employees carrying items in and out. He had a football under his arm, headphones around his neck, and he looked just like Lara; the silent wife; curly brunette hair and a steely blue gaze. He was young, attractive, and balancing precariously on the cusp of manhood. These were the traits Julian fell for like a fly to a spider's web, the same traits he once cherished in me, the ones I faked to get what I wanted, which, at the time, was him. The kid ran past us as if we weren't there and headed for the street, blind to any danger at his age.

'Be careful on that road, Tyler,' Lara yelled, and I was strangely relieved to learn that she did indeed have a voice. The kid ignored her and kicked the ball into the road anyway, and images of blood dripping from crushed metal filled my head. A car wreck, mangled flesh, a flat football. Little horror shots that some people call intrusive thoughts, only I didn't find them intrusive, I welcomed them.

I took a final drag of my cigarette and held it up as if

to ask where to discard it. Melissa pointed to a plant pot a couple feet away so I went over to it, dropped the butt in, then picked up two stacked boxes from the floor. Melissa tried to stop me, a worried expression on her otherwise placated face. 'Please, I insist,' I said, portraying someone who gave a shit. 'It's not that bad, I promise.' I was actually in agony, but whatever, little lies make big explosions. I walked to the front door. 'Want me to leave them on the doorstep?'

'Oh, no, you can go on in. Thank you, darling.' It was the invitation to my inner vampire. Inside the house, I placed the boxes on the floor, and the whole place was exactly as I remembered: mundane cream walls; dark wooden floors; an out of place ceiling fan; glass sliding doors leading to the pointlessly small back garden; a Victorian fireplace; a winding staircase; and a crack in the drywall near the door, from where Graham had thrown me into it when I was fifteen attempting to leave after a one-night stand. The one-night stand that turned into years of blackmail and ultimately, his death. I smiled fondly at the memory and traced my fingers over the crack, and something struck me, a distant feeling of longing. Graham was so much fun to play with, I almost found myself in a state of regret that he wasn't around anymore.

I glanced in one of the boxes I brought inside. In it was a photo frame with a photograph of Lara next to someone who looked remarkably like Ashley, and my interest peaked. If it was indeed Ashley in the photo, and she and Lara were friends, it easily explained Lara's behaviour towards me. Mine and Ashley's dislike for one another was no secret, and I wouldn't put it past her to play her own games to get what she wanted, which was to get me to leave Julian, or vice versa. It was a bit of a long shot, and I guess you could call it paranoia, but you're not paranoid if you're right, and I usually was.

I returned to the women outside to make conversation, mundane enough to give me the larger picture without making me come across as invasive. Melissa kept to her role of keynote speaker while Lara pretended to be occupied with the boxes still left in the boot of their Jeep, which I knew was theirs because it had a tacky, rainbow-coloured Pride sticker stuck to their bumper, with the words 100% PROUD. 0% SHAME. She was probably making sure there were no obvious indicators of them being connected to Ashley, but she was too little too late on that front. To be good at the game you have to know the rules, you can't go in oblivious.

'It's a nice house,' I said, like it was my first time viewing it. 'I was starting to wonder why it's been empty for so long.'

'Yes, we heard about that,' Melissa replied, lighting up another cigarette. 'I wonder the same. I don't think we would have known about it if it wasn't for Lara's friend sending us the listing.'

'Well, they did you a favour.'

'So what do you do, Matt?'

'I'm in university at the moment. And I work on the weekends as a pianist.'

'Oh, that's impressive!'

'It's not as glamorous as it sounds,' I said. Lara returned to us, holding a box.

'Babe, we better get moving. I don't want to be here all day.' She was talking to Melissa, but I took it upon myself to intrude.

'I'll grab those boxes there,' I offered, pointing to the stack near the Jeep. Lara wanted me gone, which only incentivized me to stay. I walked to the Jeep to get the boxes and when my back was turned I heard her muttering to Melissa. She thought I couldn't hear her, but I have the hearing of a bat.

'Stop telling people our business,' she whispered. 'We don't know him.'

'What's the matter with you today?' Melissa asked. 'He's a kind young man. He's helping us out. Be grateful.'

'I'll be grateful when strangers stop going through our stuff. You're too trusting, Mel.' I had to give it to her, Lara had a point, but that's what I was counting on.

I carried more boxes inside for them, and after a couple of trips my wrist was killing me. The kid kicked his football into the road again and Lara demanded he get back on the drive *right this minute*. He rolled his eyes but listened that time, approaching us like a scolded child would: head down, shoulders slouched, dragging his feet.

'Who are you?' he asked me, apparently only then realising I had been there the whole time. I smiled at him, extended my hand. He shook it. I gave him the whole speech again: I'm Matt, I live right across the street, the house with the bumblebee-yellow Mini cooper on the drive. I saw the vans here and came over to introduce myself and help your parents with your things, yadda yadda.

'Cool,' he said. 'Your car is, uh, bright.'

I laughed agreeingly. 'It is bright. My husband drives a red Jag, I imagine you'd like that one a bit more.'

'Is it fast?'

'Fast as hell.'

'Cool. What did you do to your hand?'

'I got too drunk and fell over.'

'Cool.'

'It *was* pretty cool, actually. If I was playing football it would've been a hell of a save.'

'Do you play football?'

'No, I'm more of an arts and crafts person myself.'

'Matt here plays the piano,' Melissa added.

'Well,' Lara said, finally breaking the invisible wall she had put between us. 'I don't imagine you'll be playing much of anything with an injured hand.'

'Just try and stop me.'

'He's been helping us carry some boxes,' Melissa said to her son. 'You hear that, Ty?'

Her sarcasm wasn't lost on him. He rolled his eyes, 'Whatever, Mum. I didn't want to move in the first place. And I told you my head hurts.'

'Funny, you're still capable of kicking that ball about and listening to loud music.'

'Aunt Ash says exercise is good for headaches.' I paused at the name. Lara stiffened, and she was looking at me like I had a knife to her throat. Melissa sighed, oblivious to her wife's sudden terror, and Tyler walked away and waltzed into his new house.

'Teenagers,' she said, but I was looking at Lara. The coldness in her had vanished and been replaced with something else, fear, anxiety, *shit, he knows.*

'Thank you for your help, Matt,' she stammered. 'We really appreciate it.'

'You're totally welcome,' I replied, smiling at her for an unreasonably long time.

Back at home, Julian was still out. I wrote his number on a sticky note and put it on the fridge in the middle of everything else: photographs; a calendar; magnets; piano chords; deadlines; addresses; bills; appointments; things that made our lives seem accessible from the outside. Open books don't draw undesirable attention.

Not long after, Julian returned from his sister's, dawdled into the kitchen with his head down and shoulders hunched, just like the kid had when Lara demanded he get off the road. Tyler had an excuse: he was a kid, but Julian's behaviour was all self-pity, a spoiled man losing control. He told me about the visit even though I didn't ask, and I was barely listening to him as he rambled on about Ashley this and Ashley that. Apparently, she thought I was dangerous, which was nothing new. She had hated me since day 1, and day 1 was 6 years ago now. It never ceased to amaze me how Julian could turn an old issue into a brand new one. You could tell him you were going to stab him in the back and he would still be surprised when you did. He was selfish through and through, he didn't even ask about my day, he thought the world paused until he pressed play again. In his mind, nothing at all changed when he left. But no one put Matty in the corner, and Julian knew better than to think he could silence me. He had tried, again and again. I even got the bandage to prove it.

'Well,' I said. 'My day has been great. I met our new neighbours. A couple and their son are moving into Graham's old house.'

'They are? I didn't notice.'

'You don't notice a lot,' I said, teasing. 'Anyway, the son is pretty young, like 13 or 14. I think you're gonna find it difficult living so close to him.'

'What are you talking about?'

'You'll see,' I said, winding him up tighter.

'Matt, I've had a day. Just tell me what you mean.' His olive-green eyes stared into mine as intensely as they had on that first day, and I grinned. He was, by all accounts, so easy. He was impulsive and pathetic and a slave to his own hypocrisy, I knew his next move before he did. I admired him once, when I was young and he was self-assured and easily the most gorgeous man to walk in my line of vision, the one man I couldn't kill with my bare hands, despite how much I wished I could.

'I think you know exactly what I mean,' I said, and he didn't say anything else as he filled a glass up with whatever wine was his choice that evening. It all tasted the same to me.

I didn't bother telling Julian anything about that day. The photo of (maybe) Ashley, Lara's bizarre behaviour, or the fact that I had declared a silent war on him. What happens when you break the hand that feeds you? I couldn't wait to watch him starve.

# Two

Greece. Of all places to go on our honeymoon, it had to be Greece. Not like I had a choice in the matter, though, because Julian got what Julian wanted, and anyway, what better way to make him believe he had cracked my impenetrable shell than to go along with his every single whim like the obedient puppy he desired me to be. The more he thought he had me wrapped around his fingers, the tighter he was wrapped around mine.

We were in our villa in Santorini after a night of heavy drinking and heavier drugs, fucking like wildebeests, hurting each other. Bite, scratch, choke: these were a few of our favourite activities, and sometimes, not even those were enough to satisfy. Sometimes, one of us wanted to go further: throw a fist; pull out a knife; ignore the words *Stop* and *No* and tighten the rope until we were blue in the face. That night in Santorini was one of those times, and it was Julian who wanted to take it to the limit. He wanted to see me cry, really cry. He wanted to hear me scream in genuine pain.

I was on my knees on the floor, thoroughly enjoying myself as Julian thrust into me from behind, when he pulled my arms behind my back and whispered, in his drug addled state, 'Howl for me, Matty.'

I was the type of person that found it difficult to cry, though I had managed to perfect faking it. When I was younger I would pinch myself hard on the inside of my arm, or force my eyes open for as long as I could manage to make them water. My personal favourite trick when I was a kid and wanted attention from my mother was The Onion: I'd go to the kitchen, stab an onion a couple times while leaning close to it, hide it in the bin, and away I went. Mother caught me in the act one day, so I put a stop to it, but hey, it was fun while it lasted.

It was a real cry Julian was after, not one of my tricks, not a performance, just honest to god tears. I didn't have the advantage needed to stop him as he held my arms there behind my back, and he started twisting my wrist, as if it was a dial and he was tuning into my ever-increasing pleas to stop, and I heard something crack before I felt it. The pain came next, then a rush of nausea hit my chest. My knees were burned from trying to crawl away, my skin was burned from the blazing sun outside, and my lip was stinging from where I bit down on it to stifle a scream. It was no use, I couldn't get away, and I couldn't hold it in. Julian won. He kept winning until he was done, and when he finished I stayed there for a long time, sobbing into the rug in our villa, cradling my throbbing arm as Julian dripped from between my legs.

'Now, we're even,' he said. Sure, I stabbed him once, whatever. All I took from him was a pint of blood. He took my music from me, my art, my job, the freedom to drive, the ability to play the piano without pain. What he didn't take was my ability to play him.

# Three

I was in a music lecture at university when I got a text from Julian. It was a photo of Tyler sitting in my kitchen, reading a book of mine, and I thought: *So it begins*. Julian wasted no time, as ever. The text informed me we were having the boy over for tea, and it included a request that I pick up some snacks on the walk home, which I did. I walked to the nearby Tesco's after uni and then headed back, equipped with crisps, chocolate, and a bottle of gin.

When I entered the kitchen, Julian looked like he was having the time of his life. There was a spring in his step, a reddish flush to his cheeks. Tyler looked the same, more boyish, like a regular teenage boy receiving some attention from someone other than his nagging parents. He had no idea how easily Julian would ruin him, and not a clue how much easier it would be for me. Luckily for Tyler, I didn't want to ruin him. Ruining Julian was what I wanted, it was just unfortunate that I was counting on him hurting the boy to do so.

The 3 of us ate burgers and made small talk. Julian told me about his generous offer to take the kid football training, and I shot him a look of discouragement because that's what one husband is meant to do when the other is attempting to groom a child. Julian's predictability was as tedious as it was mesmerising. He had gained Tyler's trust already.

When it was time for him to leave, Julian wanted to walk him home, but I did it. I had shoes on, he had taken his off already, too bad.

'You don't need to walk me,' Tyler said when we left, mumbling into his football. 'It's right there. It's cool.'

'You never know what creeps are lurking the streets,' I replied. 'You can't trust anyone.' We stopped at the beginning of his drive and he turned to me with a grateful smile.

'Thanks, Matt. Tonight's been cool.'

'See you soon, mate,' I said, and that was that. Yeah, I could have warned him about Julian, given him a lesson on stranger danger and predators and whatever, but where's the fun in that? Julian already had a spell on him and I wasn't trying to be a hero.

Melissa came over a couple of days later with a homemade vegetable lasagne to thank Julian and I for *taking Tyler in and feeding him,* as Julian described. It made me think of the boy as a cat, and I doubted that was how Melissa worded it but it didn't warrant mentioning. Domesticity and vegetable lasagnes and loving thy neighbour as one loves themselves was a place I didn't belong and probably never had.

\* \* \*

Ruining people. I loved the way the phrase felt inside my mouth, rolling around on my tongue. It was delicious, it made me hungry, I wanted to consume it.

Football training was twice a week, Monday and Thursday evenings. Every time Julian got home he had a repulsive glow about him, a palpable pleasure, a radiating nervousness I couldn't help but play with. I spoke to him about the boy just enough to keep him on edge.

*How is he? He's a sweet kid. How did the training go, did you both have fun? Is he any good at it? Do you think he will keep it up? Are you sure you can commit to taking him twice a week? You're awfully busy, Jules. You can't be everyone's best friend.*

Additionally to the two days a week Julian saw Tyler, he had started spending his days with his face glued to his phone, texting, texting, texting. When he was asleep one night I took his phone, and lo and behold there had to be hundreds of text messages to and from Tyler. I scrolled to the beginning.

Julian: So how did you get my number, Mister?

Tyler: Your fridge, duh.

Atta boy.

# Four

I couldn't stand being cooped up on the weekends for any longer. I needed to go to work, I needed to play music again. It was the only thing that kept the urges at bay. The need to hurt someone was always there in the back of my mind, but without music to drown it out it was slowly crawling to the front.

I started practising again to strengthen my wrist, and it hurt like a bitch but the pain was familiar enough by then to push through it. It was an empowering feeling to notice my strength growing gradually, and what first seemed insurmountable became simple, as easy as it had always been, and if anything, I think the pain helped. It became my muse, the thing to beat, my opponent. After all, a step backward, after making a wrong turn, is a step in the right direction.

Julian was surprised to learn I had been playing again, and even more taken back to learn that I planned on going back to work. Frustrated was probably a better fitting word; he couldn't control the uncontrollable, and he couldn't stand that I never stayed down for long. I wasn't like him, I didn't wallow in my own self-pity and expect the world to come to my aid.

'You can't possibly go back to work,' he told me, his body tight, his jaw tighter. 'You won't be any good, Luca could fire you.'

'I have enough dirt on Luca to own that place if I wanted to,' I said. 'Call it tenure.'

'You need time to heal, Matt—'

'What I *need* is to play my music. We all have a crutch, Jules. Allow me mine. Please.'

'It appears I don't have a choice in the matter.'

'It would seem so,' I said, smirking. Suddenly his hand was around my wrist, squeezing, and he was looking at me with those hungry emerald eyes. I bit back a whimper, fought the urge to grab his tie and strangle the life out of him. 'I'm going to work, Jules. Break the other wrist, break my fingers, it won't stop me.' There was a moment where I thought he might follow through on my offer, but he dropped his hold and stepped away from me with a sigh.

'Fine,' he said reluctantly. 'You can drive there, then, since you think yourself so capable.'

Jimmy had texted Julian earlier in the day to ask if he could come with us that evening. He tagged along now and then, when he was feeling particularly alone and sorry for himself, and I didn't care who was there, the more eyes I had on me the better I played, and the higher my pay check would be. Jimmy always tipped me a ridiculous amount of money, and depending on how out of his mind he was, I would take more from his wallet when he and Julian weren't looking. Sometimes I got a free pill or two, or a baggie of coke.

I picked him up on the way to work, and he was already drunk when he got in the back of my car. He asked about my wrist, and Julian took charge, told him it was an accident, that I did it in Greece, that it looked worse than it was. Lies, lies, lies. Driving one handed wasn't as difficult as I thought it would be, but it wasn't exactly easy eithe, and Julian, to spite me for not falling in line, offered me no help when I struggled. Jimmy was upset about something or other, and Julian was trying to goad it out of him as he always did. I zoned in and out of the conversation, focusing on hiding from Julian how much changing gears hurt.

At work, Julian and Jimmy sat at a table by the window while I caught up with Luca before my set. He was my boss, but not really my boss. Bosses have power, and Luca had none, not over me. I knew too much about his secrets, his second life, his deepest regrets. When he clocked the splint around my wrist he went into full blown panic mode, yelling in Italian about how I should have called him and given him time to get another pianist in as a replacement. He rambled on and on about unreliable musicians and being kept in the loop yadda yadda, and when he finally came up for air I told him, in Italian, I would still be playing that night, why else would I be ridiculously dressed like I was going to my mother's wedding? I added, in English, 'Chill out, Boss.' Luca was looking at me like I wasn't real. I laughed, took my splint off, and handed it to him. He was always rushed off his feet, even if things at the bar were quiet, and I had considerably wound him even tighter.

'Are you positive you can do this?' he asked, shaking my splint around as he spoke.

'With my eyes shut.'

At the piano, with all eyes on me, it was all I needed to prove to Julian and Luca that I could do anything if I put my mind to it. Luca, who was watching wearily from the bar. Julian, who was staring hungrily at my freedom. Jimmy, gazing at Julian like he was Michelangelo's David. Me, controlling the audience and their emotions with the simple press of a set of keys.

That night, in bed, while Jimmy slept in the spare room, Julian was texting Tyler next to me. I pretended to be asleep when he checked on me, but I was wide awake.

# Five

Tyler was hooked on Julian. His football found its way into our garden almost every day, and on the occasions I answered the door he looked disappointed, like a lost little puppy searching for his master. There was something amusing about the way his face would drop upon realising Julian wasn't home, something exciting, so I couldn't help but prolong our time together—there was so little entertainment in the world, I had to get it where I could. On one of these occasions I was feeling particularly playful, so I sent Tyler through the house to get his football instead of retrieving it for him. I shut the door behind me, waited in the kitchen for the boy to return, and when he did, I stood in the doorway so he couldn't leave. I wasn't trying to be menacing, per se, but I could tell from the way he stiffened up that I was.

'When does Jules get home?' he asked. It was impressive to me he could feel so safe in the presence of a man who had such ill intentions towards him. But that's what groomers do, after all, and Julian was excellent at it. I imagined Tyler had the whole thing playing out in his mind as some forbidden, fairy tale romance. Boy meets a married man, an affair ensues, and they run away together because they're in love, happily ever after.

'About seven, tonight,' I said to the boy.

'Cool.'

'Why do you ask?'

Hesitating, Tyler replied 'I… I'm just wondering.'

'That's fine, I'm pretty curious myself,' I said. 'Can I ask *you* something?'

'Yeah, sure.'

'How come your aim hasn't gotten any better, what with training and all?' I smiled at the stiffening of Tyler's posture as he tried and failed to think of an excuse.

'I—I don't know,' he replied. He was too shy and dumbstruck to ask me to move out of his way, so there he was, speechless, terrified. I thought he might actually cry. He stood there, holding his ball as if it was made of lead; swapping it from one arm to the other and back again.

'Relax,' I whispered, smiling. 'I'm joking, mate.'

'Oh, good, cool.'

'Can I ask you something else?' Tyler nodded. 'Is it just you and your mums, or do you have any other family?'

'It's just us, really.' He was confused at my question, but relieved at the same time. 'I've got grandparents, if that's what you mean.'

'Yeah, yeah that's what I mean. What about aunts and

uncles?'

'No, my mums don't have any brothers or sisters.'

'Really?'

'Well, I call my mum's friend my aunty, but she's not really related or anything, and we hardly see her.'

'Yeah, that doesn't count,' I said dismissively. 'Sorry about the weird questions. Like I said, I'm just curious.'

'It's cool. We're a pretty small family, I think.'

'Mine is too.' I smiled, and the atmosphere was less tense than it had been. I pretended to notice I was in his way of leaving only then, stepping aside to let him pass.

'Thanks for letting me get my ball,' he said.

Following him down the hallway, I asked, as if it was an afterthought, 'What's the name of that aunt who's not really your aunt, by the way?'

'Ashley,' he replied.

'Hey, be careful with that ball, okay? If you hit my car, I won't be happy.'

'I will, I'm really sorry, Matt.'

'Don't worry about it.' Tyler left the house, and when he was walking down the drive, past my car, I said 'Oh, and FYI, Ty. If Julian's car isn't here, it means that he's not either.' The boy nodded and kept his head down as he crossed the road, wee-wee-wee, all the way home. I shut the front door and burst into laughter, it was the hardest I had laughed in a long while, and later, when Julian was home, he asked me what had me so amused, and I told him it didn't matter, he wouldn't get it, he had to be there.

# Six

It was Jimmy's birthday party, and I was there, at his place, because I was obligated to be, despite not being remotely bothered. When Julian and I first arrived there, Jimmy was strung out on his couch, and the whole place looked like a crime scene in Vegas, not that the state of the place was a shock, by any means. I had the urge to slap him to wake him up, but Julian opposed, of course, like a proper killjoy, so I wandered to the kitchen to get a glass of water, switching on the lights as I went. The whole place had been drenched in darkness, and Jimmy's cat announced her presence by clawing at my leg in an attempt to climb me. She was getting older, so Jimmy always made sure to remind visitors not to let her outside anymore, as if for some reason those things correlated. With this in mind, and the increasing itch to cause mayhem, I filled a pint glass up with water and opened the back door to let the cat out. Back at the crime scene, Jimmy was awake, though barely, and Julian looked defeated.

'The hell's the matter with you now?' I asked when we were alone.

'Jimmy just told me he invited Ashley tonight.'

'So what?'

'Will you stay away from her?' he asked.

I rolled my eyes. 'She probably won't turn up anyway, Jules.'

'If she does. Don't antagonise her, alright?'

'Would I do such a thing?'

'Please, just *listen* to me. For once.'

'Like you listened to me when I asked you not to get involved with the kid?'

'It's just football training, Matt,' Julian snapped back.

'Sure it is,' I said, nodding, smiling. 'Until it's *just* something else.'

Later on, the usual suspects turned up: Josh; Abraham; and Harris; and 2 other people I'd never seen before, a girl and a guy who looked as out of place as I felt for my whole life. Ashley walked into the house an hour late, and I was slightly buzzed by then on the sangria I made, so I couldn't help myself when I said, 'Hey, sis. Nice of you to show up this time.'

'Hello, Matthew,' she replied, smiling falsely. 'I see you're still just *terrible*.'

I laughed. 'Have a glass of sangria, won't you? Try not to choke on the ice.' Julian abruptly pulled me by my good arm, and it hurt, but it was nothing I couldn't handle. He did it so roughly that people noticed, and I could see the regret in his eyes, the guilt ridden, puppy-dog look he got every time his own rage surprised him. No one said a word about it, better to sweep it under the rug than get involved with other people's bullshit.

Ashley and I avoided each other for most of the night. I kept to the back of the room with Josh and Harris, talking about music and concerts, while Ashley stuck with Jimmy and his work friends. Julian was twitchy, shifting his eyes around the room and bouncing from group to group like a mute referee. The noise started to make my skull ache, and I was full of sangria by then, so my bladder was ready to burst. I went upstairs to take a piss, announcing my departure as I went.

In the bathroom, with my cock in my good hand, mid-stream, I heard the door click open, and I looked to my left and there was Ashley wearing her signature scowl.

'Bathroom is occupied,' I said.

'I see,' she replied. 'I'll wait.'

'Do you want to close the door, or…?'

'Not particularly.'

'What are you doing? You want to suck my dick?' I asked, trying to get a rise; no pun intended.

'You're disgusting, I hate you,' she spat.

After the non-conversation started itself, we entered into an awkward silence, and I was staring right at her as I continued urinating into the toilet bowl. After a couple seconds I was finished, so I asked her what it was she thought she was doing. She ignored me. I tucked my shirt into my jeans, did my buttons and belt up, all while Ashley was looking at me in such a way that she looked

227

just like Julian did when he was about to lose it. 'Don't pull that face,' I said. 'You look like your brother.'

'Fuck you,' she spat.

'What are you doing, Ashley? What do you want?'

'You just asked that.'

'And you didn't answer.'

Ashley looked around the bathroom briefly. 'I'm looking for painkillers. I've got a headache.' I didn't reply that time. I hadn't taken my eyes off her since she walked in. I could tell she was getting unnerved, then frustration kicked in when she couldn't pinpoint the reason behind her sudden fear. 'Stop staring at me like that,' she said. 'Stop it, Matt.'

'I'm not doing anything. I've no idea what you're talking about.'

'I really fucking hate you.'

'That's not news to me. It's no secret we don't like each other, Ashley. It's been common knowledge for years now. You need to get a hobby, you're a broken record.' Ashley's face told me she was contemplating what to say, then she seemed to pluck up a bit of courage.

'I want you to leave Julian,' she blurted out. 'I want you to leave my brother alone.'

I laughed at that, I couldn't help it.

'Well, that's not going to happen.' I was no longer interested in the conversation, so I went to walk out but Ashley blocked me from doing so. My immediate thought was to grab her by the hair and drown her in the toilet bowl, but the more I thought about it the less it made sense. Can you drown someone in a toilet bowl? I'd never tried that one. 'Move out of my way,' I said as politely as possible. 'You're boring me.'

'You really don't have anything there, do you?' she said, looking at me as if something was suddenly confirmed to her. 'Do you?' she asked again, but I was still standing there, not saying anything, and the longer I didn't respond, the more enraged she got, until she was calling me a *fucking demon*, *psychopath* this and *dangerous* that.

'You're a freak,' she added. She was seething, almost vampiric, and I wanted to get back downstairs but she wouldn't let me past. 'I think you're a murderer.'

'Do you have evidence to back your accusation up?' I asked, genuinely curious.

'You're intelligent, charming, cunning. You see people as nothing but toys, toys you create to fill your empty world. I don't need to be a psychologist to know you're dangerous, Matt. Just call it a gut feeling.'

'Well congratulations on your psychic abilities,' I said. 'I hate to break it to you, but your *gut feeling* isn't proof of anything.'

'I'll find proof.' Ashley was sure of herself, and it almost put me on edge. Almost. 'I'm going to prove that you're up to no good, and when I do, you won't have anyone.'

'If you truly believe me to be this dangerous, psychopathic murderer, do you think it's wise to have me cornered in a bathroom?'

'You wouldn't do anything to me, not with everyone here. You're too clever for that, too calculated. You'll do anything to keep your pretty boy image.'

'Or,' I said, as I loomed tall over her, 'you're full of shit. I think you're grasping at straws, and I think you're doing it because you know deep down Julian is not the angel everyone thinks he is. You're trying to blame me for the darkness that's been inside him since the day he was born.'

'*You* put that darkness inside him. He is a far better person without you around, everyone can see it.'

'You don't know who your brother is,' I said, highly amused by the whole development. 'You only see what he wants you to see. The sooner you open your eyes to the truth, the easier it will be for you. Leave us be, Ashley. The truth, no matter how badly you crave it, will ruin you.'

'You're a liar,' she said. 'All you do is lie.'

'Yeah, you keep telling yourself that.' I pushed past her this time, and I was willing to hurt her if she tried to stop me again, but she didn't. I turned around once more, not quite satisfied with the ending of our conversation. She was angry and upset, sure, but I wanted her to feel stupid too. 'Oh, and Ash? Say hello to your friend. I do hope her and the wife are settling in well.' Ashley went silent, lips glued shut. Her usual tan, freckle-filled face went crimson red from shock, and her eyes were wide open, as was her mind. I had her plan figured out, and oh so soon. She didn't confirm I was right, nor did she deny it, just stood there like all of her energy was sucked dry. I walked away without another word, satisfied I ruined at least one person's night, but when I was back on Jimmy's landing, Julian was standing there, so furious it was all I could do not to laugh. To avoid any more drama for the time being I ignored him, but he grabbed me by the back of my shirt so I couldn't go any further.

'What the *fuck* did you tell her?' he snarled.

'I'm not having her barge in on me and call me a murderer while I'm taking a piss,' I said. I realised Jimmy was on the landing with us, swaying at the other end by the stairs. He was upset, slurring his words and asking me what the hell I was talking about. Julian let me go, Ashley came out of the bathroom with mascara all over her face, and I knew it was a ploy to make the guys believe I had done something to her. It backfired miserably. 'You heard me, Jim,' I said. 'It's true, that's what she called me. Can you believe that?'

Jimmy was yelling, drunker than everyone else and talking like he had just come back from the dentist. Ashley tried throwing me under the bus by calling me a liar, but Jimmy had already heard enough, so she couldn't get a word in edgeways. Then Jimmy was screaming, calling Ashley a bitch, telling her to get the fuck out, and why would she say that, why Ashley, why? He got more and more emotional until he was sobbing on the floor.

'I think he wants you to go, Ashley,' I said.

'Go and fuck yourself.' She stormed down the stairs leaving shortly after, calling us insane as she went.

'You too,' Julian said to me. 'You caused this mess. Give me a minute with James.'

I left the two men on the landing and walked down

the stairs that Ashley had just walked down, but I stopped on the last step and stood there, silent, listening. I could hear them talking, hear Jimmy's sobs and Julian's soothing voice.

'Mate, what the fuck just happened?' The voice startled me only slightly, and I turned to Josh, pressing a finger to my lips.

'Jimmy lost his shit,' I whispered, my breath hot against my hand. 'I'm trying to listen.'

'What's he saying?'

'Not a lot,' I replied, shaking my head in disappointment. 'He's just blubbering like a little girl.'

'I heard the cat's missing,' said Josh. 'Maybe that's why.'

'Maybe.' We both walked away from the stairs and into the lounge, where everyone was gathering their belongings, preparing to leave. 'What did Ashley say before she left?'

'Nothing. She came in crying, grabbed her bag, and fucked off without a word.'

'Jimmy threw her out.' Josh's eyes widened in amusement. 'Yeah, tell me about it. She said something he didn't like, and he lost it.'

'Makes it a change from the two of you arguing, eh?' I nodded at him, not really listening. 'Have you seen the cat? I told Jimmy I'd find her. She's disappeared, dude.'

'I let her out,' I said. 'Earlier on, I let her out the back door.' It was just the two of us in the conservatory, everyone else had filtered out by then. Abraham was waiting for Josh in the car.

'You weren't supposed to let her out,' he told me, mildly worried. I was smiling. Then his face changed. 'You can be a real cold bastard, you know?'

'Yeah, I know,' I replied. 'I'm sure she'll be fine.'

'And if she's not?' Josh asked. I shrugged my shoulders. 'Cold bastard,' he repeated. 'You got a fag on you?' I handed him my pack and a lighter from my pocket. He lit one. 'Are you still coming to London next month?'

'Of course I am.'

'What about your arm?'

'It'll be fine. I worked last week, you know?'

'You didn't tell me, I would have come to watch you.'

'You had that band playing in the club,' I said. 'You were swamped.'

'Right. Forgot about that.' Josh offered me a cigarette and I took it. 'I still can't believe you fell down the stairs on your honeymoon.'

'Yeah, me neither,' I said. Julian came into the room and announced we were getting a taxi home because we were both too drunk to drive my car, so I went outside to park it on Jimmy's drive. I spotted Taffy, the cat, wandering around the road, and I didn't aim for her intentionally, nor did I make an attempt to avoid her. Natural selection, and all that.

Later, Julian and I got into a fight. He heard some of the things I said to Ashley, blamed me for the way things ended at Jimmy's house. At first, he tried making me leave, said he didn't want me in the bed. When that didn't work, he tried flipping his argument. Instead of being mad at me, he pretended to be concerned.

'You gave Ashley more ammunition tonight,' he said. 'She was already suspicious of you. I just don't want you to get in trouble, Matty. I'm only looking out for you. What's so hard to understand about that?' But it wasn't about me. He was concerned only for himself. He was angry at me for casting a cloud of doubt over his perfect image. How dare I tell the truth about him for once? So began the same see-sawing conversation we had all the time: if one of us got caught, so did the other.

Things escalated quickly after that. It got physical, as it often did, but that night I was less interested in participating, so I cut it short. Julian was always a dreadful fighter, so I waited for my moment, the moment he would get carried away and let his guard down, and like magic, he put both his hands around my throat, leaving his entire body vulnerable, and I kicked him, hard, in the nuts. Temporarily disabled, Julian writhed and howled from the hallway floor while I went upstairs to bed, leaving him there alone to screech like a banshee.

All in all the night turned out to be quite theatrical. Ashley's reaction earlier in the evening, when I mentioned saying hello to Lara, confirmed the strong inkling in my mind that they knew each other. It explained her immediate disliking of me, and it was actually the *only* thing that made sense, when I thought about it—Lara must have made up her mind about me before we even met because someone had made it up for her. There was not a single person I couldn't charm into thinking I was their best friend, not a single one apart from Ashley, and now Lara. On top of that, there was the whole Jimmy debacle, the crying and the despair and the confession I heard him tell Julian while I stood at the bottom of the stairs. An 8-year-old girl was killed in a hit and run, and Jimmy was the driver. Secrets: they were everywhere, and I kept my knowledge of them all to myself.

# Seven

Melissa knocked on our door the morning after, and Julian and I had to practically draw straws on who would answer the door, because our fight the previous night had left marks on both of us. I drew the short straw. I was hungover and in desperate need of hydrating as I threw myself downstairs, and Melissa asked if Julian and I would have Tyler over for a couple of hours that night. I agreed because I couldn't decline, and when I told Julian about it, he pretended to be annoyed, even though his eyes sparkled like emeralds.

We ordered pizza when Tyler arrived at seven, because what else do you feed a 14-year-old, really? The three of us watched TV, mostly in silence, and I ignored the fact that Tyler sat on the floor so he could be near Julian. He could have sat in the armchair, but god forbid he be more than an arm's length away. I pretended not to see the boy's hand rubbing Julian's calf, pretended not to see Julian's attempts to hide his pleasure. It impressed me how quickly he had sunk his teeth into the boy, so imagine my surprise when Julian chose to drive me to Jimmy's place to get my car, instead of the obvious choice of staying in the house, unsupervised, with his new plaything. I was disappointed in him. There I was, handing him a golden opportunity, and he didn't want it. In the end it didn't really matter, there was always next time, and with Julian, there was always a next time.

Julian stayed in the car with the kid when we got there, and I went in to check on Jimmy briefly, who was in as much of a mess as he had been the night before but for a totally different reason this time. His neighbour woke him up that morning with the sad news that Taffy, the cat, was dead. She was found on the road, squashed into the tarmac. Hit by a car, apparently. A hit and run, you might say.

'Accidents happen,' I said. 'I'm sorry for your loss. If there's anything we can do, just ask, okay? You know we're here for you... Hey, Jim, how the hell did the cat get out in the first place? And what kind of person would leave her lying in the road like that?' Jimmy didn't answer me. He looked at me like I knew something I shouldn't, but he kept quiet. Better to not say a word than to incriminate himself.

Julian got home before me. He was busy clearing the pizza boxes and the glasses from the lounge when I walked in.

'Where's the kid?' I asked.

'Upstairs. Bathroom.' It was coming up to midnight

and the boy would be leaving soon. When Tyler was back with us his demeanour was different: he was quieter than usual, kept his head down and his eyes averted. I wondered what happened in the time before I got in, but it didn't matter, not really. What mattered was that *something* happened, be it big or small, and things would soon start to shift.

I forgot all about Jimmy's dead, squashed cat until we were settling down for bed. Julian was obviously quite upset by the news. He managed to make it my fault before he even knew the truth, so I decided, in spite, to keep to myself that it was my hand that opened the door and my car tyre that flattened the cat.

* * *

*I'm sorry about earlier, kid. I got carried away.*

That is what one of the texts from Julian to Tyler said. Once those kind of messages started they didn't stop and I made sure to keep a record of them, screenshotting and forwarding the photos to myself, then deleting them from Julian's phone before putting it back where I found it. He remained none the wiser, and so did I.

*I shouldn't have touched you like that.*
*I'm sorry. I can't keep my hands off you.*
*Are we okay?*
*I miss you.*
*Did you like what I did to you in the car earlier?*
*God, you drive me crazy.*

Some of the texts Julian sent Tyler, stored for a rainy day.

# Eight

Julian went to see Jimmy with chocolate and a card, consolations for the whole dead cat thing. We got into a slight argument before he left and I let slip I was the one who let the cat outside. He kept pushing me, and that morning I wasn't in the mood for his mood. Julian acted shocked at my admission despite knowing the worst of my transgressions, asking me why I would do such a thing, *why, Matthew, why*, and I gave him the same answer I always gave: I was bored, wanted to see what would happen. It's safe to say he was raging when he left, telling me how much he wanted to hurt me, slamming the front door behind him. I gave it no more than ten minutes before following him in my car. And I did it without a thought, really, as if guided by something other than my own mind. I stayed far enough behind the Jag to remain invisible, parked at the end of Jimmy's street, and waited. Call it intuition, I could feel it in the air: Julian would be looking for ways to get back at me, and Jimmy would be desperate for comfort. I listened to the radio for ten or so minutes, then I exited the car and strolled up the damp and cold street, like I had all the time in the world, nodding politely to a neighbour of Jimmy's, stroking a dog out on a walk with his owner. Outside Jimmy's house on the road was a dark red stain with patches of fur still ground into the tarmac, and I wondered how much rain it would take to wash it away.

I crept up Jimmy's drive, like a cat, ironically. The motion light on his porch flashed on, barely missing me as I hid from view of the window. I waited for the light to flicker off, and after a minute of standing still and silent, I shuffled carefully to the window. A laugh escaped my lips—I was being ridiculous, *looked* ridiculous, and for what? Knowledge. I craved it, hunted it, consumed it. And when I craved knowledge on Julian's comings and goings, I never had to hunt for long. I peeked through Jimmy's front window and there they were, fucking on Jimmy's white, whiskey-stained sofa.

I didn't go straight home, I decided to fuck with Julian myself, which never required more effort than I was willing to give. I drove around Oxford for an hour or so, contemplating what to do with my newfound knowledge, settling on nothing. Not yet, anyway. I kept my cards close to my chest, where I preferred them, where I could keep them safe.

Julian was beside himself with anxiety when I got home, firing questions at me about my whereabouts, as usual, but with feeling this time, paranoia and jealousy and anger all rolled up in one pathetic mess.

'Where have you been?'

'Out,' I said. 'Did you enjoy yourself over Jimmy's?' Julian looked at me like I knew something I shouldn't. The way everyone looked at me. Don't trust Matty.

'You're a real piece of work,' he snarled.

'A masterpiece,' I replied.

\* \* \*

There was an event coming up at a club called *Luxe* in London that Josh and I bought tickets for, and I invited Julian but didn't really want him to come, and he declined anyway, of course, because it was the first time he would have the house and the teenager all to himself, for a full night, with no distractions. The day before the event I got home from university early, and sat in my car waiting for Tyler to get home from school.

'What's this?' he asked in response to the key I handed him, completely bewildered.

'It's a key to my house. It's yours.'

'Why?'

'Just in case you ever need to get out the back for your football and we aren't home. Or if you ever need to get out of the house.'

At that, Tyler looked at me like I was insane and asked, 'Why would I need it to get out?'

'If you ever got locked in.'

'Why would I be locked in?'

I sighed, shrugged my shoulders and said, 'Just take

the key, yeah?' and he shook his head, no, and held the key back out to me. I backed away from him, hands up, saying, 'You'll be sorry if you don't take it.' Tyler, speechless, watched me walk away. 'Make sure you have it on you at all times, okay?' I said, loud enough for him to hear me. 'And don't tell Julian I gave it to you. You know how he gets, right? He'll freak out.'

# Nine

I left my laptop on the sideboard in the bedroom, plugged in, open, with the camera facing the bed, recording. I told Julian it was updating, it would take approximately 16 hours, and he wasn't to touch it because I needed it to turn my assignment into my professor, Camille, when I got back from London. I knew he would be too antsy about having the kid over to think too much about it.

I got a taxi to Josh's place and he drove us both there. He had insisted, since my arm was still touch-and-go, despite my having driven since the week after I did it. At least I didn't need a bandage or a splint anymore. We merged from the A40 to the M40, which was a total drag because there was an accident that afternoon, so what should have been 90 minutes turned into a 3-hour drive. Josh was stone cold sober so his road rage was at a peak, and I remarked how ginger people really did have red-hot tempers, which just made him worse, swearing at me while I laughed and lit cigarette after cigarette and sang along to the radio until we were entering the city. Josh told me to turn it off, like a real killjoy, because, 'I can't listen to your shit singing for any longer, and I can't concentrate on the fucking roads, Matt. I don't know where the fuck we are. Where are we? Do you know where we are?'

Someone almost drove into the side of the car at a junction, and Josh put the window down and screamed, 'It's my right of way you fat fucking bitch!'

'Chill out, mate,' I said. 'Want me to kill her for you?'

'Yeah, please. Where do I go next?'

'Put the satnav thingy on… Where *is* the satnav?'

Josh looked at me like a naughty child. 'I broke it. I ripped it out the other week.'

'Why?'

'It told me to take a left turn into a fucking river bank.' The image of that palaver entertained me to no end, and we eventually made it into London without a body count.

Josh parked in a car park a short walk away from Luxe, and we went for lunch at a pub and drank bottles of Heineken and smoked more cigarettes. We were pretty buzzed by the time we left, and on the way to Luxe, Josh asked to borrow my lighter. There was a brief moment of panic as I almost handed him my pocket knife instead, but it reminded me to hide it in my Dr Martens—there would be security at the doors of the nightclub, searching people for drugs and weapons. Josh lit his cigarette as I pretended to re-tie my laces, sliding the pocket knife into my sock.

'Thanks, Mate,' he said as he handed the lighter back.

'Welcome.'

Growing up, I never understood the whole *friend* thing. Friends were something *normal* people had, so like everything else in my life, I knew I had to mimic the concept, but that's not to say I wanted to. It was more of a need, something I had to have in order to fit in and not become the next Jeffrey Dahmer. The creepy, gay loner that parents warn their daughters and sons about by the time they can talk. Despite having people around me that would class me as their friend, I really only had one, one person who didn't overwhelm me with the urge to hurt them, and that person was Josh. My oldest, and only friend. Freckle-faced-red-head with a red-hot temper and an unexplainable respect for my utter cold-heartedness. Josh was the only person I never imagined killing, and that included my own mother, and Julian too. I wished I could just passively watch people without being expected to participate myself, like a TV, but if I *had* to participate, Josh was fine company.

Luxe was packed. The dance music was bouncing off the high ceilings, and raised voices were beaming across the bar at the bartenders, who were all uniformly dressed in black leather, looking exhausted already, like they just came from a hard day of shooting for a BDSM movie. I posted a couple photos on Instagram along with a short recording of the heaving club, featuring an already drunk and disorderly Josh, who had just ordered us the strongest cocktail on the menu. He literally asked for 'Whatever is strongest, mate,' and on the way to a spare table he pointed out a guy that was sitting in a VIP booth, surrounded by boys that didn't look old enough to drive, never mind drink. 'That guy is famous,' Josh said, but I didn't recognise him. Cameras were flashing like a strobe, and there were actual strobes, too, beaming multi-coloured lights across the club in different directions. I had an amusing thought: If someone with epilepsy was there they would be dead, and no one would notice.

A woman dressed in the same black leather as the bartenders came up to our table holding a tray of double shots of tequila, and Josh and I gave her a tenner, which bought us 5 each. After we swallowed the shots and the waitress had moved onto the next group of people, I launched into a spiel about how I had been robbing Julian for months, how he had absolutely no idea, and I was going to take the money and buy myself a nice apartment overlooking a beach somewhere, and I was going to ruin Julian, leave him with nothing, which meant I might never see Josh again, should my plan work out. I asked Josh how he would feel about that, if he never saw me again, if I just disappeared, and Josh was nodding along, pretending he could hear me over the music, saying, 'Yeah, mate. Totally. I get it. You're my best friend, mate. I support you no matter what. Go get us another drink, will you?'

On the way to the bar I was feeling particularly agitated, but not necessarily in a bad way; more like I was close to a breakthrough; a man on the cusp of something brilliant; itching to get there. I needed a release, the water break before the final mile. With the pocket knife in my boot and the yearning for chaos in my blood, I switched directions and made my way to the so-called famous guy in the VIP booth. It was lit in a neon pink as I walked in, and I sprawled myself across his table, a needy and wanton thing. I had no interest in adding fanfare to the situation. After all, I had a thirsty mate waiting for me on the opposite end of the club, which gave me no more than fifteen minutes to get the job done before a search party would be launched, and by search party I mean a worried ginger and whatever strays he caught in the meantime. No one would be looking for the famous guy, though: no one knew he was there apart from the select few who recognised him, and the uncomfortable looking teenage boys who accompanied him. They didn't say a word as I swooped in and flirted with the master of their table, and I thought I was probably their saving grace of the night. Not that I'm saying I was their hero, I couldn't think of a less truthful word than heroic to describe my actions that night. I was simply doing what I felt like doing because I could get away with it.

I looked the famous guy in the eyes as if I'd never seen a greater god. 'I can't believe it's actually *you*,' I said, though I had no idea who he was. 'I'm a huge fan! I literally *love* you. Would you come dance with me? *Please?* Just for a minute? It would make my night, it really would.' He didn't take much convincing, really. Not once I added, with a seductive smile 'I'll make it worth your while. I have a few talents of my own.'

The dance floor was heaving with so many people we could barely move, and the flashing lights were the only source of light we had in an otherwise dark club. We were like sardines in a tin, cramped together, pulsing and rubbing against one another whether we liked it or not. The famous guy told me to call him Dave, but I wasn't really planning on spending much longer with him. I needed to let off some steam, that's all, and despite my promises to show him a good time, he was nothing but a game piece to me. He was the dart to my board, the ball to my bat. His arms were around my waist, mine were over his shoulders, looped around his neck. I leaned closer to his ear.

'Can I tell you something?' I asked. He assumed I was going to compliment him again. He smiled, unaware of the peril he was in.

'Yeah, you love me. I've heard it, kid. What else do you want, an autograph?' I laughed, focused my eyes on his, drawing him into an intense stare off. 'What's so funny?' he asked.

'I lied to you,' I said, lifting my knee to reach into my boot. 'I have no fucking idea who you are.' Before the supposed celebrity could answer, the pining inside me crested a giant wave of hate, and I pulled the knife out of my boot and stabbed him, quickly, in the neck.

Bewildered, Dave, or whatever, tried backing away, gurgling like an infant, unable to scream or cry out because of the blood spurting from the wound in his throat. Though I wanted to watch him die, I was running out of time, so I thrusted the knife in his stomach for good measure and let him drop to the floor, then casually mingled with the rest of the crowd. Behind me, Dave the celebrity, flapping around on the floor like a fish out of water. Everyone was too high and drunk and cramped together to notice the blood pooling on the neon-lit dance floor, and the music was loud enough to hide the sound of an explosion, so any gargles of death would surely be drowned out. I pocketed the knife, wiping the blood from my hands over everyone's clothes as we bumped and danced into each other. I moved through the crowd and back to Josh, which is when the crowd finally noticed something was wrong, (they were slipping in blood by then). There was a commotion, but I was already far away from the scene of crime; back at the bar ordering two of the strongest drinks on the menu again, which I learned was a special cocktail called *The Luxe Luthor*; then mingling back with Josh at our table, and some strays he managed to pick up.

'You good, Matty?' Josh asked, unaware of the increasingly concerned crowd behind me. Rowdier and rowdier.

'Yeah, mate. Never better. Was I long? There was a queue at the bar.'

'Nah, not too bad. You're glowing, mate.'

'It's the glitter,' I replied, giggling like a child, but I knew what he meant, I could feel the glow myself, adrenaline, euphoria. I managed to scratch an itch, at least for the time being. It was extraordinarily easy to take someone's life and get away with it, especially when you've grown accustomed to it. I liked using my knife, but it was messy, though I guess that's why I liked it so much. Paint the room red.

'What's going on over there?' Josh asked, standing on the tips of his toes to get a better look at the ever-growing swarm of intrigue.

'God knows, probably a fight.'


The screams started shortly after that, and security quickly got involved, cutting the music off and blocking the dance floor. We were told over the speakers that there had been an accident; there was a man seriously injured; the police have been called; remain as calm as you can and don't leave until the police get here. There were too many of us and not enough security, so people naturally didn't listen. Some of us left the club like Josh and I, some panicked, some fought with the security guards, and some drunkenly tampered with the scene of crime, making it impossible to determine what really happened at Luxe that night. The ambulance turned up too late, the police had no leads, the evidence was smeared all over the place, and Josh and I got a twin room at a nearby hotel, where we watched the story unfold on the news and Josh expressed disappointment at missing the whole thing.

# Ten

I got home the following afternoon. Julian had cleaned
the house from top to bottom, and it was so thoroughly
done that it would have impressed an OCD patient. He
was restless, jittery, and he was walking around the house,
checking his phone, trying his best not to act like a guilty
dog. Thing is, Julian's *best* was awful. Upstairs, my laptop
was exactly where I left it, still open on a black screen
with a blue decoy buffer, like a snake chasing itself
around and around. There was an app for everything. A
spy camera in the form of a buffer screen. Who would
have thought? I didn't watch the recording right away, I
saved it to a memory stick, sent it to my phone, and hid it
in a folder on the laptop titled *Piano stuff*. I didn't yet
know if the video had caught anything at all. I closed the
laptop and inspected the bed: Julian had washed and
dried the sheets and put them back on, I could tell by the
still-damp corners of the bedspread, and the white
bottom sheet had been replaced with a light grey one.

Back downstairs, Julian asked me all about my night. It was great fun, I said, Josh and I had a blast. How was your night, Jules? A flash of regret revealed itself on Julian's face, or maybe it was disgust, and he said 'Uneventful. I cleaned, watched something on the telly. But mostly, I missed you.'

The next day I took the bins out and there was the white sheet, sitting in the bin outside. I unravelled it from the ball Julian had bundled it up into, and there were reddish brown stains on it, which were obviously blood. I put it back where I found it, put a black bag on top, and went about the day as usual.

*** 

Something had changed. That week, Julian didn't take Tyler to football training as he usually did, and Tyler stopped showing up at the house at random. I didn't see him at all, actually, and Julian wasn't late coming home from work anymore. His drinking got heavier, his temper got shorter, and I couldn't help but wind him up tighter. I would ask him, 'Where's Tyler today? No football?' and he would shake his head, say, 'He's still not feeling very well.'

'What's wrong with him?'

'No idea.'

'I haven't seen him around.'

'Me neither.' Another glass of wine, short, chewed off nails. At night Julian would stand at the bay window of our bedroom and glare across the street at Tyler's house, and I hadn't watched the video yet but I knew exactly what I would find.

Jimmy started showing up at the house instead of Tyler. He was in a state, as always, and Julian would go outside to talk to him—or yell—instead of inviting him in like usual. This was obviously suspicious behaviour, but Julian was so wrapped up in his own little world that he didn't seem to notice me noticing him.

'What's happened between the two of you?' I asked more than once.

'Nothing,' Julian replied. 'I'm just... Well, I'm sick of him. He's a mess.'

'Want me to have a word?'

'No!' Julian snapped. 'No... Leave him be. He needs to learn to look after himself. We can't keep doing it for him. He needs help, but not from us.'

'Are you sure? What kind of help?'

'Not the kind you can assist with.'

'Just say the word—'

'Stay away from him, Matthew. Promise me you won't talk to him.'

Since he was so concerned about the two of us communicating, I didn't tell him about the numerous texts and calls Jimmy left me, nor did I inform him about our conversations. They were all the same: *Tell Juju to ring me. I need to talk to him. Please, Matt, please.*

254

# Eleven

Julian crept his way out of bed earlier than usual, tiptoeing around me so as not to disturb the sleep I was faking. I had a day off uni, and I heard the central heating starting up which told me it was just past 6am. Julian left his phone under his pillow when he went to shower, so I unlocked it, wincing when the screen lit up and threatened to burn my retinas. I read through some texts between Julian and Tyler with one eye protectively closed. The most recent texts were sent from Julian's phone—though it looked like he was having a conversation with himself. Tyler stopped replying to him the weekend I gave him my key, in fact, it was the night of Luxe, and the texts were all variations of the same thing: apologies and regret. *Please talk to me, you're killing me here, how did you get out of the house?*

I heard the shower turn off and the glass doors sliding open, so I slid Julian's phone back where I found it, still pretending to be asleep when Julian came back in the bedroom to get dressed for work. After he left, twenty minutes early, I waited for the familiar sound of the Jaguar starting, and when it didn't I got up and went to the window. I saw him across the road talking to Tyler, only he wasn't really talking. The kid was pinned against Lara's car on their drive, and their faces were almost touching as Julian loomed over him while Tyler struggled to get away, refusing to look Julian in the eye. A car, an Audi, was driving up the street, and it irked Julian into backing off from the kid. Suddenly Melissa opened the front door, and her expression was one of clear shock, I could tell even from where I was in the warmth of the bedroom. I could see her because she was facing my way, but I could only see the back of Julian. I was briefly disheartened that I missed being witness to Julian's attempts of worming his way out of how bizarre it was for him to be talking to a teenager so early in the morning, not to mention how the teenager looked like he would rather be dead.

# Twelve

When Julian eventually left for work after chatting to Melissa, I decided to watch the video. I was on my phone because it was easier, really, and I forwarded through hours of footage within seconds. The video stumbled onto the sick scene I was hoping for, and I say *hoping* because it's the closest word to how I was feeling, but it wasn't exactly the right one, just the one I empathised with the most in the moment. To get through it I had to pretend I wasn't watching it, and I'd seen a ton of fucked up videos on the internet growing up. I stopped forwarding when I saw a shadow just out of frame, which soon revealed itself as Julian's, then the screen burst with a warm orange glow from my Himalayan salt lamp. Julian's full form came into the frame, closely followed by Tyler, and I noticed their height difference—startling—only then. Both of them were wearing boxers and nothing else as Julian led the boy to the side of the bed, and Tyler got in, under the sheets, and shuffled over to make room for Julian, who climbed in next to him. I forwarded through another couple minutes of foreplay: touching; kissing; grinding against each other; Julian, rolling on top of the boy. I pressed play as Julian was asking, 'Are you sure about this?'

Tyler whispered three yes's, one after another in quick succession, and suddenly Julian flipped him over so he was lying on his stomach. Tyler made the noise of a shocked animal, but didn't protest other than that. It was when Julian grabbed his arms and held them behind his back that the boy started to panic. It was funny how quickly Tyler changed his tune.

'No, Jules, not like this, stop,' he pleaded. Julian didn't listen, why would he? He had the boy exactly where he wanted him. There could be no take backs. Instead, Julian soothed Tyler's cries, telling him to breathe, then there was a blood-curdling scream coming through my phone, so loud I nearly dropped it. The Himalayan salt lamp flickered, the bed frame squeaked and rocked faster and faster, and Tyler cried and whimpered while Julian ignored him. This went on for longer than I could bear, but my eyes were glued to the screen. I was lucky I hadn't eaten yet. Tyler went quiet after a couple of minutes, probably from shock, and Julian let his arms go, knowing the boy was too traumatised and weak to do anything else. The fight had drained him, his cries reduced to mere whines of pain, and Julian took what he wanted from him until he was satisfied. He collapsed next to Tyler on the bed, and everything was suddenly so still I thought I'd accidentally paused the video. I skipped forward again, looking for signs of life, then the little silhouette of a curly-haired boy emerged from the bed. Julian didn't stir, so he must have fallen asleep right after to protect himself from the guilt. It shouldn't have surprised me, really: Julian never could face up to anything.

Tyler limped to the foot of the bed, and he stared at Julian's sleeping form for—and I double checked this—five whole minutes, before disappearing out of frame. He didn't return at any point that night, and Julian was none the wiser, as ever. He woke up a couple hours later in a complete fluster, yelling Tyler's name over and over, frantically searching the house and then coming back to the bedroom as if the boy would magically appear. He picked up his phone and though I couldn't see what he was doing, it was evident he was trying to ring Tyler, talking at the phone, saying, 'Pick up. Pick up Ty, come on, come on!' and, 'How the fuck did he get out of the house?'

I forwarded through the remainder of the video to make sure I didn't miss anything. There was nothing of grave importance, just Julian pacing like a loon in and out of frame; stripping the bed; trying to phone Tyler again; re-making the bed minus the bloody sheets. He didn't sleep at all that night, which didn't surprise me, really. When I got home from Luxe he looked like he hadn't slept in days. On my laptop, I cut the video down from 20 hours of unworthy footage to 15 minutes of pure gold. Julian texted me as I was finishing up: *Bumped into Melissa this morning. She invited us over for drinks this Friday. I said yes, but what do you think?*

I texted Julian back: *Yeah, saw you both talking earlier*, for no reason other than to scare the shit out of him. He would wonder all day what I meant by that; how much I saw and how much I knew. *Drinks sound great, babe,* I said. *Can't wait.*

After that I found Ashley's number and texted her too: *Do you know what you've done?* She replied a couple hours later: *Who is this?*

I text her right back: *It's a secret.*

# Thirteen

I was packing some of my things into the boot of my car: boxes of shoes; jackets; art supplies; books; candles; a backpack full of thousands in cash that I stole from Julian. I found most of the money hidden in the globe in his study, along with a white box with a label that said Flunitrazepam, the medical name for Rohypnol; commonly known as the date rape drug, which I also took. My guess was that he planned on giving it to Tyler one day, or another unsuspecting boy.

My phone was blowing up with messages from Jimmy that afternoon, all the same; all desperately begging me to get Julian to answer his phone calls, but I ignored him. I had far more important things to be getting on with, plans to be plotting and a life to be packing away, and I should have known better, really. Jimmy didn't take no for an answer; he was quite like me in that respect, and he caught me off guard by turning up at the house while I was moving my stuff. Red handed. I shut the boot but it was too late, Jimmy saw everything.

'What's going on? Where's Juju?' he asked. *Why* are you moving your stuff out? You getting a divorce *already*?'

I could have probably let it go, lied my way through the questions, denied ever having anything in my car, made Julian and Jimmy both think they were going nuts. I could have taken my things to Josh's house to hide and pretended it never happened. There was no real need for any harm to come to Jimmy, but where's the fun in that? Maybe it was the frustration of being caught; or the affairs Julian was having all over town; or how pathetic Jimmy was, how fucking weak and pitiful his cries for attention, how invasive he was; or the itch that had crept back tenfold. Maybe it was none of these, and merely being presented with the opportunity to destroy him was enough.

So, why *was* I moving my stuff? The answer was simple.

'I'm having a clear out, selling some of the new clothes I've never worn. They still have the tags on. I've got some Hugo Boss, some Ralph Lauren. I can bring them over tonight for you to have a look, if you want? No charge. Mates rates.'

'Boss, you say?' Jimmy said, interested. I nodded.

'There's a brand-new Armani watch, too. And a new bottle of Versace aftershave.' I was making it all up, of course, but Jimmy fell for it like I knew he would.

'Yes, do. Where's Juju? He's been ignoring my calls and I need to talk to him.'

'He's at work,' I said, checking the time on my

phone. 'He should be on lunch break by now. You can catch him if you hurry.'

\* \* \*

I met up with Josh for lunch, where we talked about the famous guy who got killed at Luxe and any recent updates of the investigation. There were none, really, no leads, no CCTV, no witnesses, no valid evidence. The conversation drifted into a debate over the perpetrator: Josh's theory was that it was a victim who was abused by 'Dave'; my theory was that it was a knife-happy criminal who saw an opportunity to cause chaos and took it. After some back and forth I leaned forward, laughing, and said, 'I did it, I stabbed him twice and then ordered our drinks.'

'You're lucky I know you're joking,' Josh replied, chuckling like it was the funniest joke he'd ever heard.

'Does your drug guy sell heroin?' I asked, sipping cold coffee. Josh nearly choked on an onion ring.

'You're kidding, right?' My face clearly portrayed that I was not, in fact, kidding, and Josh shook his head. 'Why do you want that?'

'I don't, I'm curious that's all.'

'Well, I mean, yeah, he probably does, he's a drug dealer. And if he doesn't sell it, I'm sure he knows someone else who does...' Josh leaned back in his chair, observing me. 'If I find out you're doing heroin, I'm signing you into rehab, mate.'

'I swear, I'm not,' I laughed. 'It's just one of those

intrusive questions I had to ask.'

'Well, I'm glad I could answer it for you,' Josh said sarcastically. 'I don't know what that says about me, but there we are.'

'It says you're fun—you've got a guy for everything!'

'Any more intrusive thoughts for me to answer today?'

'Yeah, actually. I was thinking about Jimmy's cat this morning. She had diabetes, didn't she?'

'Yeah, think so. He was injecting her every night before she died.'

'I'm sorry I let her out,' I lied, to keep up appearances.

'Nah, I think you did Jimmy a favour, Mate. She was old, and he couldn't let her go. It was cruel by the end, she was suffering.' So I was a hero, after all.

Josh and I finished our food and smoked a couple cigarettes outside in the carpark. He told me he and Abraham were going on holiday to Mexico in two weeks, which made me aware of the fact that it would be the last time we saw each other and the last cigarette we would smoke together. On the way home I stopped off at Josh's drug dealer's house and bought a gram of heroin for £80, which in retrospect seemed a little steep, but I didn't care, it was Julian's money anyway.

# Fourteen

I waited for Tyler to get home from school at 3.30pm. It's crazy what you can get done in a day when you put your mind to it. Julian was still at work, and so were the kid's parents, so there would be no further interruptions.

I got out of my car, where I was waiting, out of sight, like a stalker, and walked towards him, calling out his name. He didn't hear me the first time, so I called him again, and when he turned around he looked startled as I approached.

'Good afternoon,' I said.

'Oh, uh… Afternoon,' he mumbled.

'I came to chat.' I kept nearing him. 'How are you?'

Tyler swallowed, took a step back, and another. 'Yeah, I'm cool.'

Our eyes locked and that's when I saw it: the second he understood that it was too late; I already knew about him and Julian, and it was only a matter of time before I brought it up. Tyler pulled his phone out of his pocket like it was a weapon of some kind, like he needed one.

'Why are you afraid?' I asked.

'Dunno.' Tyler thought for a moment, clutching his phone. Fear caused him to change his answer. 'My mum doesn't like you.'

I smiled. 'A lot of people don't like me.'

'I know why you're here.'

'Why am I here?'

'Probably to punch me, or something.'

'Why would I do that?'

''Cause of Julian.' A pained look crossed Tyler's face and his voice softened. 'I'm really sorry.'

'Did you take the key?' Tyler nodded. I didn't need to tell him *I told you so*. He was already there himself.

'How did you know?' he asked, tears brimming his waterline, and I figured he meant how I knew Julian would lock him inside.

I shrugged. 'I know Julian.'

'I'm sorry,' Tyler said again. He was openly crying then.

'I'm not here to hurt you, and I'm not going to tell your parents. Not unless you want me to—'

'No! Please.'

'Okay. I won't.' I would, but not yet.

'Don't you hate me? Don't you want to kill me?'

I laughed. 'No.'

'Why?'

'It's not in the plan.' Tyler's eyes were wide and wet and it was like he couldn't understand a word I was saying.

'But I went to your house,' he sobbed. 'It's my fault. I wanted to.'

'I didn't say you weren't stupid.' I smiled, and it lacked any expression but it was the most I could offer, and Tyler was lost, in a daze he had probably been in for days. I noticed the dark purple-ish hue beneath his eyes that told me he hadn't been sleeping; the red-raw bottom lip; the soulless and vacant look he gave me before his eyes filled with tears. He was not a well boy.

'He hurt me,' he whispered, as if the words would cause him great pain if spoken any louder.

'I know.'

'I asked him to stop—'

'I know.'

'I thought he cared about me.' The penny finally dropped. 'He said I was safe with him, he promised, he told me he wouldn't hurt me...' I drifted out of the conversation, all the blubbering was making me uncomfortable, and I zoned back in as Tyler was saying '...and he came over here this morning, he... he won't leave me alone. He's like, stalking me. I don't want to see him. He's afraid I'll tell my mums but I won't, I swear, I... I just want him to leave me alone. But now it's all fucked up, 'cause this morning my mum caught us talking and she invited you guys over our house to get drunk.'

'Yeah, he texted me something about that. It's good, this is good.'

'Why is it good?' Tyler was more lost than before.

'It's all fitting together,' I said, nodding.

'What is?'

'You'll see.'

* * *

'Did you see Jimmy today?' I asked Julian as soon as he walked through the front door. He put his umbrella back in the umbrella stand, hung his coat up.

'Yes, he came by the office,' he replied. 'Did *you* see Jimmy today?'

'Yepp. He stopped by the house,' I said. It was a breath of fresh air, we were both being honest with each other for once. But, as they say, all good things must come to an end.

'What did he want? Did he say anything weird?'

'Like what? Did you tell him I killed his cat?'

'No, Christ. Why would I do that?'

'I stopped questioning the things you do long ago, Jules,' I teased.

'Very funny. No, he doesn't know about the cat.'

'Well what do you mean, then?'

'I don't know, Matt. Never mind.'

'He was a mess, if that's what you mean,' I said. 'But nothing out of Jimmy's ordinary. I'm going over to see him soon, I've got some things for him that I'm getting rid of.' A look of terror crossed Julian's face before he quickly hid it, and he wrapped his arms around me in a possessive embrace.

'Don't stay too long, I miss you,' he said, but what he really wanted to say was, *I don't want you to go. I'm hiding something from you that I don't want you to find.* 'And Matty, don't listen to him if he says anything—'

'Weird?' I paused, smiling. 'I never listen to a word he says, don't shit yourself.'

I left the house shortly after, drove to Jimmy's and let myself in. Jimmy was crouched over his coffee table, crying into a bowl of cereal, and I thought it was funny how his last meal was likely the same as the little girl he killed. I pretended not to notice he was crying.

'Can I get a glass of water please, Jim?'

'*Christ!* Where'd you come from?' he said, apparently only then realising I was there. He wiped his face with his shirt sleeve. 'You're like a *ghost.*'

'I did knock,' I said, which was a total lie.

'Didn't *hear* you.'

In the kitchen I ran the tap while I looked in every drawer until I found the cat's needle and syringe. It was in the cutlery drawer, of all places to keep it, right next to the half-full vial of cat insulin, which probably cost Jimmy the same amount each month that the heroin cost me. It's strange how much effort people are willing to put in to save their pets, just get a new one.

I stood there for a minute or so, contemplating how exactly I was going to immobilise Jimmy to make my plan work, and then it came to me, like a bee to pollen: I didn't need to do anything apart from good, old-fashioned manipulation. A little bit of persuasion to a weak mind does wonders, and Jimmy's mind was in its most impressionable state—It's not hard to convince someone on the edge to jump off, see where they land. Think about it: he killed a little girl, and the thing about killing is that when it's an accident, it eats you alive. Add empathy, heartbreak, and the predisposition to drug use in the mix, and that's when it gets real messy, that's when you have a helpless soul desperate enough to take any quick fix you can offer. Julian offered him comfort, whatever good that did him, but I was there to offer him something better. Nirvana. To slip away into the quiet. I guess by Josh's logic, I was doing Jimmy a kindness, too, like I did his diabetic cat.

I sat down on Jimmy's sofa with a glass of water in one hand, the cat's needle and syringe tucked in the pocket of my hoodie, along with a spoon I got from the kitchen, and the bag of brown powder I bought earlier that day.

'How you doing?' I asked.

'*Fine*, you?'

'Did you see Jules earlier?'

'Yeah, I saw him.'

'Talk to him about what you needed to talk about?'

'Yeah—'

'Why did he come home so angry?' I asked. Jimmy paused, considering how much to tell me without giving it all away.

'I barged into his office while he was with a student. He was helping her out with something, so that probably pissed him off.'

'He told me you've been acting crazy lately.'

'What? *Why?*'

'Don't ask me,' I shrugged. 'He says you're delusional, that you need help.'

'I'm *depressed*, not crazy.' Jimmy looked wounded, weak, like he was on the verge of tears again. He shook his head. 'He's a prick.'

'Agreed.'

'He told me to *stay away* from you.'

'And he told *me* the same,' I said. Jimmy dropped his head and covered his face with his hands, crying into them. I sat quiet and still for an increasingly long time, uncomfortable in the face of so many emotions, and waited for him to calm down again.

'I'm so confused all the time,' he whispered, while rubbing his eyes.

'It's hard to find clarity with alcohol. I find it only makes things murkier. You need something stronger.'

'*Trust* me, I *know*.' Jimmy roughly pushed his bowl to the middle of the coffee table, spilling dregs of milk on the glass. He muttered under his breath, *fuck it, fuck it all,* and said, as if just remembering the reason I was there, 'So where's the stuff, anyway?'

In truth there was no Versace aftershave, no Hugo Boss clothes or Armani watches.

'In the car still.'

'Why?'

'I want to show you something else first.' I sipped my water and put the glass down on a black slate coaster, then presented the little baggie and shook it in the air. 'You ever tried H?'

'*Christ*... Is that *heroin*? What are you doing with *that*?'

'I take it sometimes, when things get too much, you know.' Another lie.

'Does Juju know?'

'He doesn't need to know *everything* I do,' I said, feigning exasperation. 'He's a tosser anyway. Fuck him.'

'What's happened between you two?'

'I was going to ask you the same thing.' Jimmy swallowed down the lump in his throat and changed the subject, like I knew he would.

'What's the heroin for?' he asked. 'It's a bit hardcore for a weeknight, no?'

'Well, I noticed you've been, like, really depressed, or whatever. This shit will knock your socks off, make you forget about everything.'

'Isn't it *super* addictive?'

'Well, yeah, but only if you do it a couple of times. Once won't hurt. Besides, addicts are weak. You're not weak, are you Jim?'

'*Where* did you even get it from?'

'I've got a guy,' I shrugged. Despite Jimmy still being weary on the subject, I emptied a generous spoonful of brown powder onto the spoon, a splash of water, and started heating it from underneath with my lighter. Once the ball is rolling, it's difficult to opt out of the game, and contrary to my words of strength, I was counting on Jimmy being weak. The liquid bubbled from light brown to dark. 'The first time you do it, it's like you're flying,' I said, putting the spoon down on a coaster, then I dropped a cotton ball into the cooling liquid.

'Yeah, I've heard that,' Jimmy replied, observing me prepare it all as if I was a professional. 'To be honest, I've always thought about trying it. Just to see what the fuss is all about.' I grinned as I presented the needle and syringe.

'Tonight's your lucky night.' Jimmy laughed. I hadn't heard him laugh for months, which was funny considering why I was there. It was like we were almost friends.

Jimmy never really liked me, the way people don't tend to like their ex's new romantic fling. In the beginning he pretended to be obsessed with me, some kind of coping mechanism or whatever, but pretty soon the realisation hit him that I was there to stay, and it killed him to see Julian so seriously involved with someone else.

'So, what do you say?' I asked, using the needle and syringe to suck up as much of the liquid as I could. 'You gonna make me fly alone?' I tapped the syringe for dramatic effect, and Jimmy considered my words for a long moment before putting his hands up in the air like he was surrendering.

'What the hell,' he replied. 'Let's *do* it.'

'Alright,' I said, standing up.

'Woah, why *me* first?'

'I can't be strung out giving you your first hit, are you serious? I could kill you. I need to make sure you don't have a reaction and, like, die on me. Once I know you're okay I'll do some, too.'

Jimmy nodded; it made sense, of course it did. I was there as a friend with offerings of peace, and I don't think he'd been thinking straight for quite some time. He took a deep breath as I moved towards him, slowly and carefully; carrying my concentration like a brimming cup.

I couldn't rush through fear of putting Jimmy off the idea; any sudden moves or wrong words could snap him out of it, and it's always easier to kill the willing. Less fun, sure, but easier nonetheless.

'Do you have something I can use to tie around your arm?'

'I'm sure there's a tie here somewhere...' Jimmy looked around, patting the sofa next to him, but came up empty.

'Okay, take off your belt,' I offered. I held the syringe between my teeth like I was a dog and it was a stick as I looped Jimmy's belt tight around his own arm. I pulled until there was no more slack, then pulled it tighter for good measure. Jimmy's pulse was hammering when I pressed my fingers to his arm, the last chorus of the choir.

'Does it hurt?'

'It stings for maybe three seconds. It's like when you get your bloods done at the doctors. Ready? Take a deep breath.' Jimmy closed his eyes as he followed my orders, and I slid the needle into the thick, prominent blue vein in his wrist and pushed the plunger down, slowly, until the barrel was empty. I pulled the needle out and placed it on the table in front of us.

'It's done?' Jimmy asked, pleasantly surprised and lucid for the moment.

'Just like that. Now, sit back and embrace it. Relax.'

'There's something you should know,' he said, taking a deep breath as the drug hit him like a freight train.

'Shh. Don't stress,' I whispered. 'You fucked my

husband, I know.' Jimmy's eyes went wide, pupils constricted to the size of a needle point, and I wasn't sure if it was the drug, or a reaction to what I said, but I didn't care either way. Within a minute Jimmy went slack in his seat. Like a balloon deflating, his breathing slowed down and his muscles went limp. Droopy eyelids fluttered open and closed as he tried to fight the high but failed, and he couldn't speak a word, despite clearly wanting to. There was a peaceful and languid expression of total bliss on his face, and though I was confident I gave him enough, I thought I best get my money's worth. He couldn't stop me at that point even if he wanted to, but I don't think he was aware of anything at all, not my name, not his own, and not hitting that little girl with his Porsche and leaving her to die on the side of the street. I kept heating and injecting the liquid millilitre by millilitre until Jimmy was totally unconscious, and even then I didn't stop. I left a small amount of heroin spilled on the table and half-cooked on the spoon, and poked the needle deep into Jimmy's arm, leaving it there. I washed and dried the glass I was using and put it to the back of the cabinet, wiped my prints from everything using a wet-wipe and disinfectant, so I was never there. I left Jimmy's belt wrapped tight around his bicep so that his arm went a plum-purplish colour, and his breathing stopped shortly after he pissed himself.

No matter how many people I killed and which method I used, it always felt like life faded so quickly. There one moment and gone the next. I could drug someone, gut someone, or choke them with their own belt, and it never seemed to last long enough.

I stood there for maybe five more minutes to make sure he didn't miraculously rise again, and, satisfied with my staging of the evidence, left to go home. No one would blink an eye to find that Jimmy, the drug-fuelled depressive, overdosed while trying to chase something better.

\* \* \*

My plans for Julian, to be truly life-shattering, needed Tyler, but Tyler needed convincing. Fortunately for me persuasion was my main attribute. I was never afraid of losing anything, except a game, maybe, which helps in getting what you want. And if at first I didn't succeed I would try and try again; I could tire a bear out, weaken God's Achilles heel, and since Tyler was only a kid—and a stupid one at that—I knew it wouldn't take a lot of effort.

The first time I asked him if he'd like to help me fuck with Julian, he said no. 'I don't want anything else to do with Jules. Why can't you do it yourself?'

'Because it's not as fun,' I said, but Tyler remained stubborn. I took my hat off to Julian, credit where credit is due, and all, because he managed to slip inside Tyler both mentally and physically in a matter of months, and even though the kid clearly despised him at this point, the strings were still attached. Fraying, but attached, nonetheless. I decided, in the end, that the best course of action was blackmail. It always worked. So the next time

I saw Tyler, I wasted no time.

'If you don't do what I'm asking of you,' I said, 'I'll tell everyone about you and Julian.'

Tyler's eyes shot to mine. 'I'll just say you're lying.'

'Well, you can *try*,' I smiled at him. 'But I have a video, so…'

'You're lying. No you haven't. You're a liar just like Julian—'

'Do you want me to send you the video? I can do it right now.' I pulled my phone out of the front pocket of my hoodie and brought up my video album, then I opened the video in said conversation and flashed the screen at Tyler, like he was a bouncer at a club requesting my ID. The video was skipped to a particularly telling moment: Tyler, on my bed, nude apart from his grey boxer shorts, knees to his chest as Julian got in beside him.

I asked again, 'Do you want me to send it to you?' and I saw the moment it dawned on him I was not there to be a hero; I was not his saving grace or the answer to his problems or the one who shall deliver him from Julian's evil, and neither was I his friend. Tyler was crying when he said, 'No. I don't want to see it. Please don't,' and I put my phone away with a sigh of false disappointment.

'So.' I smiled. 'You'll help me?'

'Yeah.'

'Atta boy.'

# Fifteen

The planned neighbourly get-together. From the moment Julian and I turned up, Lara was uptight and uncomfortable in my presence, putting on an obvious act of indifference, pretending her and Ashley hadn't spoken about the night at Jimmy's where she accused me of being a murderer and got chucked out for it, and probably also wondering how much I had told Julian about her relationship with his sister (Nothing). Julian was acting like a threatened dog, ears perked up, tail tucked between his legs, yet still maintaining a sense of high alert. When I questioned him about it he put it down to nerves: it was his first time meeting Lara, who couldn't have been any less subtle in her feelings on the four of us getting together for a drink. Melissa had obviously told her at the last minute, maybe even that morning, but her bluntness only made the night more entertaining. Anything that wound Julian tighter and made him drink faster was funny in my book.

I chatted with Melissa while Julian attempted to blend in, and Lara kept herself out of the equation by messing about in the kitchen. It felt good, being there in that house again. The memories I shared there with Graham were suspended in the air around me. I could still smell his fear, hear his pleas, see him tied up and naked on his bed upstairs, crying and ashamed that a 15-year-old kid put him in his place. It was like returning to the scene of the crime to get off on it once more. I imagined that's how Julian felt too, but with enough guilt for both of us.

I sipped on a beer while everyone else drank champagne, and eventually the conversation turned to Tyler, boy of the house. Melissa expressed concerns: he had become withdrawn, distant, not like himself, and she asked me if I'd noticed anything or if Tyler had confided in me. I said no, not really. Besides, Jules was with him a lot more than me.

Julian shot me a look and I smiled back at him as I watched him attempt to play it cool. He was sweating, jumbling his words up. 'Oh... I mean, I... I'm not with him that much... I haven't heard anything, no. He seems fine to me. He's alright... But I haven't seen him, not lately...' Smooth, Jules, real smooth. I poked at him further, like he was a caged animal and I was a curious, stick-wielding child.

'You saw him the other morning,' I pointed out. He was as guilty as sin, yet Lara and Melissa remained clueless. They were shitty parents, well and truly, I mean, how could they not put two and two together? When a floorboard creaked, Julian shuddered. When a gust of wind rattled the living room door in its frame, Julian's bones shook with it. When Tyler's name was mentioned, Julian would look around the room at Melissa, Lara, and I, nervously sipping his wine, avoiding direct eye contact. Despite it being incredibly risky, I knew it was only a matter of time before he would sneak off upstairs to see the kid. The higher the risk the better, the more he got off on it, and I guess that was the difference between us. He was sloppy, I was careful. No one had even noticed Jimmy was M.I.A, never mind dead from overdosing heroin; My mother's ex-boyfriend died the same way, almost a decade before; Catherine drowned in her hot tub, her death was ruled an accident; Graham and Will were added to the list of the thousands of unsolved murders in London; There were no leads on the actor that got stabbed to death in Luxe; and there I was, free as a bird to do it all again, plotting circles around Julian and loving watching him spin.

The plan was simple really; simple enough for a child to understand. When Julian went upstairs to see Tyler, the kid's job was to make him believe that all was forgiven. Kiss him, cry to him, I didn't care, as long as he made him believe it. And if Tyler didn't do as I said, I would show the video of him and Julian to his parents.

Later, when Julian and I got home, I got a text from Tyler, right on schedule. It said: *I did what you said. I told him I forgive him. Please don't tell my mums.*

Me: *Good lad. I'm not going to.*

Tyler: *Cool. Now what?*

Me: *Now we wait.*

Tyler: *Wait for what?*
Me: *You'll see.*

\* \* \*

The secrets were all proving to be too much for Julian. He was restless, drinking every day. He was, ironically, like an addict during cold turkey, so I told him to see a doctor like a good and caring spouse should do. The doctor gave him something to take the edge off, and that *something* was awesome. Julian was totally out of it most of the time, which made my life so much easier. It wasn't difficult to slip him more than his recommended dose; an extra one or two pills here and there, not enough to make him a walking corpse but enough to make his mind more pliable, so when he started asking where my candles were disappearing to, I said that he broke them a couple nights before, when he was drunk and clumsy in his drowsiness—*Don't you remember, Jules? It was just this week. Are those pills really helping you? I'm actually getting a little worried here.*

When he asked where my other things went, I replied, 'Honestly, Jules, if I have to keep repeating myself I'll lose my shit. I went through my stuff, remember? Had a clear out? I gave some stuff to Jimmy and sold the rest. Stop taking those fucking pills, would you? Do you have dementia? Should I be concerned? I mean this is getting ridiculous.'

Julian would apologise for forgetting things I'd already told him even though I hadn't told him a thing, and he didn't notice Jimmy's sudden absence from our lives so I didn't remind him. I was curious to see how long it would take him, or anyone else, to realise he was dead.

# Sixteen

I was in town, shopping for wine in the Oxford Wine Company's shop on Turl Street. It was Julian's birthday a couple weeks away so a gift bag of wine wouldn't raise any suspicion if he saw it. I asked for their best bottle of Caro. It was the wine from Julian's father, our wedding gift and the one Jimmy drank without bothering to ask. I held the bottle, it was heavy in the palm of my hand, and the shop assistant made a joke that wasn't very funny— 'Hey, wanna buy it before you drop it?'

I faked a laugh as I handed it over for her to scan.

'Is it for a birthday?'

'Yeah, my husband's,' I replied.

'Want me to gift wrap it?'

'Nah, you're good.' These were the conversations that made me irritable. I wanted to smash the wine bottle across the shop assistant's face.

When I got home I opened the bottle and poured about a glass full out, then crushed up the roofies I found in Julian's globe bar a couple weeks before. I ground them to powder with a mortar and pestle and put it in the bottle, replaced the handy twist-cap, and shook it around for a bit.

The next day I gave the bottle to Tyler. I told him, 'Don't drink it, whatever you do. Just hide it away until I tell you. Do you have somewhere your mothers won't find it?'

Tyler nodded. 'In my room, under my bed.'

'Nah, too obvious. What about your school bag?'

'They look in there sometimes.'

'Well where *don't* they look?'

'Under my bed, I told you.'

'Jesus, kid. Believe me, they look under your bed. You got a shelf you can put it on? Hide it behind some books or something?'

Tyler thought about it for a second, then nodded again. 'I can put it behind my speakers.' He was upset, still angry over the whole Julian thing, but he did as I asked, accepted the bottle from me and kept his head down in shame. I couldn't have cared less about the desperation in his eyes for it all to just *stop, please Matt, please leave me alone*.

There were a couple of other things I did that week: Bought zip ties from a Halfords near uni; texted Ashley *Lara says hello*; stole some more of Julian's cash; packed some more of my things into the boot of my car; spiked Julian with even more pills to keep him just below the surface of reality; wondered how on earth he was still teaching.

The text I got back from Ashley made me laugh. It said: *This is Matthew, isn't it?* That same night she sent a text to Julian that said: *Do you know that Matt's been texting me? Threatening me?* And fortunately for me, Julian was too out of it to notice, so I got there first.

As Julian, I text back: *What are you talking about? Are you serious? Can we meet on Saturday evening? I miss you, sis. I've been thinking a lot about what you said about Matt. I want to talk.*

Ashley replied: *Ok. Fine. Can you do 7?*

I deleted all traces of the texts as a precaution, but Julian was so spaced-out I don't think he would have noticed anyway.

\*\*\*

I followed Tyler to school on Friday morning, the day before Julian and Ashley's plans to meet at a Starbucks. By Julian, of course, I mean me, but Ashley didn't know that. When the kid saw me, he didn't even act surprised. He looked defeated, depressed, and his hair was damp from rain. He slumped against the wall outside the school and sighed.

'What now?' he asked. I leaned against the wall next to him and lit a cigarette.

'When I leave tomorrow, I'll text you,' I said. 'Go over to see Julian about ten minutes later, and take the bottle of wine I gave you. Have you been shaking it every day like I asked?' Tyler nodded, so I continued. 'Give it to Julian, tell him it's from your mum, Lara. It'll make sense to him, so he shouldn't really ask why the bottle is open.'

'What if he does?'

'You tell him that your mum had a glass before realising she didn't like it, which is why she wants him to have it instead.'

'What if he wants me to drink it with him?'

'Don't,' I said. 'Ask him for a beer or something. I'll make sure we have them in the fridge.' I offered Tyler a drag, he shook his head, no. School kids walked past us like we weren't even there, all ill-fitted coats and flimsy umbrellas.

'What if he doesn't drink the wine himself?' Tyler asked. 'What if he tells me to go away?'

'Believe me, that won't happen. He won't be able to resist it, or resist you. Once he starts drinking it he'll get very sleepy very fast, two glasses ought to knock him out for at least a couple hours. Bear in mind, though, he's built up quite the tolerance to sedatives, so try and get him to drink three, okay? If he passes out downstairs we'll have to carry him upstairs ourselves, so when he starts getting sleepy, persuade him to go to bed. Once he's out cold, ring me, and I'll come back and help you tie him up. After that, you're on your own.'

'What if he wakes up when you're gone?'

'He probably will. Just gag him.'

'What if he escapes?'

'If he gets free, he will kill you, so if he does, you run home as quickly as possible and lock the doors. Do not, under any circumstance, let him go. He will beg and plead and promise you the world, but you don't listen, got it?'

'Yeah.' Another boy, taller than Tyler, said hello as he walked past. 'Hey, I'll catch up with you in five.' I took a couple drags of my cigarette, waited for him to disappear around the corner, then continued.

'You said you wanted to make Jules bleed, right?' Tyler nodded, I smiled. 'That's exactly what you're going to do.'

Tyler's eyes were wide with concern as he asked, 'How?'

'I want you to carve something into his back. A word.'

'Are you serious? I can't do that—'

'Yes you can. And you will.'

'Please don't make me.'

'What would you prefer? Get your revenge on Jules for what he did to you, or have your mums find out what he did to you? I know what I'd choose.' Tyler's eyes filled with tears, and he looked like he was going to throw up. 'Hey, look at me,' I said. 'You can do this, okay? I know I'm being hard on you, but it's the only way it can work.'

'Why don't you just do it yourself?' Tyler whimpered.

'I told you, it's no fun on your own. Don't you want to hurt him back? The way he hurt you? He betrayed your trust, Ty. Are you just gonna let him get away with that?'

Tyler dried his eyes with his school tie, then looked me directly in the eye for the first time, asking, 'What word? What's the word you want me to use?'

'Pederast,' I said, turning to walk away. 'I'll see you tomorrow.'

'Matt?'

I stopped. 'Yes, Tyler?'

'Can you at least text it to me so I can spell it right?'

# Seventeen

Jimmy's body was found, finally, and right on time, too. I was getting sick and tired of hearing question after question about his whereabouts, so I urged Julian to do something about it. The dead man had, obviously, stopped stalking Julian, and you'd think it would provide him with some relief, but it didn't. He missed the attention he was getting. I guess there's nothing like a stalker to make you feel special.

'Why don't you go see him, if you're so worried?' I suggested. 'I'm sure he's just strung out somewhere, doing what Jimmy does best. He was high on something the last time I saw him. I don't think he even registered I was there.'

Julian agreed with me, and decided to take me up on my advice—he went to see Jimmy after work one day, nine days after the last time I was there. His body would be decomposing by then, his organs accumulating gases, his abdomen bloating up like a balloon. The smell of him would be enough to make Julian throw up as soon as he entered the house. I was curious how Julian would handle the matter—would he see Jimmy's dead body and freak out and run away? Would he panic and attempt to check for a pulse? Would he call the police, or just leave without a word, like he was never there? I was willing to bet on the latter. He wouldn't want the police around, asking him questions. Not when his husband was a serial killer and his boy-toy was sulking across the road.

I was right, it turned out. When Julian got home his face looked like it had been painted white, and his eyes were red rimmed as tears fell down his cheeks. He could barely speak to me, but he tried. 'He's... James is dead. He's dead.' I put on my best mask of shock, hugging him like I cared, like the news destroyed the indestructible.

'What do you mean he's dead?!' I said. 'How?'

'I don't know,' Julian replied, shaking with shock. 'I just... I found him. He... I think he overdosed...'

'How do you know he's dead? Did you call an ambulance?'

'He's dead, Matt,' he cried. 'Looks like he's been there a while. Oh, Christ...'

'Well what did the police say? Did you call them?'

Julian shook his head and sobbed into my shoulder. 'I didn't call anyone. I just came home. I panicked.'

Bingo. 'Well did anybody see you?'

'I don't know!'

'Okay, calm down, shh. We'll call it in anonymously, okay? We'll say we're concerned neighbours, and there's a smell coming from the house, and we want someone to check it out. Are you *sure* he's dead? Maybe there's a chance an ambulance can save him.'

'No, you didn't see him, Matty. He's gone. He's really gone.'

Julian was devastated, so he took the rest of the week off work. I called the police from a payphone at the university the next day, pretending to be a concerned neighbour with a strange smell coming from next door. I submitted my dissertation early and went shopping that afternoon. I didn't know where I was going but I needed some things for my road trip: A new phone; bottled water; snacks; books; cigarettes; lighters; a pocket knife; black gloves; post-it-notes; bright pink envelopes; pens.

\* \* \*

Saturday night, the big night, my last in Oxford. I thought it best Julian stayed at home to grieve when I went to work, but I wasn't really working, nor would I be again. Not there anyway, not in London. No one else knew, not Luca, not even Josh, because it was better that way, no fuss, no answering to anyone, just me, myself, and I, slipping away without the awkwardness of goodbyes.

In the afternoon I made Julian a coffee with a couple of his pills dissolved in it without him knowing. Despite him being spaced out and distraught and probably confused over Jimmy's death, I still dressed the part for work so as not to look suspicious: Shirt and tie despite never wearing ties. I guess you could say it was a premeditated move on my part, because you never know when you'll need to make your own garotte. That night's fate was hanging in the balance, there were no definite outcomes, but you have to trust the process and I sure as shit trusted mine.

I left the house at 4.45pm and parked my car just up the street so it was out of Julian's view. I sent a text to Tyler saying: *I just left, wait until 5 then head over.* In the car, I thought about writing a letter for Julian, but the idea of it all made me laugh out loud. How ridiculously mundane it was. Very Romeo, Romeo. Instead, I wrote two words on a post it note and signed it *with love from Matthew.* I put it in one of the bright pink envelopes I bought that week, slid the ring from my finger, and put it in the envelope too, before sealing it shut. I watched as Tyler, the little chicken, crossed the road, and smiled at the sudden swell of excitement in my chest.

\*\*\*

Tyler rang me at six, and he was obviously shaken up because I could barely understand him; he was panting like a dog and rushing his words. I told him I was on my way and hung up the phone. He greeted me at my own front door saying, 'He literally passed out. I can't move him, or wake him up. This isn't cool, it's like he's dead... Is he dead?'

'No, he's not dead,' I laughed.

'What did you put in the wine anyway?'

'Roofies.'

'What are they?'

'You ever hear of the date–rape drug?'

'Yeah…'

'That's what it was.'

'Where did you get it from?'

I thought about the question and whether or not to tell Tyler the truth. I didn't want anything scaring him out of the house. The answer, I realised, was in my favour. He would hate Julian just a little bit more, and he needed all the hate he could get to justify hurting Julian the way I wanted him to. 'I found it hidden in Julian's study. He was going to use it on you,' I said. 'But I saw to it that you used it on him instead. Where is he?'

The lounge was dark apart from the glare of the TV, and Julian was splayed on the sofa, out cold, with a half-full wine glass in front of him on the coffee table. 'How many glasses did he have?'

'Two and a bit,' Tyler replied. He was biting his lip, nervous.

'That's good, but he might wake up sooner than expected. If he does, gag him, yeah?'

'Yeah, I remember.'

'You grab his legs, I'll get his arms.'

'Why can't I just do it down here?'

'I can't tie him to anything down here. I told you what would happen if you didn't get him upstairs, didn't I?'

'He fell asleep before I could do it,' Tyler said, sulking, but he grabbed Julian by the ankles anyway. It was difficult, to say the least, getting him upstairs. He was a tall man, naturally heavy because of it, and I had to yell at Tyler on more than one occasion not to drop him. The boy took to shoving Julian's legs up from his feet instead of carrying him up the steps, while I dragged him by the arms with all my might. I was surprised we didn't break anything, and at one point the back of Julian's head hit the edge of a step pretty hard. When we finally got him to the bedroom and on to the bed I asked Tyler if he wanted him lying on his front or back, and he chose face down. Atta boy. I went to my side of the bed, stuck my hand under the mattress, and pulled out the pack of cable ties and the new pocket knife. I tied Julian's every limb to the bed frame, his body stretched out like he was to be drawn and quartered. I tightened the ties as much as I possibly could, and it would be uncomfortable, but that was the least of Julian's problems, really. When I handed Tyler the pocket knife, I said, 'Not too deep, just use the tip,' and the boy had this wild look in his eyes before I left, a look I couldn't mistake for anything else: crazed anticipation. He was brimming with vengeance, despite wanting nothing to do with it.

I swiped Julian's phone from the coffee table, grabbed his car keys from the sideboard in the hallway, and took in the house that had been mine for the past six years one last time. I headed to the Starbucks Ashley arranged to meet Julian at, which was a thirty-minute drive away because she refused to drive any closer, because she was a bitch just like her brother. On the way there I realised I forgot to leave the envelope for Julian in the house, what with all the excitement. I guess it wasn't my last time in the house, after all. I couldn't leave without showing him that I won, so I decided I'd drive back to the house, leave the envelope on the sideboard, and drift off into the night like I was never there. First, though: Ashley. I couldn't wait to show her what her little brother had been up to.

# Eighteen

Ashley was sitting at a table smack-bang in the middle of a very busy Starbucks, drinking from a cardboard coffee cup, biting her red painted nails, not registering my presence until I pulled the chair out opposite her and sat down. I folded my arms resting them on the table top and smiled when her eyes met mine. Her face dropped, saying, 'What the fuck do you want?'

'We have a date.'

'No.' Ashley shook her head. 'I was supposed to be meeting Jules here. *We* have nothing to talk about, Matt.'

'I can assure you we do,' I said, trying not to get ahead of myself. The suspense was killing me.

'I'm not interested in anything you have to say to me,' Ashley spat. 'Do you realise how weird it is, making me think I'm meeting my brother here and then just showing up? It's *really* fucking weird. You're a complete psychopath.'

'Maybe,' I grinned. 'But do *you* realise how weird it is

to have your friend spy on your brother-in-law by buying a house in the same street? I think you win, on a scale of weirdness.'

Ashley hesitated. 'You don't know what you're talking about,' she said. 'It's a coincidence my friend lives close to you.' I hummed as I picked up a wooden coffee stirrer from the table and snapped it in half, not saying a word. I stared at the splintered pieces of wood as if I was alone and passing the time by being a vandal. Silence makes people uncomfortable, it's surprising how much people will tell you if you just sit and listen for long enough, and it worked with Ashley too, until she was twitching in her seat. 'It's not as crazy as you make it sound. I merely *suggested* that Lara buy that house, and when she did, I asked her to keep an eye on you, that's it.' When I still didn't say anything, Ashley snapped. 'Is that why you're here? To gloat that you know about my little plan?'

'I guessed your little plan the day they moved in, Ash. You aren't as clever as you think.' I looked at her and her face was as red as her chipped nails.

'Well then why *are* you here, Matt?'

I leaned across the table and whispered. 'I've got something to show you. Let's call it… a documentary.'

Ashley shot me an incredulous look. 'You want to show me a documentary?'

'Nah, just messing with you. Let's call it a home movie.'

I got my phone out of my pocket. I brought the video up. I skipped forward a couple of minutes, until the good stuff started happening, then slid my phone across the table in front of a concerned Ashley. Her eyes drifted from me to the video, and I sat back in my chair, watching her as she watched her brother rape a boy the same age as her daughter; a boy who considered Ashley an aunt; and a boy who was once innocent, but not anymore, not thanks to her.

Ashley put her hand over her mouth in shock as tears slid from her eyes and rolled off her fingers. They landed on my phone, and it bugged the hell out of me, mini puddles on my screen, but it was fascinating to witness the stages her mind went through in such a short period of time: how her expression changed from shock to upset to downright horrified. She made it through about 3 minutes before she looked at me with wide, distressed eyes, and asked, 'What is this?' even though she knew exactly what it was, she just didn't want to believe it.

'That's what happens when you think yourself a mastermind by getting Lara to move her wife and child into my street,' I said. 'You know, I actually kinda dig your plan, or the spirit of it, anyway. It's just such a shame you put a kid at risk to get dirt on me.'

Ashley was shaking her head. 'No, it can't be, no, god no.'

I was nodding, 'Oh, yes, it is.' Her eyes drifted back to the video, and even with the volume down quite low I heard the scream clear as day, that painful screech just after the words, *stop please Jules stop please not like this I need my hands please stop it*, and that's when Ashley pushed my phone back to me like it was a live grenade. She was speechless, sitting there with her coffee going cold, her face buried in her hands as her shoulders heaved with waves of despair. It was quite amusing, really, people began staring at her, and it was all rock and roll that night so I dug the knife in deeper. Metaphorically, I mean. I had no reason to kill Ashley, she was never a real threat to me. She was a bored and lonely stay-at-home mother with nothing but time and gossip on her hands.

'This is your fault,' I said. 'If you'd just kept your nose out of my business, none of this would have happened.'

Ashley removed her hands from her face. 'Fuck you.' I waved a tissue at her, gesturing that she should clean herself up. The state she had worked herself into was embarrassing. She attempted to compose herself, whispering, 'Why would you show me that?'

'I wanted to see your face when you saw your precious brother in his true form.'

'You're disgusting.' It made me genuinely laugh, the uncontrollable kind, while Ashley resembled someone whose entire life had just been smashed into dust. If I was disgusting then I wondered what she thought about Julian, what she thought about herself.

'You're a walking fucking contradiction,' I said. 'You and Julian both.' I picked up my phone and jumped out of my chair, making Ashley nearly fall out of hers. 'I'll send you the video soon,' walking away, leaving her there, alone, to process what had just happened. I ignored her when she started yelling like a total banshee after me: *It can't be Jules, it can't be him, it can't be, he wouldn't do that, he wouldn't hurt a child, never, that... It's not him, it can't be, it can't be... It's not Julian, it's not...*

Her nonsensical rambling was cut off when I shut the door behind me and I was back in the car park, but I didn't need to turn around to know she was probably on the floor by that point, in full mental breakdown mode, surrounded by concerned onlookers trying to enjoy a coffee in peace. The tantrum wouldn't solve anything, it would have been easier for her to just accept the truth: her darling little brother was a monster, a predator of the worst kind, and it was her own fault that his most recent victim was her friend's son. What a funny story.

\* \* \*

Driving around Oxford, taking it in for the last time, Julian's phone chirped from the passenger seat with a text message from who else but Ashley. It said: *Call me as soon as you get this, Jules. I need to talk to you immediately.* I laughed, had to—an hour before that she had acknowledged that it was me who had used Julian's phone to arrange our little date. How stupid can someone get, really?

I got back to Lathbury Road at around 9.15pm, ten minutes after Tyler texted me to say he was home. I remained in the car as I took out my phone. I sent everything I had to Julian's phone: the video; photos of text conversations between him and Tyler; and photos of text conversations between him and I, where he admitted to being involved with Graham's murder. Then, with

Julian's phone, I logged into his work email account. I wrote: *Hello, all. There's something you should know about me. Kind regards, Professor J Blake.* I attached the photos and the video to the email, then added every contact in Julian's address log. These included, but weren't limited to: Ashley; Francis, Julian's father; Harris; Abraham; Julian's boss; his boss's boss; the Vice Chancellor; the whole faculty of History; and his students, some past, mostly present. 200 recipients in total, and I didn't waste time in tapping send. The only people whose emails he didn't have were Lara, Melissa, and Tyler's, but he did have their phone numbers, so I sent everything to them in a text with the same message: *There's something you should know about me.* I waited for five minutes before leaving my car, by which time there was a reply from Tyler: *You bastard.* I got a good laugh out of that, he would know it was me who sent it as Julian was still tied to the bed when he left.

\* \* \*

I fed the Koi in the pond out the back garden one last time, and threw mine and Julian's phones into it, along with Julian's car and house keys. He wouldn't be using them anymore, and neither would I. My amended plan was simple: leave the envelope on the sideboard and get out of there.

I let myself in through the back door. The house was as dark as ever as I walked through the kitchen and down the hallway until I was at the bottom of the stairs. The silence was deafening. I could smell blood, like I swallowed a mouth full of pennies, and the bathroom light was on, which was strange, but I assumed Tyler must have gone in to wash his hands and forgotten to turn the light off. I put the pink envelope on the sideboard in the hallway, and I was suddenly overcome with the desire to *know*. I wanted to *see* it. The grand finale, the conclusion to my design, the climax of my destruction. It wasn't enough to be told the job was done. I wanted more, a sneak peak, a final image to take with me when I got out of town. Curiosity will fuck even the best of us up. Build a wall and everyone wants to know what's on the other side.

I ascended the stairs one slow and steady step at a time, until I was on the dimly lit landing. I stood there for a bit, listening for sounds that never came, so I opened our bedroom door and turned on the salt lamp just like Julian did in the video that was quickly becoming infamous across Oxford, and it wasn't a very bright light but it gave me something to work with. The blood dominated the room, the red was overpowering. Julian was no longer tied to the bed and from behind me the bedroom door swung shut.

'What did you do, Matthew?' Julian said, and I laughed because he had no idea.

# JULIAN

PEDERAST. That word, so archaic and yet so current. Fresh in my mind, echoing my lecture hall, an ode to my life that was now raw and bloody on my skin. It was a message from someone, spoken through Tyler. Permanence. Penance. The boy was fourteen, for Christ's sake. I was willing to bet he didn't have a clue what the word meant. Tyler liked football and gaming. He liked *Pokémon Go*, cheeseburgers, tea. He listened to indie rock, he watched gay porn in his bedroom and cleared his search history every night as if he was doing something illegal. He liked affection, hated it when I wasn't watching him at all times. He was so sweetly pliant, so impressionable.

It hit me, that perhaps I wasn't the only person in the world who mattered. It smacked me in the face like a cast iron door. I was not the only person with talents of deception so honed that I could wrap young boys around my fingers. I told myself I was an idiot. A downright fucking fool. Matt's things going missing, the inaptness of his character, my constant drowsiness, the Caro, drugging the Caro, tying me to the bed, and that fucking word. Tyler was used and abused and discarded and not only by me, but by Matt, too. The whole thing had his name written all over it.

The exposed flesh on my back was too painful to put

a T-shirt on, so after I showered I draped a towel across my shoulders in the hopes it would soak up most of my blood and save me the carpet cleaning bills. I put some shorts on and looked for my car keys and phone to call for help. I didn't know who I was going to call, just that I needed a lifeline of any kind, but I searched the house high and low and I couldn't find them anywhere. I started panicking again, rushing, and my head was spinning and the nausea came back with a force. My back only got worse, like Tyler was digging into me all over again with a bigger, sharper blade. My car keys and my phone were missing and I knew it was no coincidence, it was connected to the whole mess somehow. But why would Tyler or Matt take my phone? Why bother stealing the car keys? What did they think I was going to do, drive to the hospital and explain that I've just been sliced open by a kid, and oh, don't mind the word, it's just an inside joke between me and my husband, no truth to it?

*Liar. Pederast. Everyone is going to know exactly who you are.*

I was pumped so full of drugs and in so much agony I wasn't thinking straight, so I drifted like a ghost back upstairs, thinking perhaps I should just sleep it off, let it all figure itself out the next day. I heard a door open downstairs and stopped, alert as a starving animal. I held my breath, tilted my head, honed in on it. I hid out of view of the door and stayed there, still and silent as a ghost, in the dark corner of the bedroom. I thought it was going to be Tyler, and I accepted that I would probably kill him if I saw his face. It was his fate.

Imagine my surprise when Matt walked into the

bedroom. I watched him for a moment, two, three. He switched on the lamp on his way in and his behaviour clarified all doubts I'd had. I slammed the bedroom door, shutting us both in.

'What did you do, Matthew?' Matt turned around to look at me, nonchalant and cucumber-cool. He laughed. I clenched my fists. 'I wouldn't be laughing if I was in your position right now.'

'That's because you're a coward,' Matt said in a sing-song voice. 'What's wrong, Jules? Don't you like your new tattoo?'

I stood there so filled with hate I could feel it physically, hot and tempting as the hell Matt came from. It was such a contrast from earlier in the evening, when he walked into the living room all dressed up for work, suit and tie and shiny black shoes, and my heart burst with warmth for him. Now, it was bursting with rage. Rage for what he had done to me. Rage at his audacity. How could he have the nerve to show his pretty face as if nothing happened?

'You're very clever, Matt,' I said, and I meant every word. 'But you know what your problem is? You're so clever that you think everyone else is stupid.'

'You. I think you're stupid.'

'Well what now? Did you think I wouldn't know that this is your doing?'

'Quite the opposite. I was counting on it.'

'So you thought you would get that poor kid to do your dirty work and then what, exactly? Come home so we could fight and fuck it out and live happily ever after?

I hate to break it to you, Matt, but you've crossed the fucking line—'

'I'm leaving tonight,' Matt interrupted, like he hadn't listened to a word. 'I'm bored with you.'

It hurt, I'll admit. His words took me back six years, back to the time he told me that he liked spending time with me because everything else was boring. I was everything else now. I was nothing to him. Boring.

Something inside me broke and I didn't give him a chance to speak another word. I ran toward him and grabbed him roughly by the hair on the back of his neck, harder than I ever had before, until he was crying out and hissing in pain, until I felt his fluffy blonde strands snapping off in my fingers, until I could see the fear in his eyes despite his attempts at hiding it, defiant as always, and even then I didn't let him go.

'You can do what you want to me,' he said, grinning wide with his face bent upwards from my grip in his hair. 'You'll never hurt me as much as I've hurt you.'

'Really?'

'Really.'

I slapped him, hard, across the face before he could respond. It split his lip. Who did he think he was? His confidence was his curse. Matt spat blood and saliva over my face and gasped from the shock, from the breath I knocked from him, and he was trying to fight out of my hold but my fist was locked like a dog's jaw.

'Did that hurt, darling?' I hit him again. 'How about that?'

Matt mumbled something, setting his jaw, looking at

me with victory. Like he was in on something I wasn't. I hit him again and he said, 'Fuck you.'

I put my hand up to scare him that time, just the threat that I would do it again and again if he didn't wipe that overconfidence from his face. I was past the point of controlling myself, and Matt never was the submissive type. He spat in my face again, more blood, and I let go of him briefly to grab his throat. I was untethered, my passion knew no bounds, and I felt nothing but a euphoric sense of calm as I slammed his head against the bedroom wall. Matt went limp, his entire weight relying on my hand. If I removed it from his throat he would have fallen to the floor before he could find his feet again. His eyes were empty staring voids.

'Did that fucking hurt?' I said. 'Did it?!'

The second time his head met the wall it was far louder and I thought I heard something crack. Matt fell to the floor with a thud, leaving a blood trail down the magnolia of the wall. He was holding the back of his head, vulnerable and in pain despite never admitting it. The boy who had been murdering in cold blood since he was thirteen years old, too clever and audacious for his own good. He should have known better than anyone never to underestimate or undermine other people, because it just happens sometimes, we lose ourselves and become something other. It can be panic, or anger, or love, or all those things combined, things that Matt could never understand or relate to. It could even be as simple as curiosity, the urge to do something your mind otherwise urges you not to.

I was standing over Matt, watching as he clumsily rolled to his knees and attempted to crawl to the door. I pushed him over so he was on his back—he wasn't going anywhere. By the smugness on his face he knew he wasn't either.

'You're pathetic,' he slurred. 'Pathetic, twitchy, small man.'

'*You* are pathetic,' I spat. 'Mr Invincible. Look at you now.'

Matt laughed. He laughed and laughed until he was coughing. 'I've destroyed you,' he said.

'Yeah?'

'Yeah. It's too late, Ju… It's already too late…' and when Matt laughed again, all blood and teeth and unrelenting opposition, it enraged me. All of a sudden I was sitting on his chest, my knees pinning his arms to the floor beneath us as I pulled his tie from around his collar and wrapped it around his neck as he struggled to get away in vain. His wide eyes were as blue as they had ever been. In that moment I decided to be the monster he had always made me out to be. The one he wanted me to be. A wolf in sheepish sheepskin.

I was shouting, *I'm the one who decides when it's too late!* and with each end of the tie wrapped around my fists I pulled and stretched until my arms were screaming and even then I didn't stop. Matt tried to breathe in reflex, instinct, but it only made things worse for him. He inhaled the contents of his mouth and started gurgling, choking—his lungs were drowning in his own blood and spit and vomit. I could hardly feel my back by then, I almost forgot about the pain, and I probably would have had Matt not got a hand free to dig his nails into it. I screamed, pulled the tie even tighter, gritting my teeth with the force of it, and pinned his arm back down.

I let him drain the best of me, even when he was close to unconsciousness, even when my fingers went numb from the tightness of the tie, and I didn't let go of it, couldn't. All I could do was pull, falling into the blackness of my brain. Matt's words and his never wavering insolence were like fuel to me, and I couldn't stop until they were both gone, until I'd finally won our game of will-he-won't-he. *I'm bored with you. It's already too late.* Well, newsflash. I finally proved you wrong, Matty.

He fought until the very end, bucked and jerked with all his might, even when the blood vessels in his face had popped, leaving a scatter of dark freckle-like spots just beneath the skin. Blood and bile and saliva and god knows what else ran from his mouth. I wasn't aware of much by that point but I knew to keep squeezing for a couple minutes. Matt had taught me that, oh the lessons he gave me, the sins we shared like a bucket of ice cream.

I'd been holding my breath with him, white spots obstructing my vision, my jaw aching from the force in which I'd been gritting my teeth, my arms threatening to give way to screaming muscles. I let go of both ends of the tie, felt the light-headedness take over, and then collapsed to the floor next to him.

On my fucking back.

I rolled to my front, on my hands and knees as I yelled and kicked and tried to ride through the pain, the word on my back exposed and beaten. I stayed there for a while, letting my breath come back to me, trying not to throw up. I was crying, I didn't know when it started but I was, and the tears came in waves. Like anger did. I could feel myself shaking but it was like I was watching myself shake from somewhere else. I tried to dry my eyes to look at Matt, praying he was okay. But I knew he wasn't. It was like my mind made me block it out. *Don't look. You don't need to look. You know what you did. You don't have to face it.*

But I did. I had to face it. I had to pull myself together and stop being such a fucking coward. Matt was right about that. I almost heard him say *who's gonna clean up your mess now? Told you it was too late.*

I didn't know what to do, because what the fuck *do* you do when your husband's body is on your bedroom floor and you don't remember being the one who killed them but you know you are? What do you do then? What would Matt do?

*I wouldn't have lost control. Because I am strong and you are weak.*

I told the imaginary voice in my head to shut up and got up from the floor, wandered downstairs in a daze, still wearing shorts and nothing else, still bleeding from my branding. God forbid anyone walked through that front door. I was heading for the kitchen to get a couple black bags and rubber gloves, maybe some bleach and towels, not because I had a plan but because that felt like the right thing to do. Too much TV. In reality, I didn't have a clue. My keys were gone so I couldn't drive away.

My phone was missing so I couldn't call for help. I thought about burning the house down, I thought about running. I thought of a lot of things that hardly made sense and then something caught my eye on the sideboard. A flash of pink in an otherwise dim hallway.

An envelope. I tore it open like it was Matt's rib cage and my car keys were buried inside his lungs. There was a small piece of paper inside and it didn't say much, but what it *did* say was everything. It was the past seven years wrapped up in two words. It was everything and nothing and all the deadly, depraved little games in between. It was the truth, no matter how much I believed that Matt had finally lost. It was the end of it all. Everything I knew. The victory was sweet, while it lasted.

*They know*

His wedding ring fell out of the envelope onto the sideboard. I crumpled the note and envelope up in my fist and punched the wall opposite me. There is a point where your body is in so much pain and distress that your brain blocks it out. The hit knocked two framed photos off the wall, both of them of Matt and I. Glass smashed, our world broken. One was from when Matt was sixteen and I was thirty-five and we hadn't even started, not really. When I'd taken him to the cinema to see a horror film and he'd shovelled popcorn into my mouth and made me laugh and it was alright, everything was fine because we were the only people in there. When things were easier. Innocent. Can you see why I like the company of young boys now? It's all so… uncomplicated. Clean and pristine as Matt's wide blue eyes. I'd rather be watching a horror movie with a boy just young enough to give me the edge I thrived on, than have my life turned into one. The other photo was of our wedding day. Matt in gold, me in white. Such pure colours, a mockery of the rotting souls inside us that only we could see in each other. If my love for you wanes, kill me.

*They know.* What the fuck was that supposed to mean? I hated Matt more than I ever had in that moment, The Riddler as ever, always vague enough to remain mysterious, even in death.

And there, in the hallway—with the smashed photos, and Matt's wedding ring, and *Pederast* carved into my back, and the pain so unbearable my mind had no choice but to make it bearable, and Matt dead upstairs, so recently dead his body was probably still warm, and the kid, the one who got away, and the lies, and the secrets, and my own stupidity, and the note, the fuckery, all of it, seven years down the drain—it dawned on me that Matt's two-worded note was not a riddle, and in fact, his vagueness was never intentional, he just said what needed to be said and he didn't dress it up in something it was not. Everyone knew.

'What have you done, Matthew, what the fuck have you done!'

I was shouting into an empty and dark house. Matt couldn't answer me, he wasn't there anymore. Yet he *was* still there. He was at peace upstairs while my life fell to

sand and slipped between the spaces of my bloody
fingers. He was still there, talking to me. But it could
have anyone's voice, really. Matt's or Tyler's or Will's. It
could have belonged to any of the people I used and kept
using and destroyed to rebuild myself over and over
again, because I was never complete, not really. The
voice, whoever it belonged to, said: *What did you do,
Julian? What the fuck did you do to that boy and so many others
that you refuse to acknowledge like they are nothing. And what are
you going to do now? You're branded. You're done, it's over. How
long do you think it will be until the other boys come forward, some
grown up by now, some not. How are you going to wriggle your way
out of this cesspit like the worm of dirt you are.*

Boys. The other boys. Boys from before, ghosts,
coming back to me. I wasn't sure I could dig that deep,
remember their names and the way they screamed mine.
Who am I kidding? There was William Smithers,
fourteen. You know Will. The first time I let my
perversions run off and do their own thing. Hard to
forget your first time doing something, especially a pupil.
In the back of your car. Over and over and over again.
And there was Oliver John, fifteen, who after four
consecutive nights of detention ended up on his knees in
front of me, my hand guiding his bobbing head and my
eyes watching the classroom door. There was George
Howells, sixteen and in his last few months of school.
Everyone called him Howie at the time, and that's what I
called him when I asked him to stay behind after class
and ravished him until he couldn't remember his full
name anymore. After Howie there was Nathan (I never

314

did get his surname, or his age for that matter, but he wasn't older than seventeen), a pretty boy I picked up one night on the way home from Jimmy's house after an argument. Nathan the smalltown boy looking for a ride home after a drunken blow out with his mates left him with no cash to catch a taxi or a train or even a bus home. And then there was Matt, and you know how that went. And Tyler, Will's image, full circle. What were the chances of the others coming forward after all that time? Slim to none until I was in the spotlight.

I was the sexual yardstick for each and every one of those boys. They spent the rest of their days trying but failing to relive the feeling of being given everything when they knew nothing, and every partner they had after me would need to pass through the gate of comparison, and it would be a losing game.

I would apologise for having led you on for such a long time now, but it's best not to be glib at this point. You knew who I was when you decided to give me the time of day a second time around. A burden shared is a burden halved, and I'll take any illogical philosophy right now. Besides, I never lied to you, not really. I just understated a little, that's all. Drip fed you just enough. Is that not what we all do, in one way or another? No one is ever 100% truthful, not even with themselves. Even the best of us are brimming with secrets, so the next time you look at that innocent angel in your life whom everyone worships, just remember that they're as full of darkness as you are, perhaps even worse. So you see, I'm not all that bad. I am you and them. I am everyone and no one. I'm the guy you least expect, which has to mean something, does it not?

Matt's voice, the one in my head, said: *No, it does not.*

It meant nothing because I was still there in the midst of it all. Because I didn't have time to clean up the house of horrors or attempt to hide my husband's body or put a t-shirt on. Because I didn't have enough energy to run. Because my life was over, and how far would I have gotten anyway? Too much of a coward to run, as Matt would have said. So overcome with self-pity and cowardice you freeze, still believing your own lies, that someone will come save you, that you're innocent, that you've done nothing wrong and those who judge you are the delusional ones. Pathetically selfish. Selfishly pathetic. Now you've got a dead boy upstairs and an abused boy across the street and a line of grown-up and damaged boys waiting their turn to carve you up like it's Halloween and everyone is going to know about it. Now you are the exposé of the year. The latest scandal and all past scandals. Another pederastic professor to make an example out of.

They would demand to know just one thing: *Why?* I wasn't sure I had the answer. You know how when people are so hungry they will be driven to eat the inedible? It was a feeling close to that kind of hunger, where I would allow myself a taste and then start devouring the whole thing. It was like being a ghost and not being able to haunt. It pushed and pulled at me until it hurt. It was an innate part of me that I had tried and failed to change so many times throughout seventeen years of corruption. It was like telling a wolf it cannot hunt and telling a mother she cannot love. Impossible, inconceivable. I was born that way, how is that my fault? It's funny, really, how human beings will punish other human beings for being human beings. Wolves do hunt, and mothers do love. They love with such enormous intensity it consumes them for the rest of their lives. Like my afflicted addiction consumed me and drove me to the far end of depravity. I was a junkie controlled by my substance, and my substance was the freshest of flesh.

Flashing lights. Knock knock. I felt my age for the first time in my life, weak muscles and heartbreak. For a moment I imagined Lara and Melissa at my door, and it may sound ridiculous but I wished and prayed that it was—at least then I wouldn't have to face the consequences of my compulsion. Death was easier, far better than being so exposed, sliced and blood slick and leaking from the mouths of everyone in England's green and pleasant land. *Have you seen the news? Another professor bites the sexual-miscon-dust.* I'd rather be dead. Wouldn't you?

Knock–Knock. I opened the front door, had to. Better than having it kicked in. Better than causing a scene bigger than the one Matt caused. That's what he would have wanted, after all.

Julian Blake? Yes, that's me, let's get this over with. Suspected of sexually abusing a minor. Yes, that's me. I did what it said on the tin (I mean skin), no suspicion needed. I come in peace. I come in pieces.

I was escorted out of the house and man-handled by

317

a police officer despite my compliance, shoved into the back of a police car in handcuffs as a couple of my neighbours watched on, drinking in the gossip, the late-night scandal, Lathbury Road lit up like Blackpool, lights on and doors open and mouths whispering, some screaming. Lara and Melissa standing outside their house across the road, wailing into the frosty night air, saying things my ears blocked out, while another police officer searched my house.

Questions, questions, questions. They had a video that I'd apparently sent to most of Oxford, another charge added to the litany of crimes. The making, possession, and distribution of illegal pornography. Not to mention the photos Matt included in the email, linking me to Will's death, to Catherine's, to Graham's. Question after question but I didn't have to answer them, it was my right to remain silent after all, and probably for the best. There was one question though, one that had me singing like a prairie bird, my one weakness, my Achilles heel.

'Can you tell us anything about the body of the young man we found in your house, Mr Blake?'

I can tell you everything about him. Beautiful, astonishing, the brightest star in the sky. Too clever for his own good. He was Matthew, my Matthew, spectacularly cunning, the air that I breathed and the words that I spoke, a part of my every decision, my every thought. Pristine blue eyes and a grin that threatened to swallow me whole, like it had again and again. I can tell you that, even in death, I feel his smugness watching me wherever I go. The prison cell, the courtroom, my dreams. He still talks to me, taunts me. I can tell you I loved him, and love often makes us do despicable things. I can tell you a million facts about that blonde-haired beauty, talk until my jaw breaks, write until my fingers bleed, and if I run out of ink I'll sooner use my blood than put the pen down. I can tell you about his love of games, a winner through and through, always ten steps ahead, a league of his own. I can tell you that he was always right—I am nothing. Without him there is nothing, I have nothing.

I can tell you that I'll sooner put a noose around my neck than spend the rest of my life alone and haunted by the ghosts of young boys in the confines of a cell, and if in another life Matt and I meet I'll say: *It's good to see you, thought about you every day*, and I'll have my way with him and kill him with my bare hands right afterwards to save myself the hassle. That is what I can tell you.

# Acknowledgments

*A big thank you to my mother, Michelle, for always supporting my dreams. To the rest of my family and dearest friends — you know who you are — I love you.*

*To Stuart Debar, and the rest of the team at SRL Publishing, thank you for giving me a platform in which to share my story.*

*To Nicky Shearsby, I am very grateful for the advice along the way and for the beautiful cover design*

*Thank you, to the fans, who have waited patiently for this sequel to be written.*

*Last, but not least, I'd like to give credit to the main characters, Matt and Julian, for refusing to be silenced.*

SRL Publishing don't just publish books, we also do our best in keeping this world sustainable. In the UK alone, over 77 million books are destroyed each year, unsold and unread, due to overproduction and bigger profit margins.

Our business model is inherently sustainable by only printing what we sell. While this means our cost price is much higher, it means we have minimum waste and zero returns. We made a public promise in 2020 to never overprint our books just for the sake of profit.

We give back to our planet by calculating the number of trees used for our products so we can then replace. We also calculate our carbon emissions and support projects which reduce $CO_2$. These same projects also support the United Nations Sustainable Development Goals.

The way we operate means we knowingly waive our profit margins for the sake of the environment. Every book sold via the SRL website plants at least one tree.

To find out more, please visit
www.srlpublishing.co.uk/responsibility

Milton Keynes UK
Ingram Content Group UK Ltd.
UKHW042115101023
430285UK00001B/4

9 781915 073266